W9-BQY-486

PRAISE FOR THE NOVELS OF SORAYA LANE

I Knew You Were Trouble

"Readers will fall head-over-heels in love with Nate and Faith. Lane's latest is filled with a huge dose of Southern Texas charm."
—*RT Book Reviews*

"First-rate writing and memorable characters prove that sometimes things are worth the trouble, as demonstrated by Ms. Lane."
—*Jenerated Reviews*

"A fun, endearing, yet heartbreaking read that kept me eagerly turning pages just waiting to see how everything works out for Faith and Nate."
—*Romance Junkies*

"For those who love a Texan man and some good flirtation, I recommend *I Knew You Were Trouble*."
—*Harlequin Junkie*

Cowboy Take Me Away

"A sexy, charming Southern read."
—*RT Book Reviews*

"Soraya Lane keeps the story going and exciting to the very end."
—*Reader to Reader Review*

"If you like steamy cowboy romances, you'll love this book."
—*Bitten By Love Reviews*

"Captivating on so many levels . . . heartbreakingly memorable."
—*Romance Junkies*

The Devil Wears Spurs

"Hot, handsome cowboys and sharp, amusing banter make Lane's latest a fun, sexy read . . . With down-to-earth characters in a Western setting, Lane tells a story that will keep readers engaged until the very last page."
—*Romantic Times*

"It's no gamble to bet on cowboy Ryder King. Soraya Lane's *The Devil Wears Spurs* is hot as a Texas summer. It's a wild ride you don't want to miss."
—*New York Times* and *USA Today* bestselling author Jennifer Ryan

"Watch out, the Devil has met his match! Sit back with Soraya Lane's *The Devil Wears Spurs* and enjoy the sparks that fly between champion bull rider Ryder and Chloe, a barmaid with a few aces up her sleeve. You won't want their story to end!"
—Laura Moore, bestselling author of *Once Tasted*

"Sassy, sexy, and so much fun, *The Devil Wears Spurs* is a cowboy fantasy come to life. With this rowdy, romantic ride from the ranches of Texas to the casinos of Las Vegas, Soraya Lane proves herself a bright new voice in western romance."
—Melissa Cutler, author of *The Trouble with Cowboys*

Also by Soraya Lane

I Knew You Were Trouble
Cowboy Take Me Away
The Devil Wears Spurs
Cowboy Stole My Heart
All Night with the Cowboy
Once Upon a Cowboy Christmas

My One True Cowboy

Soraya Lane

PAPL
DISCARDED

St. Martin's Paperbacks

NOTE: If you purchased this book without a cover you should be aware that this book is stolen property. It was reported as "unsold and destroyed" to the publisher, and neither the author nor the publisher has received any payment for this "stripped book."

This is a work of fiction. All of the characters, organizations, and events portrayed in this novel are either products of the author's imagination or are used fictitiously.

First published in the United States by St. Martin's Paperbacks, an imprint of St. Martin's Publishing Group.

MY ONE TRUE COWBOY

Copyright © 2020 by Soraya Lane.

All rights reserved.

For information, address St. Martin's Publishing Group, 120 Broadway, New York, NY 10271.

www.stmartins.com

ISBN: 978-1-250-22438-5

Our books may be purchased in bulk for promotional, educational, or business use. Please contact your local bookseller or the Macmillan Corporate and Premium Sales Department at 1-800-221-7945, ext. 5442, or by email at MacmillanSpecialMarkets@macmillan.com.

Printed in the United States of America

St. Martin's Paperbacks edition / April 2020

10 9 8 7 6 5 4 3 2 1

Chapter 1

ANGELINA Ford pushed her sunglasses up her nose and balled her fists, tightly clenching them as she stared out the window at the sunny Texas day outside. She was used to being anxious about coming home; it was a running family joke that she got the hell out of Dodge as soon as she could. But this time . . . She swallowed and blinked away tears.

No crying. No feeling sorry for myself.

She slowly released her fingers and took a long, deep breath as the beautiful post and rail fences marking the start of River Ranch came into view. She had less than two minutes to compose herself before she arrived, and she wasn't going to let anyone in her family know that anything was wrong. Not yet.

Her father had been so excited when she'd called and said she was coming home for Father's Day. He'd had their family jet sent to Los Angeles for her, and a car waiting on the tarmac to drive her to the ranch. He might be unwell, but over the phone, his voice had still sounded remarkably strong. And thanks to his excitement over her arrival, he hadn't seemed to notice the tremor in her voice.

But it wasn't her dad she was worried about fooling. She had three siblings to hide the truth from, and her sister was going to be the one to notice something was wrong.

"We're here."

Angelina nodded to the driver. "Thank you."

She got out, stretched her legs, and looked up at the big, imposing house in front of her. It was beautiful; even as a child she'd never taken it for granted. She simply hadn't ever expected she was going to have to move home again.

The driver took her bags from the trunk and placed them on the veranda, and she stood as he went back to the car, watching it disappear down the long, manicured driveway. The trees rustled as she stared at them, leaves trembling in response to the gentle breeze, and Angelina shivered along with them. It was like she was eighteen again, standing on the doorstep, bags at her side. Only this time, her journey wasn't starting; she wasn't that confident, naive girl believing she could achieve anything. This time, she was arriving back home with her tail between her legs, her dreams crashing around her faster than she'd been able to save them.

"Angie!"

Within seconds, Mia had flung the door open, Angelina's niece flying down the steps with her arms outstretched and catching Angelina around the legs. The little girl's warm body collided with hers so fiercely, with so much love, that it took every inch of willpower not to let her tears fall.

"Hey beautiful," she murmured as she lifted Sophia and cocooned her in her arms, loving the feel of her pudgy fingers around her neck. "When did you get so big?"

Angelina looked up before Mia spoke, knowing what she was going to say before the words even came out of her mouth.

"If you came home more—"

"I wouldn't notice how much she'd grown every time," Angelina quickly finished for her. "Yeah, I know. But Christmas wasn't that long ago, was it?"

She put Sophia on her feet and touched her head, smoothing her curls gently and realizing how much she missed her niece when she was gone. If only she were brave enough to tell Mia that it wouldn't be so long between visits now.

"How's Dad?" she asked.

Mia smiled and opened her arms up, drawing Angelina in for a long, warm hug. Angelina inhaled the scent of her sister's familiar shampoo mixed with perfume, the same fragrances she'd had since they were teenagers. Mia had always made her father laugh, saying how she either smelled of horses or flowers; she was either out riding in filthy clothes, or dressed in jeans and a T-shirt and smelling every inch the rich heiress. The house had always been full of the scent of Mia's shampoo after she'd spent an hour in the shower, and as much as they'd fought sometimes, Angelina had always loved going past her little sister's room and looking in on her.

"I'm great, thanks for asking," Mia teased. "And Dad's, well, who knows? He wouldn't say even if he thought he was about to die."

Angelina pulled back, quickly blinking. But not fast enough to avoid Mia's detection.

"Hey, what's wrong?" She brushed at her face at the same time as Sophia caught her around the leg again.

"Nothing, I'm fine." Angelina smiled and kissed her sister's head. "Something about your perfume reminded me of Mom, that's all."

Mia squeezed her around the waist, staring into her eyes as if she was making sure everything was actually okay. "There's something about Dad being so unwell that makes me think a lot about Mom too. Come on, let's get your things inside."

She felt bad lying to her sister, but then, it wasn't really lying. Ever since her life had started to crumble, she'd thought about their mom almost constantly, wondering what she'd say, wondering if it would be different coming home to a mother's warm arms instead of feeling like she'd let her father down. It wasn't that he wasn't warm, but he was notorious for his business success, and she'd always been so proud when he inevitably declared at every family event that the apple never fell far from the tree. He was as proud of her business successes as she was, and she'd gone toe-to-toe with her brother Cody, proving that she had all of the same business acumen as he did. If not more. It had been a competition between them all their lives that went beyond sibling rivalry sometimes.

She had this nagging feeling that if her mom were still alive, maybe she wouldn't have spent her entire adult life trying to impress her dad.

"How much luggage did you need to bring? Are you staying a month this time?"

Angelina laughed and collected the heavier of the two cases. If only Mia knew.

The first thing she'd done after she had gotten settled was look in on her father, but he was resting and she didn't want to disturb him. Now, she was sitting in the kitchen, nursing a glass of wine as she sat with her sister and Lexi, her brother Cody's fiancée.

"I can't believe you're still looking after Dad," she said to Lexi, holding up her glass as the other two clinked glasses. "You do know we can employ someone else, right? You don't have to keep doing it."

Lexi snorted and then burst out laughing. "Someone else? He refuses to let me find a new nurse for him, and honestly, I don't mind. He's good company, and I'd never leave him."

Angelina smiled as she watched her. No wonder Cody had fallen so hard for her—she was gorgeous, fun, quick to smile, and the type of woman who'd managed to deal with her dad perfectly by completely charming him. She'd been his nurse since before she'd reunited with Cody, and it didn't sound like she had any intention of giving up that work, even though she was studying to be an architect as well.

"Where are you guys living now?" Angelina asked, searching her brain, certain she should know the answer. There were so many things she'd either forgotten or not paid attention to over the past six months, and this was obviously one of them.

Lexi didn't miss a beat, though, clearly not worried about Angelina's lack of memory. "We're still living in the apartment at the moment, just while the new house is being built. Cody isn't overly impressed because he wanted to rent somewhere, but I like it there, and I'm close to Walter when he needs me."

Angelina laughed. "Cody living in the apartment? I love it. I don't think he even liked living there when Dad converted it for him and Tanner to use as teenagers."

"She stays here a lot actually," Mia interrupted. "And Cody is like a bear with a thorn when he comes stomping over here looking for her, or so Dad says. I think it's a combination of their current accommodations and having to share her that he's struggling with."

They all laughed, and Angelina had a mental image of her burly brother, all grumpy about not having his girl with him. He was too used to always getting his own way. *Just like I am.*

"How's he adjusting to living back here?" she asked, lifting her glass and taking a long, cool sip of the crisp Sauvignon Blanc. "Aside from the living situation and having to share you."

"Ahh, I'd say it's been a bit of an adjustment," Lexi replied, and Mia erupted into laughter.

"Meaning?" Angelina asked.

"That he's had trouble with not working hundred-hour weeks," Lexi told her.

"And that he quizzes Tanner about business operations here like he's the CEO," Mia said with a giggle. "There's not a lot of love lost between our brothers right now, that's for sure."

Angelina refused to let her smile fade, feeling like the Cheshire Cat as she tried to keep her composure. Hundred-hour weeks had always been her life too. It was what terrified her most, coming out of a corporate, high-stress environment and suddenly having . . . She gulped and took another sip of wine, desperate to numb her thoughts, to shut her mind the hell up.

But it didn't work.

Nothing. That's what I have.

Cody might have moved from New York to Texas, but he still had his work. His business was still growing; he'd just had to figure out a different way of operating so he could have his girl *and* his career.

Even thinking about her bank balance with its usual

six zeros made Angelina shudder. She only had her personal account now, and her funds were dwindling. Fast.

"So, how's work?" Mia asked. "I can't believe you've gone, what, an hour without mentioning it. Are you sick? Do we need to take your temperature?"

Angelina smiled. "Maybe I'm trying to turn over a new leaf."

Mia laughed, and soon, even Lexi was joining in. Was she usually that bad talking about work? She stared into her wine and took another long sip. *Yeah, I am.*

"The day you're not obsessed with work and getting out of Texas as quickly as you arrive, is the day I'll eat my hat."

Angelina almost smiled. It sounded like her sister would be eating her hat sooner than she realized. She finished her wine and stood, needing to do something. She smoothed her pants, fingers skimming across the smooth black fabric. She glanced down, admiring her silk shirt; she was dressed in her usual uniform of luxurious neutrals. She was going to stand out like a sore thumb if she stayed in River Ranch for long, that was for sure.

"Who'd like me to cook tonight? We could have everyone over."

Her sister looked at her like she had rocks in her head. "*You?* Cook?" she asked, sounding scared. "We can always get—"

"Yes, me," Angelina said firmly. She needed something to do, and dinner would be the perfect thing to keep her busy. "You organize everyone; I'll get the food. Where does Dad keep the car keys?"

Mia was silent, but Lexi pointed to a kitchen drawer. "In there. Although I've been using the Range Rover, so it's probably not as immaculate as usual . . ."

Angelina shrugged. She didn't care. She just needed to get out of the house.

"Take the Maserati," Mia said. "It's like heaven on wheels."

She grinned and found the keys. *The Maserati, fast and furious.* That was exactly what she needed right now to blow all the cobwebs out of her brain.

Logan stepped out of his car, flexing his ankle and wishing to hell it wouldn't seize up every time he drove his truck. He walked into the store, smiling at the older lady behind the counter. It was starting to become a daily habit, and he bet she wondered why he didn't plan out his groceries for the week. He ran out of milk on a daily basis, he never had anything for dinner, and he could never think of what to cook. Which was why he ended up grilling steaks almost every night. And although he'd told himself he'd never take good food for granted ever again if he made it home, he already was.

"Darlin', you ever thought of buying one of our salads to have with your steak?"

He tried not to laugh. So she had noticed that he purchased almost the same identical items every time he shopped.

"What do you recommend?" he asked.

She smiled at him as if he'd just told her she looked beautiful. Which she did, for a woman who was old enough to be his mother. He made a mental note to tell her that when she'd finished her spiel on the salads.

"Well, I'm partial to the potato salad, but if you're on one of those fancy Keto diets or whatever they are, you might not be allowed them. That why you eat so much meat, darlin'? You having to go high on the protein?"

He shook his head. "No, ma'am. I'm not the dieting

type." He shrugged. "I'm not that adventurous in the kitchen." There was no need to tell her he actually couldn't cook.

He swore she was going to hug him, so he braced for it. Thankfully it never came, but she did pat his hand.

"Maybe you could try chicken one night. You can cook it just the same as you do the steak on the grill. And I'd start with the potato salad, then be adventurous and try the noodle ones or even a roasted vegetable."

Logan nodded. "I might go down and take a look. Thanks." His stomach was starting to rumble just thinking about something different than his usual steak-and-more-steak fare.

"You be sure to tell me what you think of it next time you're in," she said.

He smiled. "I will. And, June, is it?"

She positively beamed. "Yes."

"You look lovely today."

He turned as she blushed, pleased he'd put a smile on the woman's face.

"Logan Brody, still charming the ladies, I see?"

Logan froze as a silky, feminine voice caught his attention, before spinning around and coming face-to-face with the last person on earth he expected to see in a grocery store in Texas.

"Angie?" he said, shaking his head as he stared at the most beautifully groomed, not-a-hair-out-of-place woman he'd ever seen. She looked like a supermodel who'd walked straight off the pages of a magazine. "Wow. Look at you."

"Don't trust a word he says," Angelina said over her shoulder to June, who was watching them. "He once charmed the pants off almost every woman in town."

Before he had the chance to scold her, or point out

that he'd never quite managed to charm the pants off *her*, she was crashing into him, her arms around his neck as he hugged her back. She smelled like . . . He grinned. She smelled like money, that's what it was. *Old money*. In other words, she was dripping with it.

Her shirt was silky against his hands, and he cringed when his rough fingers snagged against it. But man, she felt like heaven. All soft and warm and . . . He pushed the thoughts away. It'd been way too long since he'd held a beautiful woman in his arms, but Angie was his friend, and she'd probably smack him around the head if she even knew what he was thinking. He cleared his throat.

"It's been . . ."

"Way too long," she finished, her smile huge as she stepped back and stared at him. Her blond hair fell over one shoulder as she toyed with it. "When did you get back?"

He moved to pick up his basket, the familiar prick of discomfort finding its way into his shoulders at the mention of him coming home.

"I've been back a few months," he said. "Would you believe that my folks are traveling the world, and they even bought a condo in Florida?"

Angie laughed and just like that, his tension disappeared. "Florida? What the hell would your dad do with himself there?"

"Keep my mom happy," Logan answered dryly. "Or at least that's what he tells me whenever he calls. Apparently she put up with ranching for years, and now it's his turn to follow her."

She touched his arm, her fingers warm and almost protective against his shirt. She'd always been like that,

his fiercest and most loyal best friend from his childhood. Angelina was beautiful, the kind of gorgeous
that made most boys tongue-tied and stupid around
her. When he'd first approached her, overconfident
and used to girls chasing him, he'd expected her to
flash him that amazing smile of hers and fall into his
arms. Instead, she'd glowered at him and told him to
try harder. Just like that, she'd called him out on his
bullshit, and he'd realized that he didn't need to date
her, he was happy hanging out with her. Their friendship had weathered every storm—girlfriends, boy-
friends, fights, and one drunken kiss—although that
had been a long time ago. Before they'd both moved
away and became email friends, although in the past
couple of years they'd fallen out of contact and it had
been too easy to let it slide.

"What are you doing home, anyway?" he asked.

She shrugged. "Father's Day."

"Since when is that one of the two holidays you come
home for?" he teased. Angelina liked coming home to
Texas as much as a cat liked having a shower.

"Hey, it's not so strange, is it?" she said, but he saw
the way her gaze darted left, suddenly avoiding him. He
decided not to push her on the subject.

"I thought people like you had their shopping done
by servants," he said, waiting for her to look up and
shoot him the filthy look he knew was coming. "What
brings you to this common part of town?"

"People like me, huh? Well, this girl here does all her
own grocery shopping, thank you very much."

"According to June over there, the ready-to-go salads
are fantastic."

He watched as Angie's eyebrows shot up. "Ready to

go?" she asked. "That might be just what I need. I offered to cook tonight, and I kind of oversold my culinary skills."

"Hey, no judgment here. I've been eating steaks every night since I came home. And trust me, after the first few weeks, it's pretty hard to stomach."

She stared at him. "So if I invited you to dinner tonight, I couldn't cook steak?"

Logan stared down at her, wondering what she was hiding, knowing there was something off about her. It didn't matter that he hadn't seen her in years—she might be grown up and glamorous now, but she was still the same girl. There was a reason Angelina Ford was back, and it sure as hell wasn't for Father's Day on Sunday. "Hey, I'd be eating steak anyway, so it doesn't really make much difference to me."

"So that's a yes, then?" she asked.

"Hell yeah, it's a yes," he said with a grin. "I'm sick of steak *and* my own company. At least you'd be curing me of one of those things."

"Well good, then," she said, linking her arm through his. "Now, show me where these salads are, and tell me what I need to use to cook a decent steak."

He leaned in close. "Well, you start with this thing called *meat*."

She punched his arm. "I got that part, you idiot."

"Seriously, you don't even know how to grill a steak?"

Angelina gave him a death stare. "You knew I was kidding about the servants, right? I usually do have other people to do things for me!"

"Come on, seriously?" he said, shaking his head. "You know, I thought out of the soldier and the CEO, it'd be the CEO who'd know how to cook."

Angie marched ahead of him. "Well, you'd be wrong.

Now, hurry up and help me get this dinner sorted. I've got a family to feed, and they won't be impressed if I serve them an empty table."

Logan laughed like he hadn't in weeks. Hell, *months*. He'd missed Angie. Only he hadn't realized how much until today.

Angelina glanced sideways at Logan. She hadn't seen him in so long, but that easy smile had drawn her straight back in. Aside from her siblings, he'd been the one person she'd always been able to count on, and it was like nothing had changed between them. Other than the fact they'd both been terrible at communicating over the past couple of years . . . She stopped walking. How many years had it actually been since they'd seen each other? Ten? Twelve? She wasn't even sure.

"What is it?"

"I was trying to figure how long it's been. Since we last saw each other properly."

"We left here twelve years ago," he said. "You were first. I was a couple months later." He rubbed the stubble on his chin, which she found impossible not to notice because he'd never had much facial hair when they'd been teenagers. He looked rough around the edges now, but in a sexy kind of way, whereas back then he'd been cute with a clean-cut look—his hair had always been done and his cheeks shaved. "And then we maybe ran into each other, what, a handful of times since then?"

She smiled. "You came home for my mom's funeral," she said quietly. "I'll never forget that."

"Hey, don't forget that I also took you out drinking to numb your pain. In fact, I think I carried you home one night over my shoulder."

She grimaced. "Trust me, I haven't forgotten."

They walked in comfortable silence until they reached the salads. She was mildly impressed. Not as good as her Whole Foods in California, but not bad either.

Since she'd run into Logan, she hadn't thought about what a failure her life had become. She was starting to think that inviting him over for dinner was a great idea. He could keep her mind off reality and distract her family from asking too many questions about why she was home.

"So, how's work?" he asked.

She grimaced. "Next question."

Logan just raised a brow. "I don't have any other questions."

"Just help me choose the salads, would you?"

She smiled to herself as he held up different options for her to consider, and she wondered how on earth a gorgeous, easygoing man like him was still single. *Shit, he is still single, isn't he?*

Angelina darted a quick glance at his ring finger, but realized that wouldn't tell her much. Plenty of ranchers didn't bother wearing a wedding band, and she bet a whole lot of soldiers didn't wear them either.

"Logan, I presumed, I mean, I guess I thought I would have heard, but . . ."

He stared at her, waiting for her to spit her words out. "What?"

"You're single, right?" Was that why he'd stopped emailing her, because he was married?

He grinned. "You finally want a piece of this?" He gestured at his body and she rolled her eyes.

"As if."

"The answer's no. There's no wife."

She didn't try to hide her relief; she was certain he could see it.

"But there *is* someone important in my life that you need to meet," he said with a wink. "If we're going to be spending time together, that is. I could even bring her for dinner if that's okay?"

Angelina did her best to hide her reaction this time. "Oh, sure. Anyone I know?" So he didn't have a wife, but he did have a girlfriend. She hoped she looked like she was happy for him.

He shook his head. "Nope, no one you know."

"Blonde? Brunette?"

He made a face. "Ahh, I'd say brunette if I had to pick a color. She's a beautiful girl."

Angelina smiled politely, when what she wanted to do was bare her teeth and scare this girl—whoever she was—away. She selfishly wanted Logan all to herself now that she was home, at least for one night, to reminisce and enjoy his company. She busied herself with choosing the salads and finding the meat she needed, before heading to the counter. The woman there, the one Logan had been flirting with, chatted away about the salads again until Angelina thought she was never going to stop, before they were finally done with shopping.

"You want to come over about six? Hopefully Mia has asked all the others already."

"Sounds good. Hey, do you want to meet her now?"

"Who?"

"My girl. Ella."

"Oh." Angelina nodded, probably too hard. "She's here?"

"Yup. She's waiting in the truck."

She looked around, waiting for him to point her out. When he did, she couldn't see anyone.

"Come over. She might be asleep."

"What? *Asleep*? It's only mid-afternoon." Angelina laughed. "Don't tell me, you're into older women these days? She sounds like your grandma."

As she snorted with laughter, crossing the road behind Logan, a dark brown head popped up at the window, followed by a lazy yawn.

Logan opened the door. "Angie, meet Ella. Ella, meet Angie."

A beautiful chocolate-brown dog with white spots held up a paw, her head cocked to one side as if she could actually understand what was being said.

"You asshole," Angelina muttered as she obliged and shook the dog's paw.

"What? Were you jealous?"

Angelina didn't give him the satisfaction of an answer, but if she'd been honest, she would have told him she'd never been more relieved in her life.

"Let's just say she wasn't what I was expecting."

Logan slung his arm around his dog's shoulders. "She's more beautiful, right? Is that what it is?" he teased.

She watched as the dog looked up at Logan with so much love, and for the first time, she wished someone looked at her like that. Business had always seemed to be enough, her career the most important thing in her life, but when everything had crumbled around her, she'd never been so acutely aware of how alone she was. And it hurt. She didn't even have a pet, let alone a significant other.

"You're right—she is beautiful. Feel free to bring

your girl to dinner tonight," she called over her shoulder as she walked away.

Logan's laughter made his eyes twinkle, and she smiled back at him. Maybe being home wasn't as bad as she'd thought it would be.

Chapter 2

OR maybe it was. Angelina had tried to busy herself in the kitchen and keep everyone talking about themselves, but somehow the conversation kept turning around to her. Had she spent so much time talking about herself in the past that it was such an anomaly for her to talk about others?

"I see you've dressed for the occasion," a deep, gravelly voice that unmistakably belonged to her brother, said from behind her.

Shit. Now Cody was here, which meant there was definitely more work talk coming her way. She'd usually craved the company of her younger brother, desperate to talk shop with someone else, but not today. She gulped.

She spun around, laughing when she saw Cody standing in jeans and a plaid shirt. "Holy crap! I was going to say you can't talk about my choice in clothes; but you kind of can. You're really rocking that rancher look."

Cody scowled at Tanner, who was sitting at the table eating all the snacks she'd put out. "Apparently I can't dress like a city asshole now I live here, so I save the Armani suits for New York." He chuckled. "And trust me, I can't wait to dive into my work clothes the second I get on the plane. But for now, this is my new look."

"And how is the more relaxed pace of life suiting you, brother?" she asked, as she rinsed and then dried her hands before crossing the room to give him a big hug.

"Don't tell the others," he whispered in her ear, "but when Lexi's asleep, I get back up and work all night. It's the only thing that keeps me sane."

Angelina laughed. "You and I never could handle a forty-hour work week, could we? The workaholic life is tough, but it's a hard habit to change."

She felt the familiar prickle of tears and quickly turned away, at least able to busy herself with dinner. All her life, she'd prided herself on never being a crier—she'd be the first to roll her eyes at a woman tearing up and want to yell "toughen the hell up" in her direction. But now, well, she was starting to feel a whole lot more sympathetic to people who showed their emotions. Or at least those who tried their best to stifle them when all they wanted was to turn into a human waterworks.

"So, how's work? What's new?" Cody asked, opening the fridge and pulling out a beer. "Liven up this party for me by talking business, *please*."

"Ahh, nothing new, same old thing," she said, not looking up as she emptied the salads into nice white bowls.

"Any exciting new deals?" Cody asked. "Come on, Ange, give me something. These guys kill me with their lack of enthusiasm about—"

She was saved by Lexi walking in, which seemed to take Cody's attention in an entirely new direction. He set his beer down, arms open wide as she stepped into him, kissing her like he hadn't seen her in months.

"Ahhh, are they always like this?" Angelina asked no one in particular as she stared at them.

"Ewwww," Harry, Lexi's son, groaned, covering his eyes as he pulled away from his mom and went to sit by Tanner.

"Yup," Tanner called out. "All. The. Freaking. Time."

Lauren arrived then too and gave Angelina a big hug before slinging an arm around Tanner's shoulders. "It's so nice to have you home," Lauren said.

Angelina nodded. "It's good to be home."

She laughed when Lauren rolled her eyes at Lexi and Cody, happy that Cody was happy, even if she wasn't a fan of public displays of affection. He'd sworn for years that he was too busy to have a partner in his life, let alone having children one day, but he was as smitten with Lexi as he was with his business, and that was saying something. She bet he'd even changed his mind about the kids part.

When they finally broke away, Lexi turned to face her. "Someone's looking forward to seeing you," she said. "He's awake."

Angelina nodded. She'd been waiting to see her dad, and she wasn't going to lie and say she wasn't worried about how much he was sleeping. She had no idea if that was normal or not, and part of her almost didn't want to know, because it was easier just pretending he was okay.

"Thanks. I'll go through now."

She picked up her glass of wine and took it with her, walking through the wide hallway to her father's library. They used to call it his office, but it was more like a big library, filled with endless numbers of books, two enormous leather club sofas, and his workspace. It was one of her favorite rooms in the house, because it was what she associated with her dad, the place that he always seemed most content.

Angelina lifted a hand and knocked softly before opening the door, seeing everything exactly as she'd remembered the moment she walked in. She didn't shut the door behind her, inhaling the faint aroma of cigars that seemed to permanently cling to the walls and finding her dad sitting on one of the sofas, waiting for her.

"Hey, Daddy," she said, setting her glass down and bending to hug him. His big hands were still warm and solid against her back, but she knew that him not standing when she entered the room was a big thing for him. His manners were old school, and he always stood when any woman entered the room, especially one of his daughters.

"How's my gorgeous girl, huh?" he said, still gripping her tight.

She dropped to sit beside him, keeping hold of his hand. "I'm good."

He frowned. "Why are you here? Is something wrong?"

Angelina knew it was going to be almost impossible to hide her problems from him, but it wasn't going to stop her from trying. Perhaps she should have just tried to lay low in California so it wasn't so obvious that something was wrong.

"Nothing's wrong," she said quickly. "It's Father's Day this weekend, and I wanted to come home and see you."

Walter nodded. "Worried it's going to be my last, are you? Trust me, I know the feeling."

She lifted his hand and pressed a kiss to it. "It's not going to be your last, Daddy," she said firmly. "I just wanted to see you."

"I noticed you took money out of your trust fund," he said, shifting his weight and reaching out a hand for his drink. She moved forward and got it for him, not even bothering to scold him about drinking whiskey in his condition. It was probably his only guilty pleasure.

"Ah, yes, I did." She knew her face was flushing, the heat in her cheeks not something she was used to, and she reached for her own glass and took a gulp of wine. "I didn't think you'd even notice."

"It's none of my business. It came up as an alert because you've never drawn out of that money before, and my bank manager thought it might have been theft." He chuckled. "You must be one of the only people in the world so stubborn about taking money from their family."

Angelina felt her eyebrows shoot up. He made out like she was the only one to refuse it. "Does Cody take his?"

Walter looked amused. "Of course he does. I presume he used it to help build his own property portfolio, but I've never asked. For all I know, he's just used it to whet his appetite for fast cars."

"Huh." She sipped her wine. Here she was, refusing to take Ford money all these years, other than the small seed money she'd started with to help build her company, thinking her brother was doing the same, and all the time he was happily using it. "I suppose I just thought he earned enough without needing it."

"None of you need it, which is precisely why I gave you access to it," Walter said. "If you were lazy and didn't work, I'd have cut you all off until you proved yourselves, but I never needed to."

Angelina cringed as she realized how stubborn she'd been, and for no good reason. Maybe if she hadn't been so determined to make it on her own, she'd have been able to save her company, but deep down she knew that wasn't true. The truth was, no amount of extra cash was going to save the sinking ship that had been her business.

"So, did you suddenly decide to donate to charity? Buy a new car?"

"What?" she asked, pulled from her thoughts as she realized her father was talking to her.

"With the money," he said. "I hope that after all this time, you at least spent it on something good."

Angelina could feel the heat of his gaze, knew she needed to say something to get him to drop the conversation. "Um, a car. You're right. I thought I deserved a treat after all these years working my ass off."

Walter drained his whiskey, coughing a little as she helplessly watched on, knowing he didn't want any help. He might have terminal cancer, but he didn't want to be treated like he was anything less than capable.

"I've really missed you," she said, suddenly emotional at seeing her dad and the way he was suffering. He'd always been such a big, room-dominating, proud man, and on the phone she still imagined him that way. But he'd deteriorated a lot since she'd come home for Christmas, and it was terrifying.

"You sure you're okay, Ange?" he asked, studying her face as she stared back at him. "Everything going okay in California?"

She nodded. "Everything's fine, Dad, thanks."

"Because if you need to talk, about anything, I've got all the time in the world."

Angelina smiled and rose, holding out her hand to

help him up. In her heart, deep down, she knew she could open up to him, but she didn't want to. Not until she'd found a way to fix at least some of what she'd lost. Failing was not something she was used to, and it wasn't a word she wanted her dad to associate with her either. She'd prefer to tell him once she'd figured out how to get back on her feet.

The sound of the doorbell ringing echoed down the hall, and she met her father's surprised gaze. Family always just walked straight in, so it was obvious they had a guest.

"Are we expecting company tonight?" he asked.

She grinned. "Yes, we are. Do you remember Logan?"

He squinted for a moment, as though he were trying to see something in the distance, before smiling. "Ah, yes. The soldier."

"That's the one," she said. "I bumped into him at the store. We haven't caught up in a long time, so I asked him to join us."

"Nothing better than young people at the table. It's good for inspiration."

Angelina had no idea what business deal her father might be cooking up, and she was almost too scared to ask what he needed inspiration for, since age certainly hadn't slowed him down.

"You might need to bend your rules on dogs being allowed in the house tonight, though," she said as she walked out of her father's den and into the hall.

"Why's that?" he grumbled.

"Because Logan's date is his dog, and I don't think there's any way in hell she's being left outside."

Logan stood at the door, Ella at his side, wondering if running back to his car and accelerating down the driveway would have been a better idea. Seeing Angie had caught him off guard earlier. He'd fallen straight back into being who he *used* to be, and he wasn't entirely sure that felt any better than usual these days.

He rubbed his temples as the start of a headache niggled, promising to be pounding by the time he went to bed.

Ella whined at his side, and he dropped his hand to touch the top of her head. She was his lifeline—without her, he had no damn idea how he'd manage to get out of bed in the mornings. But if he wasn't around to feed her, no one would, and there was no way in hell he'd let her suffer. Not for a second. He guessed that's why his therapist was so happy he had a pet depending on him.

"It's okay, girl, they're nice," he muttered, as if she could understand exactly what he was saying. "They're *real* nice."

The dog sat, ears pricked, and just like that, the door swung open.

"Hey!" It was Angie, looking every bit as goddamn stunning in the same silky blouse and tight-fitting pants. She'd always been a knockout—he'd had to stare plenty of guys down who didn't get the message that she just wasn't interested—but now? Age had made her more beautiful, in a self-assured kind of way. And he liked that she still had her own style, refusing to dress like everyone else simply because she was on a ranch—she'd never liked the jeans and plaid shirt combo even as a teenager.

"Hey, yourself," he said, not sure whether to kiss her or hug her. She did neither, just reaching out to touch his arm and squeeze it, so he left it at that.

"I see you brought your date," Angie said, bending down and looking at Ella. "She's a beautiful dog."

"She actually doesn't know she's a dog," Logan whispered, holding up his hand and grinning at Angie. "She's convinced she's human."

"Well, I warned Dad that you were bringing a four-legged date, but she better not be expecting a seat at the table. He's not exactly a fan of animals in the house."

Logan gestured for Ella to step in with him, and she walked perfectly at heel through the house and into the kitchen. He smiled when he saw Angelina's brothers, holding out his hand and shaking first Cody's and then Tanner's.

"Long time no see," said Cody, slapping him on the back.

"It's good to see you guys again."

"I didn't even know you were back," Tanner said, frowning. "How the hell did my sister find you on her first day home, and I haven't run into you once?"

He gratefully took the beer Angie held out to him. "I guess I've been busy. My folks up and left, then our ranch manager retired, and I've been thrown straight back into ranching. It's been one hell of a job to come home to." He laughed. "The only time I'm not on the ranch is when I'm having to go into town, looking for something to eat."

"It must have been a big adjustment," Cody said. "You doing okay?"

Logan nodded, wishing he could even figure out a way to tell them the half of it. But he knew firsthand it was easier to pretend everything was okay. "Yeah, you can say that again. But I'm doing fine, thanks."

"You'll like Sam," Tanner said. "He's Mia's husband. Sam's a horse trainer now, but he's a veteran too, did a tour in Iraq years back before he came home. He'll be around later."

Logan nodded. He appreciated the thought, but he didn't need any reminders of the military. Right now, he was doing everything he could to forget it. *If the guy's half as fucked up as I am, he won't want to talk about his past either.*

"Thanks, but I live with a vet, so I get plenty of contact." He heard Angie's snigger as the others looked back at him, blank-faced. Clearly she wasn't falling for his jokes again. "Ah, this is Ella, she did six back-to-back tours before being forced into early retirement."

He gestured to the dog beside him, her eager face looking expectantly up at all the people in the room, and when he looked up, everyone was smiling, suddenly focused on Ella. There was something incredible about the way an animal could change the mood of an entire group of people, but he'd seen it firsthand when he was serving on multiple occasions, so it didn't surprise him anymore. Men who were down about being away from their families, about serving so far from home, changed almost instantly when they had the chance to care for a dog on base.

"She was a *military* dog?" Angie asked. "You didn't tell me that when I met her earlier."

"Hold up a minute, you're telling me we're having *three* army veterans to dinner tonight?" Walter's booming voice cut through the room, and Logan turned, shocked to see how slight the once-formidable man was now. But there was nothing slight about his voice—he still had full command over the room.

"Ah, yes, sir, I guess there will be three."

Walter walked slowly toward him, and Logan watched as one of the women hurried toward him, taking his arm and guiding him toward the table. His own children didn't move, and Logan knew instinctively that it wasn't out of laziness or lack of caring, but more likely something to do with their dad retaining his pride.

"Lexi's his nurse," Angie whispered in his ear. "And also Cody's fiancée."

Logan glanced down at her, surprised at how easy it was between them after so many years.

"Got it," he murmured back.

"So, tell me about this dog," Walter said once he was seated. "The kids were never allowed to have a working dog inside, but I think she's worth making an exception."

Logan pointed. "Go see," he said, pointing at Walter. Ella happily trotted off, but her limp was obvious.

"She's injured?" Angie asked, her voice low as everyone seemed to hold their breath watching Ella cross the room.

"She was one of the most valuable dogs we had in our unit, a true one of a kind," Logan said, clearing his throat as his voice went husky, the way it always did when he talked about his military career. "She could sniff out not only bombs, but all the parts used to make them. Mobile phones, you name it, she could find it. This dog saved so many lives, I don't think we could even keep count, and we even loaned her out to the British Army when they needed a specialized dog for an assignment."

Ella was sitting at Walter's feet now as he stroked her, and Logan felt a familiar rush of protectiveness as he looked at her.

"Is that how she hurt herself?" Walter asked.

He nodded, steeling himself against the weight of his memories. He was only going to scratch the surface telling them this part, but it still hurt. "She alerted us one afternoon, and we thought we had everything, that we'd done a thorough sweep. But then she went nuts, giving us the signal, and we cleared the area immediately, but it was too late." Logan balled his fists tightly, gripping them, riding through the accelerated heartbeat and surge inside his head as his thoughts went back to that day. He'd become expert at telling people just enough—to satisfy their curiosity without losing his mind. "We lost men that day, and we almost lost Ella, but she's a goddamn fighter and she refused to give up."

Walter silently met his gaze.

"Excuse my language, sir," Logan apologized.

"Nothing to apologize for, son, and stop calling me sir." Walter chuckled. "You're the war hero, not me. If anything, I should be calling *you* sir."

"Will she ever serve again?" Tanner asked, as he moved closer to Ella and pulled out the chair beside her to sit. Everyone laughed when she held up her paw and Tanner took it, shaking it exactly like he would a human's.

"She's invaluable to the military, but she wasn't cleared for work again. She's completely deaf in one ear, although I still verbally say her commands as well as gesture with my hands, and she had a shattered hip. There's no way she could work again, and her prognosis wasn't great, but I stumped up the money to save her."

"And how did you end up with her?" Walter asked. "If you don't mind me asking, of course. Were you her handler?"

That was the trouble, he *did* mind. This was the one question he always did his best to avoid.

Logan cleared his throat. "She means a lot to me because my friend was her handler, and I worked closely with her on tour. I was prepared to do anything and everything to get her rehomed back to Texas with me." That was all they needed to know; he didn't have to tell them anymore. "I guess I was lucky I had the resources to save her. Although I'm not sure my old man was as impressed with the expenditure on a dog that can't work. In the past, most retired dogs were left overseas or euthanized unless their handlers could afford to bring them home, but now the military will at least pay for their ticket home."

They all smiled, and Ella came back to sit beside him, so close she was almost sitting on his foot. He dropped his hand, letting her touch him, knowing how much she needed the contact. Although sometimes he thought that maybe it was he who needed it, and she obliged. He blinked away tears, hoping no one had seen them.

"She's a lucky girl," Angie said. "All those incredible service animals deserve to make it home, and have a nice retirement to boot too."

Everyone in the room seemed to agree, all staring at Ella still.

"I think we need to toast the canine war hero in the room," Tanner said, before going to the fridge and getting out more beers. Logan took the chance to drain the one he had, happily reaching for another.

"She looks like she's easy to have around," Cody said as he stroked her.

"So long as she's with me 24/7 and there's nothing around to chew," Logan said, chuckling as he thought about how naughty she'd been in the past. "She had a reputation for eating everything when she was younger, even when we were on a helicopter heading into a mission. Once she ate part of a backpack and a gun holster without the soldier even knowing until we'd landed." He glanced down at her. "But she was pampered like a princess, with a temperature-controlled kennel and boots to keep her feet safe. She was treated better than most of the soldiers there because men were easy to replace." He swallowed the lump in his throat. "But she wasn't, until she was injured."

Angie touched his arm then, and he jumped before realizing it was only her. He hated that, how he almost leapt out of his skin these days at the slightest noise or touch. It made it damn hard to sleep.

"Any chance you could do the steaks tonight for me?" she asked, wide-eyed at his reaction but not saying anything. It was as if she knew he needed a break from all the questions.

"Is there any part of this dinner you're planning on cooking?" he asked.

She grinned. "Not a chance."

"And that's why you're so successful. You're good at outsourcing."

Logan expected her to laugh, but she didn't. And there was no way he was falling for the tight smile she gave him.

"You okay?"

She took a big breath. "Me? Yeah, I'm fine."

Still not buying it. But he wasn't going to pry. When she was good and ready, she'd talk, and if he pushed her, then she had the right to do the same to him, and some things were just better left unsaid.

Angelina stared at Logan as he fired up the grill, his face perfectly composed as he worked. But it hadn't been so composed before. It might have been years since they'd spent time together, but she still remembered everything about him, knew his tells and when he was hurting. And right now, he wasn't right. Something was troubling him, and she was fairly certain it had to do with his military career, or maybe even the dog. He clearly adored Ella, but it was almost like she'd triggered something inside of him too, and Angelina wanted to know more.

She opened her mouth, her own troubles on the tip of her tongue. If she could talk to anyone, get it all off her chest, it should be Logan. But suddenly her financial woes and the collapse of her company seemed insignificant in comparison to whatever he'd been through. His life had been on the line, whereas what had she had to lose? Her bank balance? Her pride? Her problems seemed to pale in comparison. Her scars might disappear one day, but his might never leave him completely.

"You know," he said as he turned around, "I thought you'd have some fancy banker husband by now. Hell, maybe even a film producer fiancé from Beverley Hills."

Angie snorted, fighting the urge to roll her eyes. "I don't need a man, Logan. And besides, I've been too busy for love."

"Says no woman ever," he muttered.

She slammed her hands to her hips and stared him down. "So, it's okay for a man to say that, but not a woman?"

Logan shrugged. "No one's too busy for love. *Scared* maybe, but not too busy. I don't buy it for a second."

She laughed. "Fine, I'll tell you the truth, then. After a handful of assholes who thought they were okay with who I was and the money I earned, maybe it's wasn't time that I was lacking. But I sure as hell wasn't scared. Maybe I just couldn't be bothered again."

"Your brothers sort those assholes out for you?"

Angie glanced over her shoulder at her brothers laughing and talking inside. "They didn't even know I was dating anyone. I've kept to myself the past decade, flying home when I needed to, but otherwise just doing my own thing. After Mom died, Cody and I both seemed to find it easier to stay away, and we don't exactly stay in touch 24/7."

She watched as Logan put the steaks on the grill and reached for the salt and pepper, grinding both over the meat.

"It's easier avoiding pain than facing it head-on. I get that," he said. "I see a red flag when I'm with a woman, and I run, so trust me when I say that I understand."

Angie leaned back against the house, listening to the sizzle of the steaks as she watched Ella investigate the backyard. There were post and rail fences separating the closest field from the sprawling lawn and garden, enough to keep horses and stock out, but certainly not enough to stop a dog from going on an adventure. She had a feeling that Ella was working, though, checking the area, and she seemed to be keeping an eye on Logan. It seemed unlikely she would make a run for it. The poor animal was probably bored and craving work again, desperate to be given a job.

"She's lucky to have you," Angie said, suddenly feeling emotional for the dog she'd only recently met. "Would she actually have been put to sleep if you hadn't intervened? The handlers must be heartbroken when that happens."

Logan grunted. "Yeah, she would have. In the past, the dogs weren't offered to their handlers at all, and sometimes those guys, sometimes two of them, have taken turns with the dog on tour. They'll be desperate to come home to see their families, but they're heartbroken at leaving the dog they love back in the Middle East or wherever the hell they've been posted. Let alone if they're injured in the course of duty." He turned the steaks as she watched. "I've been fighting to change things, because even though the laws have improved, those working dogs deserve more. It shouldn't matter if our soldiers have two legs or four, they should be treated the same."

She didn't ask him any more. He looked as if a dark cloud had passed over his face, and his attention turned back to the meat he was cooking.

"She's probably the longest relationship you've ever had," Angie teased.

"Yeah, you could say that," he said dryly.

"It's really nice to see you again, Logan," she told him as the mood changed between them.

He turned, the cloud seeming to lift as he held out an arm. She happily tucked beneath it, looping her own arm around his waist as she leaned in close to him in a sideways, one-armed hug. Logan had been her person, the one person in the world she'd been able to trust. They'd never argued, never betrayed one another, never let anything come between them. There was no baggage, no dirty history, just a genuine friendship that she wished she hadn't let slip.

"I'm sorry I was such a crap friend all these years," she said, still hugging him. "We did so well emailing and calling for a while, and then we both kind of gave up."

"Yeah, I'm sorry too." He laughed. "At least we were *both* terrible though, right?"

She smiled, wondering when exactly he'd gotten so big. She was barefoot and she was able to comfortably rest against his chest. He'd always been tall, but she was guessing he'd had a late growth spurt, and he'd filled out. A lot.

"I think you missed my thirtieth," she said. "That's one thing I wasn't planning on forgiving you for."

"Happy birthday?" he replied, looking down at her.

She smacked him and headed for the door. "It was over a year ago!"

Angie laughed to herself as she walked back inside, her feet like blocks of ice, they were so cold.

"Here's my girl," her father called out. "Come sit with me. I want to hear all about California and what you've been working on."

She swallowed and wondered if it would be too obvious to reach for more wine. Again. At this rate, she was going to be drunk before dessert.

"There's no hurry," she said, hoping her voice sounded even. "I want to hear about all the rest of you. What's new on the ranch?"

"Hey, everyone," said a deep voice, at the same time as little feet thundered across the wooden floor and Sophia hurtled at Angie again as if she hadn't already seen her earlier that day.

Saved by the kid. Again. But she knew there was only so long she could keep avoiding what was usually her favorite topic of conversation.

"Soph, there's a dog here! Want to come meet Ella?" Angie asked, pausing to say hi and kiss her brother-in-law Sam on the cheek, as he stood holding a sleeping baby Isobel in his arms.

And just like that, she managed to escape her family and head straight back out the door, with her niece and Harry both running fast after Ella.

"Oomph!"

"Sorry!" She reached for the tray of meat as she crashed into Logan while he was coming back inside.

He gave her a strange look, but true to his former best friend status, he never said a word as she disappeared into the garden, calling his dog.

Chapter 3

ANGELINA woke as sunlight streamed into the room. She reached for her phone, squinting at the digits and groaning as she realized it wasn't even seven yet. She was so used to waking up early that even without an alarm clock, she couldn't sleep in anymore. She lay there, listening to the wind outside, the creaking of the house, willing herself back to sleep even though she knew there was no use in trying.

What was she going to do with herself? She wasn't going to set foot on the ranch—horses held no appeal to her and she'd never enjoyed being outside anyway. Which left her with inside. In other words, her father and little else. If she were more like her sister, she could have curled up with a book and read, or gone out horseback riding, but neither of those things held any appeal to her. She liked being busy, and she wasn't good at sitting idle with nothing to occupy her mind.

She stretched and got up, making her bed and then walking over to the window. Angelina held up her hand and touched the cool glass pane, leaning forward and looking out over their sprawling property. She caught sight of Tanner disappearing into his truck, up early and working already, but other than that, it was as peaceful and quiet as could be. Perhaps if she'd shut her drapes the night before, it would have helped her to stay asleep. Or maybe it was the fact that it was so quiet, it had woken her. She was used to more noise where she lived.

She went into the adjoining bathroom and turned on the faucets, stripping out of her pajamas and waiting for the water to get hot. She stared at herself in the mirror as she stood, studying her face, seeing the little lines that hadn't been there only a year or so ago. Were they from age or stress? She sighed. Probably both. Without her full face of makeup on, she looked so bare, younger and more vulnerable, even with the fine lines feathering from her eyes. It wasn't the reflection she was used to.

In fact, Angelina barely recognized herself. Who was she without a business to run? What was the point of her life if everything she'd sacrificed, if everything she'd worked for, had been for nothing? What did she have left when the one thing she loved more than anything else in her life, was gone? She loved her family, of course she did, but it was the all-consuming 24/7 love she had for her work. It had been like the husband she'd never had.

She was grateful when the mirror started to steam over, and she didn't bother flicking the switch to de-mist it. Right now, she'd rather not see herself. She took the few steps from the vanity to the shower, slipping beneath the stream of hot water and holding her breath as she put her face under.

An hour later, she was back at the mirror again, but

this time she was laughing at herself. So much for not wanting to see herself. She'd blow-dried her hair and given herself a full face of makeup, and she was back wearing one of her signature silk shirts. It was ridiculous attire for a casual day at home, but she had no idea what else to wear. Not to mention the fact that she hardly owned any casual clothing. What she did have was a pair of jeans, and she'd put them on with a belt and tucked her shirt in—it was as relaxed as she was going to get. And she was barefoot, which was virtually unheard of for her.

After a final spray of perfume, she left her room and walked down the stairs, noticing how quiet the house was. When she was usually back, it was the holidays, which meant there was usually someone else staying, whereas this time it was only her and her dad.

At the bottom of the stairs, she almost ran into Lexi. No wonder it was annoying Cody—it was barely eight o'clock and she was already *leaving* Walter's library.

"Everything okay down here?" Angelina asked.

"Everything's fine. I was just doing my first check in of the day," Lexi said, yawning as she glanced back at the room. "I like to get him ready for the day nice and early. He's such a proud man, he couldn't stand anyone seeing him before he was looking like his normal self."

Angie nodded, wondering how much sleep Lexi was getting. "Are you studying today?"

"If I can keep my eyes open, I will be," she said, stifling another yawn. "It's tough burning the candle at both ends some days, but I'm fine. I wouldn't have it any other way."

"Yeah, I bet it is."

Lexi wasn't only looking after Walter and keeping

Cody in check, she also had Harry and a full schedule
with her studies from the sounds of it. But Angelina
wasn't about to counsel her. If she wanted to do it all,
then Angelina had no doubt she could.

"Have you had breakfast?" Angie asked her as they
started to walk down the hall together. "Want to join
me?"

"No, but I need to go back and see Harry before he
goes to school. Rain check for another time?"

"Sure." Angelina watched her go then went into the
kitchen, wondering what time their housekeeper started
or if she even worked every day now. But she was
guessing most days, as when she went into the oversize
walk-in pantry, it was fully stocked.

She decided to make coffee and toast bagels, spread-
ing them with cream cheese and jam and piling everything on a tray and carrying it into her father's library.
She pushed the door open with her bottom, bumping it
and walking through.

"Morning, Daddy," she called as she entered.

He looked pale, his eyes slightly sunken as she caught
sight of him, but he managed to muster a bright smile
when he saw her. She could see his blankets folded
away, and she wondered if he'd be better staying warm
with them over his legs, instead of trying to hold on to
some misconstrued sense of pride in anyone seeing him
looking unwell.

"Look at you, so beautiful this early in the morning,"
he said. "You're not all dressed up because you're leaving, are you? I don't want you coming in here to break
the bad news to me that you're flying straight out."

She set the tray down on the coffee table and kissed
the top of his head, like he'd always done to her when

she was a little girl. "I'm not going anywhere. I just thought we could eat together this morning."

She hadn't thought about whether he might have already eaten, and she could see an untouched bowl of fresh fruit on the side table by his chair, and a tall glass of juice, or perhaps it was a smoothie. She hated to think he'd lost his appetite. It made his illness feel that little bit more real.

"Did Lexi get you breakfast already?"

He nodded. "She sneaks in here early and gets me all sorted for the day, including making me that"—he waved his hand at the drink—"*concoction*."

Angie laughed. "What's in it? I thought at first glance it was just orange juice."

His grimace told her she was wrong. "Turmeric, ginger, pepper, coconut oil, cinnamon, lemon juice." She laughed at the look on his face, reminding her of a baby with its mouth twisted in disgust at a new sour taste. "It's gross, that's what it is."

"She only means well."

His face softened. "I know. Trust me. I know how lucky I am that she's still here. I have your brother to thank for that. If he hadn't shown up here with that big diamond, she would have been long gone by now."

Angelina poured him coffee and nudged it in his direction, knowing he'd be grateful for the strong black brew. They both liked their coffee as strong as tar.

"Now tell me, what are you really doing back home?"

She forced herself to laugh at her father, as if it were the most ridiculous question in the world. "I'm worried about you, Dad. I wanted to spend some time here with you, that's all."

She hoped she'd done a better job of convincing him this time.

"Logan have anything to do with it?"

His voice was gruff, like she was a teenager he had to worry about all over again.

She passed him a bagel, pleased to see him take a small bite straight away.

"Honestly, Logan and I haven't seen each other or even been in contact for, I don't know, months, years even? We used to be so good at keeping in touch, but then we kind of drifted apart," she said, taking a bite of her own bagel and slowly chewing it. "I didn't even know he'd retired from active duty."

"That dog of his was something special, wasn't she?" Walter said with a chuckle. "I think she was the most intelligent being in the room."

Angelina laughed along with him, happily chatting as they finished their bagels and sipped coffee.

"Want to do some work with me?" Walter suddenly asked, his eyebrows raised and telling her she was about to become a co-conspirator in something.

"Daddy, you do know you're supposed to be relaxing, right?" But she stood and closed the door, making sure it was shut firmly. "I don't want to face the wrath of Mia just because you've plotted something terrible for us both to do."

He had a twinkle in his eye now, and she sat beside him as he opened his laptop, excited about whatever he had to show her.

"What are you working on?" Angelina asked.

"I'm trading in currency, and it's not for the faint-hearted, that's for damn sure."

"Currency trading?"

"Don't tell Mia—she'd be furious with me—but

Cody knows. It can be our little secret." He grinned. "Your sister thinks I should be focused on my health, but what she doesn't realize is how badly I need something to work on all the time."

Angelina knew very little about currency trading, which meant it was exactly what she needed to sink her teeth into. And she also understood *exactly* how her father felt too.

"I want to know everything," she said. "Don't spare any details."

"That's my girl," Walter said with a chuckle. "Now grab that iPad there, and I'll show you exactly how I choose where and what to invest. It's as thrilling as gambling, but makes far better business sense."

"So do I call her or just see if we run into each other again?" Logan asked his dog, glancing down at her as she trotted alongside him. He was mounted on his favorite horse, Woody, but he was thinking more about Angelina than he was about riding. Or about the stock he was supposed to be moving.

Ella kept looking back up at him, and he had a feeling she was trying to tell him something.

"You liked her, didn't you? I knew you would. I mean, why wouldn't you? She's a nice girl."

Except that *girl* sounded all kinds of wrong. She was very much a woman now. Angie was a goddamn knockout, and he couldn't stop thinking about how good it had been to see her again. Or maybe it was the whole night out he'd enjoyed—it had been just him and Ella for a long time now.

He kept thinking back to what Cody had said to him, pointing out that he could easily hire ranch hands to do all the grunt work around the place, but the truth was, it gave him something to do. He'd climb the walls if he didn't have a purpose, and right now, ranching was keeping him busy. He had two ranch hands out doing some of the lighter work, but when it came to moving animals and being out on the land, he needed it. If he employed a new ranch manager, he'd be redundant.

And without the ranch to work on, he'd been back spending way too much time inside his own head. And he already knew how dangerous a place that could be.

Crack. He jumped, making his horse spook as he overreacted to a gun shot in the distance.

Just Bud shooting rabbits, he told himself. His young ranch hand had already told him he was doing some pest control, but the noise still caught him by surprise.

Pop. Pop. Pop.

Logan reached down a hand to stroke his horse, feeling the tension in his neck. "Sorry, Woody," he muttered. "Didn't mean to startle you."

Ella usually would have been excited by the noise, but her hearing seemed to be deteriorating, and she didn't appear to even hear it at all. Or if she did, she was way smarter than him and knew instinctively that they weren't in a war zone—clearly her brain didn't play tricks on her like his did.

Sometimes, he could still smell it. The gunpowder in the air, the man next to him, the humidity. And then he'd feel it. A buzz of a fly on the back of his neck would propel him straight back there, the weight of something he was carrying, the heat of the sun as it made a bead of sweat trail across his skin.

Crack.

But it was noise that tricked his brain more often than anything else. The sound of someone creeping up behind him, the almost undecipherable brush of his own boots against the dirt, the pitch of Ella barking. That's what took him back to that day.

"Brett!" he yelled, his eyes burning as he tried to see through the dust and smoke that spiraled around him. "Brett!"

No one yelled back. The men around him were gone, he already knew that. But Brett—Brett had run the opposite direction. Brett could still be alive.

"Brett!" he yelled until he was hoarse, until no more sounds would come out of his parched throat.

But he heard the yelp. Even through the ringing in his ears, he could hear the whimper of an animal, and he ran, clawing his way through rubble, fingers bleeding until he saw a patch of dark fur and realized it was Ella. He dug so frantically, knowing another IED could go off at any second.

"Ella," he gasped, seeing her fur slick with blood, her leg at an unnatural angle as he carefully lifted her out of the stones and hefted himself to his feet as she cried. And that's when he saw Brett too. His lifeless eyes staring straight back at him, body mangled. Gone.

He gasped, blinking through the dirt in his eyes, trying to unsee his friend's face. Ella whimpered in his arms, and he started walking, putting one foot in front of the other as he carried the dog, refusing to let his body give out on him until he got her to safety. She'd tried to tell them. She'd done her job, but it had all happened too fast.

Logan's horse jittering beneath him jerked him from his thoughts, and he breathed deep as his heart started to hammer away. He needed to blow out the cobwebs, go for a damn good gallop, and keep his memories at bay. The last thing he needed was to tumble back into the past, because they were dangerous memories,

memories that could drive a man crazy. And he had too much to live for.

He had Ella. And he had Brett's family to provide for, to care for, to be there for if they ever needed him.

"Come on, Woody, let's go," he said, nudging him in the side and leaning forward, pushing him into a steady canter. He'd let him stretch out into a gallop when they reached the bigger field.

Logan glanced behind him and saw Ella loping along at her own pace, and he wondered how the hell she was so smart. When she tired, she'd find her own way back to the barn, and he knew he'd return to find her asleep in a puddle of sunshine, unimpressed with the fact that he'd left her for so long.

Angelina opened her laptop and took a deep, shaky breath as she entered the log in and password for her personal banking. She felt like her heart was actually going to stop beating as she stared at the figure. It was almost at zero.

How the hell had she managed to lose so much money? She hadn't been drawing a wage from her business for more than a year, funneling all her own money in to keep it afloat, and now she didn't even have enough to make the utility payments. She fought the urge to access her trust funds, still too stubborn, even at her rock bottom, to draw on them again. What kind of woman would she be if she took the money, if she ignored her failures and simply cashed in on family money? It certainly wasn't something she saw as an option.

Instead, she picked up her phone and decided to do what she'd been meaning to do for weeks. There had been that little voice inside her head telling her that things might come right, that she might find a way to save everything before it all came crashing down, but she'd walked away from her company now and her house was merely collateral damage. She could pay off her outstanding debts and buy or rent something smaller. *Something much smaller.*

Which was exactly why she needed to contact her realtor and see if she couldn't get her place sold as quickly as possible.

"This is Mary from the Oppenheim Group."

Angelina sat up straighter and cleared her throat, switching straight back into work mode.

"Hi, Mary, it's Angelina Ford, how are you?"

"I'm great! How are you?"

"I need you to sell my house," she said, refusing to sound anything other than confident in her instructions, skipping the small talk. "I know I might have to take a hit financially, but I need an offer as soon as you can. I need to put the funds into a new project."

"You want to list it today?"

"Yes. Email me the paperwork, and I'll get my assistant to . . ." Her words trailed off as she realized she no longer had an assistant to delegate to. "I'll have the keys sent to you immediately. I'm in Texas, but they'll be with you as soon as I can get them there."

They went through a few more details, and then she shut her laptop, not wanting to see her emails or be drawn into the web of what had once been. It wasn't worth falling down the rabbit hole and being sucked back in.

"Hey."

Angelina jumped at the sound of Mia's voice. "You frightened the life out of me!"

"Sorry." Mia grimaced, but Angie saw the baby sleeping over her shoulder and realized why she'd been so quiet.

"I didn't mean to eavesdrop, but I was waiting for you and she fell asleep and . . ."

Angelina swallowed. Slowly. But it felt like a lump of stone in her throat. "How much did you hear?"

"I thought you loved that house?" Mia said, her cheeks flushed as if she were embarrassed at being caught out. "You said you'd never sell it, that it was the place you'd always dreamed of."

Angelina forced herself to shrug, even as tears pricked her eyes. "It's just a house, Mia. Real estate is an asset, nothing more, nothing less. Sometimes we have to let things go to make for other opportunities."

Mia looked anything other than convinced. "You're sure?" she asked. "Because if something's going on, if you need to talk—"

"I'm fine. Like I said, it's only real estate. I'm going to buy something else."

Mia didn't look convinced, but Angelina stood and left her laptop on the table beside her bed. As far as she was concerned, the conversation was over.

"Could you believe that dog of Logan's last night?" she asked, trying her best to change the subject. "It's hard to comprehend what she's been through. What they've *both* been through."

Mia nodded, taking the bait. "I know. Sam was really quiet all night. I think it kind of brought a lot of those memories back for him even though it was such a long time ago."

"Does he ever talk to you about it much? His time serving?" She'd thought about Logan a lot since the night before—what he'd been through and how he'd dealt with it. He'd just seemed so . . . *raw*. That was the only way to describe him when he'd been talking about his time in the military. His appearance was more rugged, his disposition different than she remembered. He'd been fun and open to talk to most of the time, but it was also obvious he was holding something back, that there was a darkness lurking there below the surface. It was his eyes that gave it away, the glint that told her not all was as great as it seemed. Maybe it took one to know one.

"Never," Mia said, rocking back and forth as the baby started to stir. "And he told me that we need to go easy on Logan if we start seeing more of him. He said it'll be really raw for him still, especially given that he lost his unit."

"It was really good seeing him again. It's like nothing between us has changed even though everything has, and I know that makes absolutely no sense at all."

"Did you two ever, I don't know, have feelings for each other?" Mia asked.

Angelina pretended not to notice the smile hovering over her sister's lips. "Never," she said firmly. *Well, that's if you don't count the one drunken kiss that we shared.* "He's a gorgeous man, but we started out as friends, you know? Logan's more like a brother to me."

"Only he's not," Mia whispered.

"Not what?"

"Your brother, stupid. He's a gorgeous hulk of a man who happens to be single," she said. "Logan's like a broken bird who needs to be nurtured and loved."

Angelina laughed, slapping her hand over her mouth

when the baby stirred and Mia shot her a sharp look. "I've never saved a baby bird in my life, Mia, and I'm not about to start rescuing them now. I think you've confused me with you."

It was the perfect end to their conversation, and she touched her sister's shoulder as she passed.

"I'll see you later on."

"Where are you going?" Mia asked.

Angelina smiled. "Just into town to run some errands." What she needed was to get out of the house, and taking a look around town seemed like a good starting point. Was it so crazy to think there might be a business opportunity for her here? A business for sale that she could buy and later sell maybe? It was what she'd done as a young businesswoman, buying fledgling small businesses and making them profitable. Starting over that way, with such a small goal, was hard to get her head around, but the only way she was going to get back on her feet was to start at the bottom and build her way back up again.

She needed her house sold, and then she'd have her seed money.

Angelina picked up the keys to one of her dad's cars and headed for the door.

"Ange, wait up!"

She cringed, feeling terrible but hoping her sister wasn't about to say—

"We're coming with you! Sophia's at preschool for the next few hours, and we can have lunch somewhere. I'll just grab Isobel's car seat."

She forced herself to smile. "Of course, that'd be great."

Only it wouldn't be, because what she needed was some time alone to process her scrambled brain full of thoughts. But Mia was her sister, and she was probably finding it hard going from competitive show jumper to stay-at-home mom, so she wasn't about to tell her she couldn't come.

Angelina was doing her best to keep the conversation light, but she was starting to realize her sister was actually enjoying her company. Her sister who'd always been so different to her, who'd always been so busy and focused on her sport, now seemed to like talking to another adult instead of being at home alone with her children.

"Mia, have you thought about getting a nanny?" Angelina asked. Hell, if she were better with children, she might have even applied for the role herself just to have something to do.

"A nanny, why?" Mia asked, clearly perplexed.

"Because you and I have never gotten along so well, and that tells me you need to get back to work. Aren't you going stir-crazy baking and playing with kids all day?"

Mia laughed. Which was better than her going red-faced and angry. "I used to spend my day with my four-legged babies, and now I'm hanging out with my two-legged babies," she said. "I'm used to not putting myself first. Unlike you."

Angelina scoffed. *"Unlike me?* I'm always putting myself second when it comes to my business!"

Her sister looked far from convinced as she cradled her baby. "Yes, but you can do that from the comfort of a plush office or gorgeous house, all the while sipping expensive shakes and still fitting in yoga and eating great food. You don't have someone else needing you more than you need yourself."

She had no answer to that, even though she felt like a wolf with its hackles up.

"My entire life has revolved around my horses, and that's meant getting up early to feed them every day, no matter the weather or how I feel. I've rugged and stabled them in all weather, and I've put their well-being before my own." Mia shrugged. "So parenting has honestly been like an extension of that for me, because I'm used to putting others first and nurturing them. I'm not the most important person in the room, or even in my world."

As if to make her point, she snuggled her daughter, kissing her forehead. "Honestly, this is the best job in the world. It's worth it."

Angelina wasn't entirely convinced. "So, you don't miss the excitement and adrenaline of show jumping? Of being an elite athlete instead of—"

"Of course I miss it," Mia said quietly, at the same time as she fiercely hugged her child. "I miss the ache of my body from pushing myself physically every day, the excitement of working with a young horse and getting them ready to compete. I miss every little thing about it."

"Then why not start riding competitively again?" Angelina asked. "You know the old saying: if Mom is happy, the kids are happy."

"It's different when you're a mom, Angie," Mia said quietly. "You can't understand the emotional pull, the enormous guilt; it's overwhelming sometimes. And I'm prepared to do this for my family. I *want* to do this."

She watched her sister and saw the truth of what she was saying. Angelina had never wanted children, or more, she'd never been one of those women who'd spent their life thinking about being a mom. Maybe she'd imagined it would just happen one day, if and when the time was right, but Mia, well, Mia was right. She'd always been a nurturer, and she was a great mother to her two girls.

"You're right. I don't know what it's like, but I do know what it's like to need an outlet. And for you, that outlet was always riding," she said. "Just promise me that when you're ready to start competing again, you find a way to make it happen. You don't let anyone hold you back, okay? Make sure it's always your choice."

Mia smiled even as tears glinted in her eyes. "Thanks, Ange. I needed to hear that."

"Hello, ladies," a deep drawl said from behind them. "Fancy running into you again."

Angelina felt a familiar warmth wash over her as she recognized the voice. She turned and saw Logan standing there, hands shoved into his jean pockets and a smile on his face that could melt ice.

"Hey, yourself," she said. "What are you doing in town again?"

"Did I not make it clear that I'm useless and end up at the grocery store almost every day?"

Angie laughed. "I thought you were exaggerating."

She couldn't believe he made the drive in every day, but then, maybe he liked coming in and seeing people. She couldn't imagine being on a ranch day in, day out, especially when he'd been used to being part of a team. It was the same as her, facing being alone after so long having a regular team around her all day, every day.

"Unfortunately not."

The baby was fussing, and Logan leaned in close, his lips next to her ear as he spoke. "You need rescuing? I don't remember you as the baby-loving type."

She couldn't help but smile. "I'm not, but she is my

niece so I'm having to make exceptions. I'm not a total ice queen."

"Want to come for dinner tonight? I have my father's wine cellar to make my way through, and I think I mentioned I grill a mean steak."

Angelina nodded, liking the idea of spending more time with Logan. "Sounds good. What time?"

"Any time," he said. "You still remember how to get there?"

She slapped his arm. "Of course I remember. I'll see you later on."

"If I'm not at the house, make your way down to the yards."

Angelina laughed. "Not a chance. If you're not there, I'll start making my way through that wine cellar."

Logan said goodbye and touched Mia's shoulder on his way past, smiling down at her, and Angie watched him walk away. She missed men like him. Men who looked like they could wrangle a grizzly with their rough, work-worn hands, but would leap over hot coals to open a door for a lady. Hard on the outside and soft on the inside, which was virtually the opposite of all the men she usually met.

"Sounds like someone has a date tonight," Mia teased, grinning at Angelina over her coffee cup.

"A date? Don't be silly. We're just friends."

"Two nights in a row?"

"Friends who haven't seen each other in a long time. It's just dinner."

"Yeah, right." Mia laughed. "It's a dinner date and you know it."

"You're lucky you're holding a baby," Angelina muttered.

"Why?'

She shook her head. "It's not a date," she said firmly.

"Sure, okay. It's not a date."

Angelina stifled a groan, trying to convince herself that it most definitely wasn't a date. Or was it?

Chapter 4

ANGELINA stared at herself in the mirror. She'd never tried to impress Logan before, so why was she so worried about her appearance now? She applied a dark pink lipstick and pushed delicate diamond studs into her earlobes, then promptly laughed at herself. She was made-up enough to be having a photo shoot, and she was dressed as if she were on her way to seal the deal on a corporate takeover.

"Knock knock," came a soft voice.

She looked over her shoulder and found Lexi standing there, leaning against the doorjamb.

"Hey," Angelina said, turning to face her. "Everything okay?"

"Everything's fine," she said, smiling. "You look beautiful. Is there a lucky man, or do you always look like that in the evening?"

Angie laughed. "I'm going to Logan's for dinner. But I think I've completely missed the mark, given that we're just hanging out at his place."

Lexi entered the room and stood behind her, as Ange looked back in the mirror.

"May I?" Lexi asked.

Angelina shrugged, not used to letting someone into her personal space like that. She and Mia had always been so different that it wasn't something they'd ever done, but Lexi was as sweet as pie, and she was gorgeous too. Angelina had really warmed to her.

"You look so naturally beautiful, as if you just wake up like that," Ange muttered.

Lexi smirked. "If only you knew how long it took to blow out my hair like this." As she spoke, she reached up and unpinned Angelina's hair until it fell loose around her shoulders. It tumbled haphazardly and Lexi ran her fingers through it and made it fall to one side. Then she passed her a tissue. "Here, blot some of that color off your lips, just a little," she said.

Angelina raised her brows when Lexi unbuttoned her shirt, showing off far more chest than she'd usually show, then proceeded to unbutton and roll up her shirtsleeves too.

"Wow, that actually makes a difference," Angie said, admiring herself in the mirror. "I definitely approve of you as my future sister-in-law."

Lexi's smile was warm. "Pleased to be of assistance."

"You know I already approved of you, though, don't you? After the way you've looked after Dad, it'd be impossible for anyone not to love you."

Angelina blinked away tears, which wasn't easy given that Lexi's eyes were suddenly full of them and reflecting back at her.

"I actually came up looking for you because he wanted to see you," she said. "I hate to say this, but I don't know how much longer he has. He doesn't want any of you to know, but . . ."

Lexi's words trailed off and Angelina watched her, waiting for her to finish.

"What is it?" she whispered.

"His pain levels are worse, and he won't tell me all of it, but after seeing his oncologist the other day, I think he received bad news," Lexi said. "And he's worried about you, for some reason. Thinks there's something not right."

Angie gulped. Trust her father's radar to pick up on her troubles. "He said that?"

Lexi nodded, before asking: "*Are* you all right? I mean, it's none of my business and I know we don't know each other well, but if you need to talk, I'm good at keeping secrets."

Angie considered her. "Thanks, Lexi, but everything's fine." She picked up her bag and dropped her makeup in, in case she needed it later for touch-ups. Lexi might have made her look more natural, but there was no way she was going out without it.

"That time we met at Lauren's, when you were home for Christmas, I was honestly terrified of you," Lexi said.

Angie spun around to face her again. "Terrified? Of me?"

"Well, equal parts terrified and angry, I guess. Angry because I blamed you for encouraging Cody to leave me in the first place, and terrified because you were the opposite of me. Beautiful, successful, wealthy, and confident. You're everything I thought I'd end up being."

Angelina reached out to Lexi, touching her arm. "You don't think you're beautiful or successful?" she asked. "You are all of those things, along with compassionate and genuine, and . . ." She took a deep breath. "Honestly, Lexi, appearances can be deceiving. And I didn't tell him to leave you. I encouraged him to be bold and take every opportunity he could. I didn't know the two of you were so close."

Lexi gave her an impromptu hug and Angie hugged her back, surprised at how nice it felt to be held like that. She should have added warm and loving to the list of endearments too.

"Enjoy your night," Lexi said.

"I will. You staying in or heading out?"

She pulled a face. "I'm staying in and trying to make it up to your brother for leaving him so often."

They walked down the wide staircase together, side by side, and Angelina watched as Lexi waved to her and disappeared out the front door. It was only her and her dad in the house now, and she felt guilty about leaving him. Why had she said yes to Logan when her father was going to be alone? She'd come home to see him, and yet here she was disappearing as soon as a better offer came in.

"Hey, Daddy," she said as she entered.

"Hello, darling. You look beautiful tonight." He looked her up and down. "I like the new look."

She only smiled, not telling him it was the brainchild of his favorite nurse.

"I was heading out, but I think I'll stay in with you now," she said, settling down on the sofa beside him. "We can binge-watch something on Netflix."

He patted her hand. "Not a chance. This old man is ready to sleep. You go out and enjoy being young."

She hesitated. "You're sure?"

"I'm sure. But I do have a question before you go."

Angelina froze. She reminded herself to keep breathing, dreading what he was about to say.

"My workaholic daughter has been home for more

than twenty-four hours, and yet you've been more interested in heading into town and cooking than working. What's going on?"

She gulped. "I'm trying to enjoy some downtime, that's all."

"I'm no fool, Ange. You haven't mentioned work since you arrived here, and you're usually holed up in here telling me all about your latest project and tapping furiously away at your laptop at all hours of the day and night."

"Honestly, Dad," she said, rising and placing her hand on his shoulder. "Everything's fine. I'm trying to disconnect for a few days, that's all."

He clasped her hand, holding her there as he looked up at her. "You're sure?"

She nodded and kissed the top of his head. "I'm sure."

Angelina tucked his blanket around him and made sure his water and the control for the central heating were within reach. Then she turned off the lights, leaving only the lamp going, watching him for a few moments before closing the door behind her.

It was only a matter of time before he'd either figure it out, or she'd have to tell him, but she wasn't ready yet. She hurried into the kitchen and found a bottle of wine to take to Logan's, and five minutes later she was in her father's Range Rover and heading down the River Ranch driveway.

Logan had just stepped out into the fading sunlight when Ella signaled they had a visitor. She'd never rush out to greet anyone, but she would always let out one loud *woof* to tell him they had company. Sometimes he wondered if she could even hear her own bark now that she was almost deaf.

"Good girl," he said, touching her head as he passed before wiping his hands down his jeans. He'd intended on showering and changing before Angelina arrived, but his afternoon had ended up more difficult than usual.

"Hey," he called out, as Angelina stepped out of her father's car and waved.

Damn. He admired the long legs clad in skintight jeans and the way her hair was all long and beachy. He was used to her looking so perfectly, over-the-top put together, but there was something about her looking more casual that caught his attention. Her sleeves were rolled up, tanned arms on show along with an impressive-looking diamond Rolex, and she was wearing expensive-looking sneakers instead of her usual sky-high heels. He chuckled as he walked closer, realizing her height was actually an illusion. She wasn't short by any means, but without her stilettos, she wasn't even close to his six-foot-three.

"Glad to see you dressed up for me," she said, grinning and holding out a bottle of wine. "On second thought, I'll keep hold of this until you've washed up."

He glanced down as she wrinkled her nose, realizing he was covered in more than mud.

"Is that poop?"

"'Fraid to say it is," he said, grimacing at how he must look. "I've got a good excuse, though." He noticed Ella was staring up at him, waiting for a command, and he pointed at Angie so the dog knew she could greet her.

"There's a valid excuse to be covered in poop?" she asked, bending to stroke Ella.

"I have a few late cows still calving. We're usually done by June, but this year we had . . ." He laughed at the expression on her face. "Sorry, forgetting you're not a *rancher* as such. Let's just say I had to help birth a calf today, and I got a little dirty in the process."

Ange shook her head. "You lost me at birth. Please don't ask me to go down to the barn to help."

He held out his arm and walked closer. "Come on, give me a hug. You know you want to."

"Eewww!" She leapt out of the way. "Don't even think about it."

"What's that saying: you can take the girl away from the ranch but you can't take the ranch out of the girl?"

She sighed. "You know that saying doesn't apply to me."

"Yeah, but you're so fun to tease." He jogged ahead of her and opened the front door, gesturing for her to enter as he kicked off his boots.

"Your mom would have a heart attack if she knew you were doing that here and not around the back."

"I know, but considering they landed me in this position, I'm doing it anyway."

Logan fell into step beside Angelina, liking the fact that his filthy appearance rattled her so much. She'd always been so fun to tease, and he was starting to see that some things simply didn't change.

"Make yourself at home, I'm going to go change."

"And shower," she said with a grin.

Logan winked and watched as Ella looked between them, deciding to stay with Angelina. It was nice to see the dog settling into civilian life—hell, she was doing a better job of it than he was.

He went into his room and stripped down, tossing his clothes into a pile and walking naked into the adjoining bathroom. It didn't take him a minute to get into the shower, and soon he was standing beneath a stream of hot water, the steam rising around him.

He leaned against the tiled wall, letting the water run down his back, smiling to himself as he thought about Ange waiting for him. She'd been a silver lining for him, getting to see her again after all this time, and it had certainly lifted his spirits. The closer he got to Brett's anniversary, the day he'd died, the harder it was to keep the memories at bay, so his old friend had been a welcome distraction.

He soaped his body and lathered up his hair, finally stepping out of the shower and toweling off, before going in search of clean clothes.

"Logan?"

He spun around at Angelina's soft voice and found her standing hesitantly at his open door. Her eyes widened and he glanced down, pleased that he at least had his jeans on even if his chest was bare.

"Get bored waiting for me?" he asked.

She held out a phone he hadn't even noticed her holding. "I hope you don't mind, but I answered the phone."

He took it and wished he hadn't. Because these were the phone calls that broke his heart, and sometimes he wondered if he'd ever be able to move on from the past.

Logan reached for it, fingers brushing past Angelina's. There was a chance it could be his folks, but he doubted it. Especially at this time of the day, when they were probably sipping cocktails with other retirees, and besides, his mother would have talked Angelina's ear off if it were her.

"Can you give me a minute?" Logan asked, voice low.

"I don't think it's a lover," Angelina teased.

He just shook his head slightly, and she backed down, nodding and walking away. But he didn't miss the hurt look in her eyes and the quick fade of her smile.

"Hello," he said.

"It's me."

"Hi, darling, how are you?" He smiled sadly as he listened to the little voice on the other end. It was so sweet, so innocent, and every time he heard it, it almost broke him in two.

"We have a daddy-daughter dance at school in two weeks. Can you come?"

"Yes, darlin', I'll be there. You get Mom to send me all the details."

"Okay. Bye."

He waited, knowing her mom would come on the line. He cleared his throat, choking up just thinking about the dance he'd been asked to go to.

"Logan?"

"Hey, Kelly, how are you?"

"I'm good. Sorry she called you out of the blue like that. You know how she gets when she wants to talk to you."

"It's fine. We still on for our date?" he asked. "It's been a while, and I'm looking forward to having a day with her."

He could almost hear her nodding on the other end of the line. "Of course. Lucy would kill me if I cancelled."

"And how are you? How are you really doing? No bullshit, tell it to me straight."

"I'm fine, Logan. Honestly, we're doing great," she said, but he could hear the heaviness in her voice, the weight of what rested on her shoulders now. "I'll see you next week. We're both looking forward to it."

Logan hung up the phone, wishing he could do more, that he could be better at seeing Lucy, even though looking into those beautiful big blue eyes almost broke his heart sometimes. He left the phone on his bed and finished getting dressed, before walking out to find Angelina. He bypassed her bottle of wine and went looking for something stronger, returning with a bottle of whiskey.

"What do you say?" he asked, holding it up. "For old time's sake?"

Angelina shook her head and laughed. "By all means, go ahead, but I'm starting with wine."

Logan took a wine glass down for her and a tumbler for himself, opening the wine and pouring hers, before dropping ice into his, followed by a big slug of whiskey.

"Cheers," Angelina said, clinking her glass to his as she stood on the other side of the kitchen counter.

"Cheers," Logan said, taking a sip, enjoying the sensation of the liquor trailing down his throat and pooling like fire in his belly. He watched her tip her head back slightly as she sipped her wine, the smooth, tanned skin on her neck, the way her eyes closed as she swallowed. "Now tell me, Ange, and no bullshit this time. Why the hell are you really back in Texas?"

Her eyes met his, warm but strong, cutting through him. And right there, he saw why she'd been so successful, the way she stared straight back at him without even a hint of intimidation. She was the kind of woman who wasn't afraid of anything, and it showed.

Angelina took another sip of wine, buying time. She wasn't about to confess to Logan, but at the same time, she knew he wasn't going to fall for any lies. He was smarter than that, and they'd known each other too well in the past to fall for any crap.

"The longer you hesitate, the more I know I'm right."

She sighed. "Honestly, I don't know why you think

there's anything going on. I'm just here to see Dad and spend some time at home. Maybe I'm feeling a little burnt out."

He narrowed his eyes, and when he moved around the counter and headed for the sofa, dropping down into it, she thought the matter was over. But as Ella sat at his feet, and he touched a hand to her head, he looked up, eyes bright and searching her out. She wasn't cracking, sticking to her story that nothing was wrong, but he wasn't buying it for a second.

"Is it a man? You can tell me. I know damn well what it's like to have your heart broken." Logan groaned. "Did you find him in bed with someone else? Did he refuse to sign a prenup?"

Angelina tried to stifle her laugh but failed. "None of the above, but I appreciate your concern about my affairs of the heart." In fact, she wished she were nursing a broken heart. It'd be much easier to deal with than what she was going through. "I'm a stone-cold bitch when it comes to money, Logan. There's no way I'd marry a man who refused to sign a prenup."

"So he did cheat, then?"

She threw her hands up in the air. "There is no *he*, Logan. I don't have a partner and I haven't had one for . . ." She had to think about that. "Let's just say it's been a busy few years at work. Actually it's been a busy decade."

He had the gall to laugh. "Okay. So it's work-related, then. For God's sake, Ange, tell me. I spend my days here on my own, with my dog for company and sometimes the other ranch hands. I'm not exactly going to gossip to someone."

She hesitated then took a big sip of wine, holding out her glass to Logan. "You need to believe me. Nothing's going on. The only problem I have right now is that I need a refill."

He stood and retrieved the wine bottle, filling her glass to the halfway mark again and setting the bottle down on the coffee table. This time, however, he sat beside her, his knee colliding with hers as he studied her.

"You've got a secret, Ange, and I'm not giving up until you tell me."

She touched his hand, looking into his eyes as she leaned forward. Two could play at this game, and she knew the second she pressed Logan for information, he'd back the hell up.

"If you're so interested in talking, how about telling me who the little girl was on the phone before? The one you had to speak to without me listening in?" she asked. It was a double-edged question—she was desperately curious and wanted to know more anyway.

Logan's gaze darkened, his eyes like a storm cloud as his eyebrows pulled low. He took a big slug of whiskey, downing the rest of the glass. "I don't want to talk about her."

"Really?" she said, raising her own brows as he scowled. "So you want to know everything about me, but you don't want to tell me a thing about why *you're* really home, and whether that little girl has anything to do with it?"

"Leave it, Ange," he muttered. "Whatever the hell fickle thing you're going through and what I've been through, what brought me home, are nowhere near the same."

Her cheeks flamed then, blood boiling as she stared back at him. It would have been so easy to let it slip, but then, that would be admitting what a failure she was. "Fuck you, Logan."

His scowl turned into a grin. "Yeah, well fuck you too, Little Miss Princess. I'm glad we're finally talking openly."

Angelina lifted her leg and kicked him, laughing when he grabbed her ankle, making her squeal as she almost sloshed the entire contents of her wine glass over herself. They kept laughing until she thought she was going to cry. But then she did cry.

Tears slipped down her cheeks, and she frantically tried to brush them away, blinking fast, but not fast enough. Logan's face had changed, his cocky, arrogant grin replaced by something that resembled horror. Or maybe it was pity.

"Hey, Ange, I'm sorry," he said, leaning forward and grabbing hold of her hand. "I didn't mean to push you so hard.'

"It's not you," she managed, horrified as a sob erupted from her. All these months of trying to keep her shit together, of putting on a brave face, and now she was going to fall apart in front of Logan? What the hell was wrong with her?

"Darlin', you can tell me. Honestly, teasing aside, you can talk to me," he said softly.

She shook her head. "I'm fine. Honestly, I don't know where that came from."

He was watching her like he didn't buy her excuses for a second, but to his credit, he kept his mouth shut and didn't keep pushing her.

"How the hell did we both end up back here like this?" she asked, shaking her head. "I mean, who would have thought, all these years later, we'd be commiserating together on your ranch?"

"Ahh, so she finally admits she's commiserating over something," Logan said, on his feet for more whiskey, smile back on his face. When he returned, he also had a bag of chips with him that he dropped on the sofa between them.

"Maybe I am, maybe I'm not. But I sure as hell didn't come here to cry over my problems." She sniffed and shook her head, as if that alone would get rid of the multitude of tears she'd been storing.

"Well, good, because the last thing I feel like doing is wiping up your tears and your snotty nose. I did enough of that in high school," he said dryly.

Angelina smiled, loving that he'd chosen to ignore her tears and treat her like he always had. If he'd opened his arms and enveloped her in a hug, she'd probably never have stopped bawling.

"Bullshit!" she protested. "I was never a crier."

"Except for the time Billy broke your heart."

Billy Elderman. Man, that was a name she hadn't thought of in a long while. And Logan wasn't wrong; she had cried over him. In fact, he was the first and last guy she'd shed tears over.

"I challenge you to a game," he said, opening the chips and holding them out to her. She never ate junk food usually, but given she was technically on vacation, and the flavor smelled so damn good, she decided it wouldn't hurt.

"What's the game?" she asked, kicking her shoes off and curling her feet up under her as she sat back against the plump cushions and watched him.

The look on Logan's face said it all. "Truth or dare," he said. "Starting with you."

She polished off the rest of her wine, drinking more in the past half hour than she usually consumed in an entire evening. "If we're playing truth or dare, we're going to need a lot more alcohol."

Logan's laugh was belly deep. "I've never heard truer words in all my life. Now tell me, is your drink of choice still tequila?"

"Not since 2009, but I suppose we're walking down memory lane, so why the hell not?"

His laughter was loud as he rose again, coming back a few minutes later with a bottle of tequila on a tray, alongside two shot glasses, salt, and some lemons. A shiver ran up her spine at the thought of drinking liquor straight, her stomach churning, but she wasn't going to back down now. Maybe alcohol was exactly what the doctor ordered.

"Are we still eating dinner?" she asked. "I could have picked up food on the way, you know. I'll get so drunk on an empty stomach."

"You have chips. You'll be fine," he said. "And it's your turn first."

"Dare," she said, not about to fall for his tricks and have to spill the beans on all her closely guarded secrets.

"You seriously think dare is better than truth?" he asked. "Sure, then, let's go. I dare you to come back to-morrow and go horseback riding with me."

Angelina laughed. "That's not how this game works!"

His eyes travelled slowly up, then even slower down, her body, and the air suddenly changed between them. "You want me to ask you a question instead?"

She reached for the salt and licked her hand, pouring a small amount before licking it off and knocking back her first tequila, followed by a quick suck of lemon. "Holy shit," she said, coughing as she tried to catch her breath. "I don't know how I used to drink them so easily!"

He grinned and poured her another one, clearly still waiting for her response as he stared at her.

"And the answer is yes, I'll go horseback riding tomorrow."

"Do you even have clothes to ride in?" he asked.

"I'm wearing perfectly good riding attire right now," she announced, wiggling her toes as she looked down at herself. "Except for my shoes, that is."

Logan moved closer to her after he retrieved his shot glass and downed his first one, pouring another for each of them. His weight changed the feel of the sofa as he leaned back beside her. He lifted her legs up and placed them over his knees, and she startled, not used to such familiarity. But it was Logan. What was weird about Logan touching her? He'd touched her plenty in the past, and she'd never once felt weird about it then.

"Come on, your turn to ask me," he said. She was surprised at how much he was drinking. He'd never been a full-on drinker when they were younger, but he seemed to be eager to consume his alcohol tonight.

"Truth or dare?" she asked, her voice barely more than a whisper.

"Truth."

"Are you drinking so much because of the little girl on the phone before?"

His stare was like stone. "Pass. Next question."

"Logan!"

"Next goddamn question, or I'll ask you about why the hell you're really here again."

Angelina took her second shot when he did, refusing to react to the burning taste this time, even though it stunned her as intensely as the first one had. She wasn't a seasoned drinker, other than having a regular glass of wine with dinner, and she'd already consumed more than she had in years.

"Do you want to be back here? On the ranch?" she asked him.

Logan's hand fell to her leg. "I dreamed of nothing else when I was away on my last tour, but then coming back here, it was"—he paused—"it was damn hard. Just coming back home, being expected to, I don't know, to be a regular civilian again after what we've been through. It's rough."

"Have you talked to anyone? I mean, a therapist or anything?"

He dropped his gaze then, his fingers suddenly strumming across her jean-clad leg. She squirmed, the touch feeling so intimate and making goose bumps spread like wildfire across her skin.

"Yeah, I still do. But that's another thing that fires me up—the fact that I'm privileged enough to afford help, when so many others aren't. If they even make it home in the first place."

She listened to him, watching as he reached for his drink and drained the glass. She wondered how often he was drinking, whether he was doing it every night to help numb whatever pain he was feeling. Or maybe it was just tonight. She hoped it was just tonight.

"Truth," she said bravely, hoping she could take his mind off whatever he was lost in.

Logan's eyes met hers. "Do you regret leaving here, or do you think we did the right thing?"

She took another drink, starting to feel the effects. Her mind was a little cloudy, the edge taken off her pain and her thoughts. No wonder so many people turned to alcohol when they were suffering—she didn't want to make a habit of it, but she was sure feeling better right now than she had in a long time.

"What was here for me?" she said. "Nothing, that's

what. In California, I built a life for myself, I went to college and did an internship, and then I jumped straight into my own business. It was the best thing I ever did, even if . . ."

"Even if what?" he asked, not missing a beat.

She swallowed down another shot of tequila. "Even if things haven't always been easy," she finished, deciding that it was about time she stopped the addictive combination of salt, tequila, and lemon.

"Truth," Logan said, as he poured two more shots.

"Have you ever been in love?"

His laugh was more of a grunt, and she watched as his eyes lifted, sparkling as his lips moved. "Maybe."

She swallowed, feeling like there had been a shift between them. She tried to shake it off, not used to being . . . She didn't even know what she felt. Uncomfortable? Unsure? This was Logan, what was there to be unsure about?

"How can you not know?"

He shrugged. "If it had turned into something, it might have been love, but it didn't. So it wasn't."

The air between them had definitely changed, and Angelina took a little sip of her drink for courage. Maybe she was drunk and not used to the light-headedness that came with it. So much for not drinking anymore.

"Truth," she said bravely, thinking that it might be the last time she responded this way to the game. But there was something about being with Logan that almost made her want to spill the beans and just be honest with someone she trusted.

His eyes never left hers even as he drank, like he was chewing over a question and trying to decide whether to ask it or not.

"Do you ever think about that night we kissed?"

Angie choked on her drink, sputtering as she gasped for air. "Logan! We said we'd never mention it again."

"We were eighteen," he said, not missing a beat, his eyes still leveled on hers, not giving up. "I think we can break our little promise now that we're all grown up, don't you?"

"No," she said, blinking and looking down at her hands. "Of course I don't."

"You're lying."

She downed the rest of her drink, shaking her head. "Do you?"

"This was your truth, not mine."

Angelina stared into her empty glass, going straight back in time, remembering the night, remembering every single thing about it. She remembered the taste of beer on Logan's lips, the gentle way he'd pressed into her, the warmth of his arms, the trust in his eyes as he stared down at her. But it had quickly been replaced with horror as they'd both realized the line they'd crossed, and they'd jumped back, mumbling and apologizing and swearing to pretend like it had never happened.

But that was then, and this was now.

"I haven't thought about it in a long time, but I'm sure as hell thinking about it right now," Logan said softly, and his fingers suddenly grazed her knee, his gaze finally dropping a little. "And I have a crazy feeling that maybe you are too."

She breathed deep, holding out her glass for another refill, but Logan took her glass and placed it on the coffee table alongside his. She was only without his eyes on her for a heartbeat, but it was long enough for her to know that when he looked back, there was going to be a hunger in his gaze that she'd only ever seen once before. Back then, it had only led to a kiss—a passionate, toe-tingling kiss, but still only a kiss. One they'd regretted instantly. But this time, there was no reason for them *not* to touch.

"We're still friends," she murmured as he turned back to her. "We promised never to do anything to jeopardize that."

Logan's hand cupped her face, and he leaned in closer to her, his gaze soft as he stared into her eyes. "We're not best friends anymore, Ange. It's been over a year since we even sent each other an email."

She gulped. "But . . ."

"You have secrets you don't want to tell me, and I sure as hell don't want to tell you mine," he said, his voice low, gravelly and sexy as hell. "But I can think of one thing that'll take our minds off everything."

Angelina saw his gaze fall to her lips, and in that nanosecond, she knew she wasn't going to bother resisting him. *Screw it.* She'd had a bad few months, but Logan was right, there was something that could make life feel a little better again, at least for the night. And he was sitting right in front of her, looking at her mouth like he was ready to devour her.

"We can't ever go back from this," she whispered, exhaling as she resisted the urge to reach for him and tug him closer.

"You'll be gone within the week," Logan replied as he inched closer. "Maybe we won't want to go back anyway. But the way I see it, we might not even cross paths again, so why the hell not?"

She wasn't about to tell him just how wrong he might be.

Chapter 5

LOGAN shifted his weight forward as he felt the change in Ange. When she'd asked him earlier if he'd ever loved anyone, he'd answered honestly. He just hadn't told her that the person he could have loved was her. But he knew that whatever they might have felt for each other, it would never have worked out. She was ambitious and determined to make a name for herself anywhere but here, and he had been as steadfast in his decision to turn his back on ranching and make a career for himself in the military.

Yet here they both were again, him back ranching with enough memories to haunt him until his final days, and Angelina mysteriously back home and refusing to say why.

But none of that mattered. What mattered was the fact that Angelina was moving closer toward him, and unlike the last time it had happened, he wasn't going to back out. She was in the driver's seat now; it was her decision whether they were taking this further—he was simply a willing participant along for the ride.

Which meant that her words were like music to his ears.

"Kiss me," she murmured, her fingers sliding around the back of his head as she moved closer.

Logan didn't need to be asked twice. He stroked his fingertips against her cheek, still cupping her face. He'd thought for a long time about what he'd do if he ever got a second chance with Angelina, berating himself for not just declaring his feelings back then. But it had been obvious she'd thought of him as nothing more than a friend. Or so he'd thought.

Logan touched his lips to hers, going slow, not wanting to rush things even though he'd drunk way too much in the past hour. The whiskey wasn't dulling his senses though—if anything, it was making him feel like fire was surging through his veins as he used every inch of self-control to slow himself down.

Her lips parted willingly, mouth opening and moving against his. Her fingers pressed into the back of his head, and he shuffled closer, arms encircling her, palms pressed to her slender back. The silk of her shirt—the one he'd teased her for being far too fancy for ranch life—was so soft, it made her even more enticing, and he decided he'd never complain about her choice in clothing ever again.

She pulled back for a second, staring at him, her gaze on his mouth as she spoke. "You're sure we should be doing this?"

Logan laughed as he kept hold of her, guiding her forward, smiling as she climbed onto his lap despite her questioning whether they should even be in this position.

"I don't think I've ever been so sure about anything before," he murmured, not wanting to waste another moment talking when he could be feasting on her pillowy lips.

Angelina's hair fell like a silk curtain against his face as she sat astride him, her body warm and supple, as she seemed to melt into him. Logan's hands were on her hips now, palms splayed as he sat back and let her take charge, happy to follow her lead. She was kissing him gently, as if she were tasting him, plucking at his lips over and over, but it didn't last long. Then, her tongue touched his, more urgently than before, colliding with his in a dance that left him breathless.

He skimmed his hands up her back, feeling her body, reaching to stroke her hair that still fell around them like a sensuous wave.

How the hell had they managed to stay platonic friends for so long with a spark like this between them?

Logan tried to slow down, but Angelina was driving him wild, her thighs clamping around him, her lips so warm and insistent, her hips in his hands . . . He slid his fingertips up to her shoulders then slowly back down again, stopping at the first button on her shirt. He waited a second, giving her the chance to say no, but she didn't. And so he carried on, impatiently popping her buttons, until they were all undone.

She sat back then, looking down at him, her lips plump and pink from all the kissing, her chest rising and falling as she caught her breath. He'd always thought she was beautiful, but looking at her right now . . . his eyes left her face and trailed down her golden skin to her lace-covered breasts. Her nipples were hard and he lifted his hands to cup them, loving the weight against his palms, thumbs seeking out her nipples and gently caressing them.

Her head tipped back then, which sent her body closer toward him. Logan didn't hesitate, he leaned in and covered her breast with his mouth, tracing his tongue over the hard peaks that were teasing him. He wanted the lace off, wanted her bare, but from her moans, she seemed to be liking the sensation of his tongue over the lace, so he kept going.

His hands were planted on her lower back, locking her in place, and when she finally tipped her head forward again, he could see the pleasure-drunk look on her face.

"You're sure about this?" he managed, his voice more of a growl than his usual tone.

Her lids were hooded as she rocked harder into him. "Oh, I'm sure."

Logan chuckled and reached around her, pushing her shirt off her shoulders and unclasping her bra. He blew out a low whistle when her breasts were bare, rounded and full, her nipples as pink as rosebuds. He went to touch them again, but she moved too fast, pulling in closer to him and kissing him again. But it was her fingers on his shirt now, her mouth still playing across his as she undid every button and finally sat back again.

"You want this off?" He laughed. "You only had to ask."

He didn't waste time stripping his shirt off so they were both bare-chested, and he sucked in a breath when she tugged him upright, her breasts warm against him as she wrapped her arms around him and kissed him all over again. She alternated between soft and whispering to more insistent with every taste, and every change in pace only seemed to make him more excited about her naked body.

Logan tried to move, but they were so low on the

sofa, it was almost impossible. He grunted and pushed up to his feet, taking her with him in his arms. Angelina laughed and locked her legs around his waist as he stumbled forward, feeling his muscles contract as he took her weight and walked down the hall.

"Where are we going?" she murmured against his mouth, biting gently at his lower lip.

"Bite me again and I'll drop you," he muttered, squeezing her butt in his hands.

She squealed and laughed, and within minutes they were edging into his bedroom.

"We're going somewhere more comfortable," he said as he made for the bed, but Angelina's hand against his crotch made him groan, and instead of getting to the bed, he ended up swiveling and pressing her against the wall. She leaned herself hard against him, squirming against his erection and making it impossible for him to think straight, to go slow like he'd wanted to. She slipped down, fumbling with his jeans, and he did the same with hers, undoing the top button and trying to inch them lower.

Angelina pulled her jeans down and kicked them off just as he was stepping out of his jeans, and the look she was giving him . . . He stared back at her, swallowing hard, seeing her rapid breath, the way her mouth was parted, the hunger in her eyes.

Maybe they were both trying to avoid something, to find a release instead of having to talk about whatever the hell was going on in both their lives. Whatever it was, he didn't care, because it was obvious she wanted him as much as he wanted her right now.

He moved closer, breathing, waiting, before reaching and scooping her up, smiling against her skin as she looped those beautiful long legs around his waist again, rocking into him hard, mouth finding his, and moaning against his lips.

Suddenly there was no time to wait.

Angelina reached down and shoved his boxers out of the way, kissing his neck, her breath hissing out as she struggled to position herself.

"Shit," he swore, stopping despite the fact that he was now pressing against her panties and ready to rip them off her. "Protection."

She groaned, legs still locked around him as he spun them and walked over to the bed. She was sucking hard at his neck now, wet lips driving him wild, but he stopped at the edge of his bed and lowered her.

Angelina groaned again as he left her, but he wasn't planning on leaving her for long. He fumbled in the drawer and, thank God, found a condom at the back, tearing it open and sliding it on.

Fingernails traced down his back, and he turned around, seeing laughter shining in Angelina's eyes.

"You sure that's not a decade old?" she asked. "I'm guessing unused from high school years."

Logan chuckled. "I cannot confirm or deny that."

"Maybe you kept it there all these years, hoping to seduce me one day?" she whispered, crawling away from him on the bed.

Logan reached for her, stretching out and grabbing her arm. He laughed when she squealed, pinning her down and covering her with his body weight.

"That'll teach you for teasing me," he murmured, grunting when she shoved him. He let her push him over, happy to be her plaything.

Logan had intended on pleasuring her. He'd intended on taking things slow. And then he'd intended on taking her against the wall where they'd been positioned before.

But just like that, Angelina was astride him, her head tipped back, golden hair falling all the way down her back as she slid herself on top of him, and rode him like the CEO she was.

What the hell am I doing? Angelina looked down at the most gorgeous specimen of man beneath her, his skin golden, body muscled, his hands on her hips. But this wasn't just some hot guy, this was Logan.

She pushed the thoughts away, not about to start second-guessing herself during the most exquisite moment she'd experienced in a long time. How the hell she'd never thought of him like this before, though . . . She groaned as he moved beneath her, shutting her eyes and throwing her head back again as she felt all the tension inside of her building into the most incredible climax.

Angelina planted her hands on Logan's chest, riding through wave after wave of pleasure. And when she finally slowed, rocking ever so gently back and forth above him, she opened her eyes and stared down.

"Well, that was unexpected," he said, making them both burst out laughing.

"Yeah, you can say that again," she murmured, leaning down and kissing him, feeling more comfortable planting her mouth on his than trying to think of anything else to say. Because this, *this* had changed everything between them.

When she finally came up for air and slipped off him, curling up beside him instead, Logan's arm found its way around her, and they just lay there, both breathing heavily. It should have felt weird, they'd known each other for such a long time, but for some reason it felt so right.

"We should have done that years ago," Logan said as his fingers skimmed back and forth across her skin.

Angelina bit down on her lower lip, embarrassed and happy at the same time.

"I kind of never thought of you like that," she admitted. "Although after we kissed, I kept wondering . . ."

His laughter was deep and chesty as he turned on his side, pushed up on one elbow and stared down at her. "I thought of you like that *a lot*," he admitted, one eyebrow raised and making it impossible for her to know if he was joking or being serious.

"But you never made a move on me," she said. "Except that one time."

"I suppose I thought you were out of my league in the end, and when I kissed you, I waited for you to continue but you pulled back."

She sighed. "Why does this feel so good? We should both be feeling remorseful about ruining our friendship right now."

He stroked her face, and she looked up into his eyes, seeing a softness, a vulnerability that hadn't been there before.

"It feels right because we both needed it. I get the feeling you've been through something, and I've lived through a lot of shit these past couple of years." He smiled. "Maybe this is simply two friends helping each other through a rough patch."

She pushed up just enough to catch his mouth in a sweet, soft kiss. "I think you're right."

But Logan wasn't about to let her kiss him like that and get away with it. It was clear he wanted more, that his appetite hadn't been sated at all. His palm suddenly covered her breast, his touch gentle enough to send goose bumps through her as her skin came to life. And his lips met hers again, slow and lazy, so she tucked her arms around his neck and tugged him over her.

Logan covered her body with his, his weight heavy and warm against her as she hooked one leg around him. She could feel him getting hard again, and she hummed with anticipation. Maybe it was the alcohol still surging through her, giving her more confidence in the bedroom than she'd had before, but she wasn't about to waste an opportunity to make love to Logan again. They'd already done it once, so what was the harm in one more time?

And who would have thought it would be the best form of stress relief? Not to mention taking her mind off everything that had been circling on repeat for the past week.

The pace was slow this time, more languid and without the haste of before, and she let herself enjoy every second of his hands on her body. Time stood still as he kissed her, over and over again, his mouth only leaving her lips to trail a warm, wet path down her neck and collarbone, stopping over her breasts.

Heat pooled inside of her as he sucked on her nipple, his mouth sending pulses of pleasure through her as she rocked upwards, both legs locked around his hips now as he moved to her other breast.

Angelina groaned with pleasure as he rocked inside of her again, mouth against his shoulder as she slid her nails down his back.

"You ruined all the fun I had planned for you," he whispered, trying to pull out. But she didn't let him, keeping her grip with her legs tight around him.

"Don't," she panted. "Stop."

Logan laughed and pushed up higher, on his knees

now, and she closed her eyes and lost herself to his touch, her head spinning as his hands stroked her breasts.

If this wasn't heaven, then she didn't know what was.

"Morning."

Angelina blinked, her head pounding as she stared at the white ceiling above her. Logan. Sex. Last night.

Oh my freaking God, I had sex with Logan.

She swallowed, her mouth dry, slowly turning to face him and pulling the sheets up with her to cover her breasts. "Morning," she croaked.

"I think we might have had a little too much to drink last night."

She laughed. "Um, yeah, I think we might have."

"And I have to apologize for not actually cooking you dinner. I was a terrible host."

Logan's lips hovered upwards into a smile, and she laughed, pulling the sheets even higher and covering her face.

"I'm so embarrassed!" she moaned. "I can't believe you've seen me naked now."

Logan laughed. "Darlin', I've more than *seen* you naked."

She kept her face hidden, knowing her cheeks would be blazing red given how hot they felt. Maybe she could just stay here a while longer, and he would eventually get up and leave the room.

"Why are you hiding?" he asked, his hand finding hers beneath the covers and sliding all the way up her arm.

She resisted the urge to jerk back, knowing she was being stupid, and then his fingertips were so soft and light that she melted and ended up wanting to move even closer to him.

"I've always loved you like a brother," she whispered. "And now . . ."

"I don't think you should use that analogy again." When she peeked out, he was grinning, and suddenly all her embarrassment disappeared. "The whole *brother* thing seems pretty weird given what we've done now."

"Is our friendship going to survive this?" she asked, inwardly cringing. She was definitely never going to use that word to describe him again!

"It's survived years of not seeing each other," he said, and she wriggled closer to him, still keeping the sheet firmly against her breasts. Logan leaned in gently and pressed a kiss to her lips. "To be honest, I think I prefer this. We both lead different lives. You're only here for what, a few more days? We know this is only sex, right? A release we both needed."

"This seemed so much easier last night," she cringed, feeling so overwhelmingly self-conscious in the light of day.

Logan must have sensed her hesitation, because when he pulled back this time, he was frowning.

"What's wrong? Was it not just sex?" He stroked her face, pushing hair back from where it was clinging to her skin. "I didn't mean that to sound callous, Ange. You know I love you. It's not that I don't care deeply for you. I just meant that—"

"No, it's not that," she said quickly. "We mean a lot to each other, but you're right, it was fun and nothing more. We both needed it, but we're still only friends. With temporary benefits."

He was studying her, his expression serious now. "Then what?"

"It's, well, I don't know if I'm only here for a few days. I have . . ." Her sentence trailed off. "I have some things going on, and I might be here longer than expected." She was so close to telling him, but in the end the words didn't make it out of her mouth. "And I'm not sure about you seeing me naked in the daylight!"

"Like a week? A few weeks?" he asked, before giving her a wicked smile. "And I wouldn't worry at all about that other thing."

Angelina knew her cheeks would be bright red, but she chose to ignore that last comment. "Maybe a few weeks, maybe even longer, and I don't want things to become awkward between us while I'm here."

His hand was suddenly on her again beneath the sheets, skimming over her hip before finding a home on her butt. "Then why don't we just enjoy it?" he whispered. "For however long it ends up being?"

Angelina felt her body start to hum again, blanketed by the pleasure that was so distinctly Logan. She hadn't been with a man in way too long, and Logan? He was something else entirely. Gentle but without treating her like she was breakable, his touch so light yet so full of passion.

But it felt different being naked with him with the lights on, making her more self-conscious. Because he wasn't some random, gorgeous man she was having a one-night stand with, he was a man she'd known for most of her life.

"Want to go under the covers?" he asked, coaxing the sheets from her tightly gripped fingers and pulling them over both their heads.

Ange giggled and slipped beneath them with him, suddenly forgetting all about her shyness as she resumed her exploration of the night before and lost herself to Logan's touch.

Chapter 6

LOGAN stood in the kitchen and listened out for Angelina. He was torn. Last night had been a lot of fun—it had been goddamn amazing—but deep down he was as worried as Ange was about what they'd done. Had they ruined their friendship in the space of twelve hours? Because when she'd arrived for dinner, she'd been definitely in the friend camp, and now he doubted he could ever look at her again without imagining her naked. And imagining how good that naked body felt against his.

He groaned.

"I think we're on the same page there. I'd prefer an intravenous drip filled with caffeine, but a cup's a good start."

He slowly turned around, coffee mug in hand, to find Ange standing in the open doorway, wet hair falling around her shoulders, and wearing one of his plaid shirts. The only disappointing thing was the fact she was wearing her jeans beneath it. She didn't look like the Angelina he knew either; she looked vulnerable, and he wasn't sure if it was the fact she wasn't wearing her usual full face of makeup and high heels, or if it was a change in her expression. Maybe it was a mixture of both.

"I don't know if we've been truthful with each other, Ange," he said, smiling when she walked up to him and stood on tiptoe, pressing a kiss to his cheek. He laughed when she stole his coffee mug and took a sip, sighing as if it were the most delicious thing she'd ever tasted.

"You realize I'm trying to be serious here, right?" he muttered.

"I know," she replied. "But you're right, we're not being truthful."

He hesitated, not sure whether she was about to say more or not. But instead, she sat at one of the barstools on the other side of the counter. He decided to make himself another coffee before leaning on his elbows across from her.

"War fucked me up, Ange, there's no other way to say it," he admitted, keeping his voice low even though there was no one else in the house to hear him. "I just, there's things in my head, things that happened to me, and I guess coming back here was me running away from everything."

She nodded and sipped her coffee. "You don't have to tell me, Logan. You don't owe me anything."

He frowned, wrapping his hands around the burning hot mug. "We used to talk about everything."

"We did," she said carefully. "But that was then, and this is now."

"Tell me one thing, Ange," he said. "Did you come home to run away from something too? Because I feel we're both hiding here, and you're keeping something from me."

He listened to her sharp intake of air. "Yeah, I did.

But I'm not running forever. I needed time to catch my breath, that's all."

Logan wasn't sure if he believed her, but he wasn't going to call her out. She was a big girl, and he was almost certain she'd had to deal with a lion's share of problems when it came to business before. He only hoped she *did* talk to him when she was ready.

"So about last night," he started, eyebrows raised as he saw color flood her cheeks. *"And* this morning." He said the last part with a grin and received a smack on the hand in response.

"We never mention it," she said instantly. "Ever again."

He reached for her hand, fingers playing across hers, but she pulled it back.

"Too much?" he asked.

"Way too much," she said, straightening and pushing the coffee mug toward him. "Now I'm going home before my family sends out a search party."

Logan laughed. "Maybe you should come back tonight, for that steak I promised you?"

Angelina laughed too, and suddenly the vulnerable girl he'd glimpsed before was replaced with the woman he knew. Her eyes were bright and strong, telling him that whatever was going on with her, it would only be so long until she was back on her feet again.

"Logan, I know we said this could be fun for however long I'm back, but I'm not so sure it's a good idea."

He shrugged. "Hey, it's a helluva good way to take our minds off our troubles. But you're in the driver's seat, so I'll wait to hear from you."

She just grinned, pausing to give Ella a smooch before waving to him. "I'll see you around, Logan. And maybe I'll change my mind."

He stood and watched her go, captivated by the girl turned woman who'd always been his friend. She appeared outside, walking briskly to the car before opening the door. But he frowned when he saw the change in her when she got in. Right up until that moment, she'd been so confident and carefree, and then when she was in the driver's seat, he saw her face fall and her forehead connect with the steering wheel. And she sat like that for at least a minute, as he quietly watched on, wondering what the hell was going through her head.

Was she regretting what they'd done? He groaned, thinking about the brave face she'd put on before, if that were the case. But he got the feeling it was something deeper, something much worse than she was letting on.

Was that why she'd broken down last night?

He'd almost forgotten about that, how she'd sobbed, a bit hazy after so many shots, but she was definitely not herself then. And what he was seeing right now was not the Angelina Ford he knew.

Logan stepped back as she finally sat up and started the engine, watching her drive away. He eventually turned and looked down at Ella, his hand falling to the top of her head.

"I guess we've all got secrets," he muttered. "Come on, we've got animals to feed."

Just like that, Ella fell into step beside him, and he went outside to work. It wasn't like they couldn't afford to employ ranch hands, but being out in the fresh air all day and working 'til he dropped was the only thing that seemed to help him.

And Angelina, he thought. Angelina had been a damn good distraction too. But she was gone and he had no idea if she'd ever be back. But even if she didn't come back, she'd made him feel lighter, his mind and heart less scarred, at least for a little while. And for that one night, for what she'd done for him, making him feel like a normal human being again, he would always be grateful.

Angelina pulled into the garage and turned the engine off, feeling more like a naughty teenager than a grown-ass woman. But it didn't stop her from creeping into the house and tiptoeing down the hallway.

"It's called the walk of shame!"

She cringed. So much for trying to sneak in without being seen or heard. Mia was calling out from the kitchen, and as Ange turned to go in and find her, a door clicked down the hall.

"Oh hey," Lexi said, looking her up and down and laughing. "Um, that doesn't look like your kind of shirt."

Angelina slowly looked down, realizing she was still wearing Logan's deliciously soft, snuggly shirt. *So much for trying to be discreet.*

"Um," she said, not knowing what to say.

But then Mia was suddenly standing in the hall too, and Ange's face was getting hotter by the second from the scrutiny.

"Looks like someone had a good night," Mia teased. "Imagine my surprise when Sam offers to mind the kids for the morning, and I get here and my sister is still out."

"Maybe I went out early," she ventured.

Mia spluttered out a laugh. "Or maybe you spent the night at a certain sexy cowboy's ranch."

Now Lexi's eyebrows were arched, looking as interested as Mia in the whole situation. "Spill. This sounds good."

"Not a chance," Angelina said, breezing past them both and quickly starting up the stairs. "I need makeup and . . ." Her words trailed off. What did she need? Anything that meant delaying the inevitable talk her sister wanted.

"We'll be waiting!" Mia called out. "This is the most excitement I've had in months!"

"Me too!" Lexi added.

Angelina listened to her sister and almost-sister laughing in her wake, and she smiled to herself as she made her way to her room. It felt nice, being back around her family, enjoying the relaxed atmosphere of her family home. In her haste to leave every time she came home, maybe she'd missed the fact that there was something strangely calming about the house she'd grown up in.

She opened her laptop to check her emails, about to strip out of Logan's shirt then changing her mind. She tied it in a knot at the side instead, leaving her jeans on and going into the bathroom to do her face. She twisted her hair up in a messy bun and then put on her foundation, mascara, and some highlighter. Then she dabbed some color to her lips, finally feeling more like herself with her mask back in place.

Then she glanced at her emails, glowering when she saw one from her real estate agent. She possibly had someone interested already. Angelina gulped, pushing away memories of her house as she thought about leaving it all behind. But it was what had to be done, and there was no point dwelling on it.

There were a few others that she didn't bother reading, and then one from a creditor thanking her for paying her debts. She'd reached into her own pocket to make sure no one was left with nothing, and as a result, she'd ended up bleeding the coffers.

But the one that caught her attention was from her old PA. Penny was asking for a reference, already applying for jobs with other property and development firms. *Of course she was.* Penny was young and talented, and she'd be a wonderful asset to any company. It wasn't like Angelina was going to be in a position to rehire her any time soon.

Angelina responded with a quick yes, deciding to mull it over for the rest of the day to make sure she wrote her the most glowing reference possible. Then she clicked through to one last email as it popped up, from her former publicist.

She groaned, her heartbeat picking up speed as she read the blast. It was only small, and she doubted it would go viral, but she'd wanted her to see it just in case.

Former high-flying CEO, Angelina Ford, heiress to one of the biggest fortunes in Texas, has walked away from the company she founded. The one-time power player failed to see a takeover bid coming after a slew of bad decisions, and has now been forced into early retirement. Even someone as trailblazing as Ford will struggle to find credibility again in an ever-competitive market. We asked Ford for comment, but she declined.

Bullshit! They might have gotten the rest right, but she'd never said no to being interviewed. She knew they wouldn't even want her side of the story, preferring to run whatever they wanted without going directly to the source.

She cringed as she left her room, heading back downstairs. It was only so long now before word spread, which meant she was going to have to come clean with her family.

"Here she is," Mia said, glancing up when Ange walked into the room. "A girl's got to be hungry after an *adventurous* night out."

Ange glowered at her. "Seriously?"

"Well, was it?" Mia asked. "*Adventurous*, I mean?"

Lexi was laughing and Ange decided to hell with it, she may as well play along and enjoy it too. What the hell use was she to anyone if she was grumpy and moping around?

"Fine, you asked, I'll tell," she muttered. "I had a great, *very* adventurous night if you must know. And we forgot to have dinner, so I'm starving."

"Forgot?" Mia asked, waggling her eyebrows. "Or you got too busy?"

Ange giggled. "If you're supposed to look sexy doing that, you don't."

Lexi was laughing behind her hand, and Angelina felt like a weight had fallen from her shoulders. There was something calming about sitting in her childhood home, surrounded by her sister and Lexi—it was good for the soul, even if she was the one they were teasing. Being surrounded by family was more therapeutic than she'd imagined.

"Cody told me you and Logan went way back, that you were best friends growing up?" Lexi asked once the laughter had died down. "So, you guys are friends with benefits or . . ."

Angelina groaned. "We've never done this before. We were really close but not like that. I mean"—she paused, thinking back—"I always thought he was hot and there was definitely chemistry, but we became such good friends that it was never worth ruining it."

"So you managed to keep your pants on through your teenage years, and bam, you hit thirty and you can't keep your hands off him?" Mia asked, cracking eggs and whisking them together. She was the complete opposite of Ange—Mia could bake or cook anything without even breaking a sweat. Angelina would be in hell if she had to whip up breakfast or *anything* at short notice like that.

"There was a lot of alcohol involved, and we both, I don't know, we're both going through some stuff and it, well, it happened."

The other two raised their brows at her, but bless them, neither one asked her what that stuff might be.

"How did he seem?" Mia asked, back turned as she cooked the eggs.

Lexi was on her feet now too, putting bread in the toaster, so Ange stood and decided to make some coffee. It was better to have something to do, to stop her thinking about . . . She smiled to herself. For once, it wasn't her business failings she was thinking about—it was Logan. Just seeing his handsome face in her mind was enough to make her grin.

"Ange?" Mia asked.

"Sorry," she said, pulling from her thoughts. "Logan was, I don't know, troubled, I guess? I mean, he's clearly functioning fine, but there was . . ." Ange hesitated, not sure whether she should say anything.

"What?" Mia asked.

She shrugged. "It's probably nothing, but I answered the phone for him when he was in the shower. I half expected it to be his folks, and I haven't talked to them or seen them in ages, so I picked the phone up without thinking."

"Who was it?" Lexi asked, putting toast on one of the white plates, before turning back to put more bread on.

"It was a little girl," she admitted. "He took the call, but not before asking me to give him some space. It was like he was expecting to hear from her."

Mia turned, holding a fry pan full of creamy-looking scrambled eggs. "Did she ask for Logan or Daddy?"

"Logan," Ange answered quickly. "I mean, I'd know if he had a daughter, wouldn't I?"

Mia and Lexi swapped glances in front of her, but it was Lexi who spoke. "Cody never knew I had a son, and I presumed he would have heard from someone."

"But Logan and I are different. I mean, we were still in touch. Granted, it wasn't often, but I would know. I'm sure I would."

"I don't mean to point out the obvious," Mia said as she plated up the eggs. "But you could have just asked him."

Ange shook her head. "It was clear he didn't want to talk about it. Or his tour of duty. He was more interested in drinking away his memories, I think, and I didn't want to push him."

They were all silent as Angelina finished making the coffee and the other two finished with breakfast. Within minutes, they were each carrying a plate and a mug with them, sitting at the kitchen table, sunlight pooling over the well-worn timber.

"Sam doesn't talk a lot about the past," Mia said quietly. "Sometimes, on the anniversary of when he came home from his tour, he goes silent and walks out to the horses, and I don't see him for hours. There's other days too, not often but every now and again, when he needs to be on his own out riding. Being in the saddle seems to calm him. But that's just his way and I make sure to respect it."

"And you're okay with not knowing everything?" Angelina asked. "I mean, don't you feel it would be better if he talked?"

She was surprised by how relaxed her sister was about it all, or maybe she'd just come to accept it.

"I'm sorry I've never asked you before," Ange added, before Mia had time to answer.

"It's fine. We've never really talked like this, have we?" Mia said, setting down her fork and touching her hand. "But yes, I'm okay with it. Sam has a past, and it's his to own. He knows he can talk to me about anything, but it's his way of dealing with it. He meets some army buddies sporadically, but he's a bit of a loner, which is why he's so good at spending hours with the horses he trains."

Angelina digested it all, thinking about Logan. Logan wasn't a loner. Logan had been the life of the party, the fun guy who loved being social, and everyone loved him in return. But this Logan, he was still fun and warm, he was still the same, but there was a sadness beneath his smile, a pain behind his eyes that she couldn't not see. It was like he was trying to pretend everything was okay, without being able to stop the tiny cracks from appearing in his armor.

Except for last night. Last night, when their lips had touched, everything else had melted away. She'd felt it inside herself, and she'd seen it in Logan.

"So, what happens next?" Mia asked softly.

Ange stabbed at her eggs, swallowing a mouthful before answering. "Well, we promised to never speak of what had happened, and I spilled the beans to you two immediately." She grimaced. "But we did also decide that we might keep this thing, this *fling*, going while I was home. Although I'm not convinced it's a good idea."

They laughed, and she groaned.

"Honestly, I think we should just try to go back to normal, don't you?" she asked.

"Look, you'll be gone within a day or two, so it's not like you have to keep running into him," Mia said.

Angelina kept eating, not wanting to lie to her sister.

"Ange? I'm going to have to call the doctor if you stay longer," Mia teased. "Seriously, what's with you? You're sitting in the kitchen wearing a plaid shirt and you're not even anxious about leaving. Where's my sister and what have you done with her?"

Ange swallowed. She lifted her head, opening her mouth, almost ready to confess.

"Who's anxious about leaving?" boomed a deep male voice.

Tanner's hands fell to her shoulders from behind, making her jump, and she stared at Mia before leaning back and smiling at her brother.

"Me," she said.

"Well, that's no big surprise," he muttered. "Any left-over eggs?"

Angelina relaxed as Mia rose, laughing and joking with their brother as she fixed him something to eat.

Her secret was safe for another day.

Chapter 7

ANGELINA let herself out of her father's library. She'd sat with him for half an hour, just watching him sleep, and she had the most gut-wrenching feeling that her family would have called her home this week if she hadn't surprised them with a visit. His health was going downhill—she knew it and she was fairly certain he knew it too. Even though neither of them would admit it out aloud.

"Hey," Tanner said, surprising her as he appeared in the hallway.

"Hey, yourself," she said.

"Nice shirt."

She knew her face would be red, but she tried not to react. "Thanks." Either Mia had told him or he was being smart.

"You know, I'm sure that looks a lot like a shirt your friend Logan used to wear," he said, looking her up and down, then giving her a wink. "Is he wearing one of your fancy silk ones since you've stolen his?"

"Ha ha, very funny," she muttered. "Is there a purpose

for you hunting me down, or did you just feel like mocking me?"

"Ahh, there she is. I thought I'd lost the real Angelina for a moment."

Ange glared at him, hands on her hips now as her temper flared. "What's that supposed to mean?"

Tanner pushed his shoulders up in a casual shrug. "You're different at the moment, that's all. You normally arrive and leave in a whirlwind, but instead, you're hanging around and behaving less like a queen and more like . . ." He grinned. "Like Mia. You actually seem like you two are related at the moment. Normally I wonder if the two of you were adopted at birth, you're such polar opposites."

Ange scowled. "Thanks. I'm pleased I'm less queenlike this time." Deep down, she knew what he meant, though. She did usually arrive and leave in a hurry, barely letting her feet touch the ground, and even though she'd thought she could hide her troubles and pretend like she was just here to spend more time, it seemed as if her family knew her better than that.

"I smell a rat," Tanner said, crossing his arms and leaning against the wall as he studied her. "Why the hell won't you tell us what's up? Something's made you come running back home, and if you won't tell me, then I'll figure it out."

The last thing she needed was for him to go digging for dirt on her, because it wouldn't take him long to find out what had happened.

"Tanner, I need you to listen to me," she said, keeping her voice low. "You do that? You go looking for answers or clues, and I'll never forgive you."

He stared back at her, but his eyes softened, making it obvious he was backing down. Or maybe he'd never seen her look like that before; she imagined her own eyes were wide and angry.

"Is it so hard to just tell me?" he asked, moving closer to her, his hands on her shoulders as he looked down at her. "I know I tease you a lot, but I love you, sis."

"Leave it, Tanner," she snapped. "Honestly, I don't know why you're all so damn interested in me. Can't you leave me to work my own shit out?"

"It's because you usually arrive like some goddamn princess who thinks she's better than us," he said, his stare like stone now. "Maybe I want to know who finally knocked you off that high horse you've been riding on."

"Screw you, Tanner," she said, kicking him in the shin as she pulled away. "And make your goddamn mind up! Am I a queen or a princess?"

With that, she stormed down the hall, knowing how childish she was being but unable to stop herself. She grabbed the keys and headed straight for the garage, not sure where she was going, but feeling she had to go somewhere.

Logan put a hand to his horse's neck to calm him as a familiar black Range Rover came speeding up the drive, stopping outside the barn. He was mounted and sitting astride his gelding, about to ride down and check on the calves he'd recently weaned. Or at least he had been until the roar of an engine had alerted him to the fact he had a visitor.

He leaned forward, waiting for Angelina to get out. It took her a few minutes, but eventually she emerged. A pang of satisfaction thrummed through him when he saw she was still wearing his shirt, albeit a slightly more styled version of it. She'd paired it with skinny faded jeans, the shirt unbuttoned just low enough and tied at the side in a knot, and an inappropriate pair of flip-flops. Still, he liked the shirt on her. She looked like a softer, more approachable version of herself, and if he hadn't been on horseback, he was certain it would have been very hard not to reach out and touch her.

We're pretending like last night never happened, he reminded himself.

"Hey," he called out. "I didn't expect to see you back here so soon."

She smiled up at him as she walked closer. "Turns out I made a dare with someone last night, and I promised to go horseback riding with him."

"Oh, now I remember!" Logan laughed, enjoying the banter between them and remembering all over again why he and Ange had been such good friends. "You do realize that you're wearing entirely inappropriate footwear, though, right?"

Angelina looked from him, down to her feet. "I kind of realized that on the way over."

"Head inside and take a look in the mudroom. You might be able to fit a pair of my mom's boots," he said. "You'll find clean socks in my room, in the drawer beside the bed. They'll have to do."

"Okay, thanks," she said, shielding her eyes from the sun as she stared up at him.

"You okay?" he asked. "I mean, riding horses is your worst nightmare, isn't it?"

She shrugged. "Nope. Being interrogated by my brother is my worst nightmare. Horses seem way less confronting than him."

Logan knew better than to probe deeper. "I'll saddle Mom's mare up for you, and we can head down and check on some cattle together."

He saw her wince. "Can't we just putter around close to the house?"

Logan laughed. "Darlin', this is a working ranch. That means there's actual *work* to do."

Angelina turned, and he watched her walk to the house, wondering what on earth was going through her head. But if he questioned her, then that would give her free rein to do the same to him, and there was no way he could even figure out where to start with all the shit in his head.

"I'll meet you in the barn," he called out.

Ange disappeared into the house, and he nudged his horse on, not bothering to call his dog back when Ella trotted off after Angelina. She was often an aloof animal, only interested in her handlers, but for some reason, she'd taken to Ange from the moment they'd met.

He only hoped his mother's mare was as fond of his friend as Ella was.

Chapter 8

ANGELINA emerged by the time he had the mare in the barn. He was making fast work of it, giving her a quick brush down before heading for the tack room to find her saddle.

"I can't believe I'm wearing actual work boots." Logan laughed and looked over his shoulder at Angelina's words.

"I take it you usually live in heels?"

"Yup." She sighed. "My feet hurt so bad some days, but it's part of my armor, I guess. I put on my work clothes and my pumps, and I'm ready to face the day."

He disappeared into the tack room and emerged with the saddle.

"You think it's stupid, don't you?" she asked.

Logan stopped beside her. "I don't think it's stupid. It's what everyone does, their own little quirks that stop anyone from getting too close or seeing their weaknesses. We all have ways of hiding ourselves from the world."

He noticed the surprise register on her face.

"You didn't expect me to understand, did you?" he asked.

Logan resumed walking and Ange fell into step beside him. "I guess I hadn't really thought about it. But no, I expected you to laugh at me."

"Come on, let's get you back in the saddle."

Ange scoffed. "I don't know if I was ever really in it."

Logan shrugged. "No excuses. There's stock to check and things to do around here, and it'll be nice to have some company for once. Come on."

He passed her the bridle, but by the time he'd thrown the saddle blanket and saddle up on the mare's back, checked it was sitting properly and tightened the girth, she was still standing staring at the pile of leather in her hands. When he blew out a breath, she held the metal bit up toward the horse.

"This goes in the horse's mouth, right?"

Logan groaned. "You seriously grew up on a ranch but have no damn idea how to saddle or bridle a horse?"

"Well, the saddle part looks the easiest. I'm sure I could have figured that out."

He took the bridle off her and untwisted the leather, before putting it back in her hands and guiding her. "You need to do this," he said, putting her left hand on the horse's nose and taking her right hand under and over. He used his own thumb to coax the mare's mouth open, and then helped Ange to slide the bridle into place behind the horse's ears. "Cheek strap first, then the nose band," he said, standing close as he watched her work. Her nails were a little too long and fumbled to find the holes, but he waited, pleased that she was actually trying.

"Wow. I did it," she said, spinning around and colliding into him. "Whoops."

"Sorry," he muttered, stepping back, but the look on Ange's face made him want to step straight into her space again.

She placed her hands on his chest then quickly removed them, her eyes flashing with confusion. "I shouldn't have done that," she said, moving away again until she was touching the horse.

"It's fine," he replied, clearing his throat. "We're friends. Before last night you would have done that, and it wouldn't have even meant anything. But now we've seen each other naked, it's kind of impossible not to react."

He knew he was lying. It was because of last night that she'd even touched him in the first place; she would never have touched him like that before, and his hands wanted to find their way to her just as bad. But they'd said they wouldn't speak of it again, and he wasn't about to be the first one to do it.

The last thing he needed was to get all messed up over Angelina. They were both adults, and they could move on. *It was just sex.*

"Come on, we've got work to do." He was surprised at how gruff he sounded, and he saw something pass across her face. But if she wanted to be here with him today, she needed to pull her weight, no matter how much he appreciated the company.

Logan checked her girth before patting the horse on the rump and signaling to Ange. "Want a leg up?"

She nodded, and he saw her take a visibly deep breath. "All the pilates in the world couldn't make me that flexible," she said, laughing as she tried to stretch her foot up. "So yes. Please."

"Give me your left leg," he said, bending and taking her weight. "On the count of three. One, two, *three.*" Logan boosted her, pushing her upwards so she landed easily in the saddle with a light thump.

"Surprisingly easy," she muttered, and he smiled as

she looked down, trying to wiggle her feet into the stirrups.

"They're too short for you, hang on," Logan said, gently pushing her thigh back so he could reach the stirrup leathers and adjust them. He let them down a few holes and then coaxed her foot into the stirrup iron. "Feel okay?"

When he looked up, his eyes collided with hers and he felt a familiar longing spur through his body. *She's just a friend*, he reminded himself. *It was a one-time thing, a release, nothing more*. And if it happened again, then what? Because he couldn't commit to anything, and he doubted she'd want to either—he had nothing more to offer her than the sporadic friendship they already had. Yet he'd been the one to suggest they keep having fun until she left.

"Thanks, Logan," she said.

He stood back and his eyes found their way back to her gaze again. "For what?"

"For letting me come here this afternoon," she said. "There's something really nice about spending time with you again. Like this."

"You must really have something to hide from if you're liking being here on the ranch with me." He knew he sounded gruff, like he wasn't even taking her seriously, but in truth, there *was* something really nice about feeling like someone needed him again.

Logan mounted up and signaled to Ella to follow them. "We'll walk the first part, but when you're ready to go a little faster, you let me know."

He nudged his horse and backed him up before turning and heading out of the barn. He glanced behind to make sure that Ange was following, and even though she looked nervous, he was confident her horse would simply follow his. He planned on taking things real slow.

Angelina didn't know what to say. Part of her wanted to spill the beans to Logan and just enjoy being able to share her troubles with someone else, but another part of her didn't want him to know she'd failed. She'd seen the look on his face when he'd first seen her the other day—he was impressed by what she'd done with her life, and she didn't want to shatter that illusion and see the look of pity cross his face. And if she told him, then it'd be real and she'd have to slowly start to tell everyone else back home what had happened.

The horse felt surprisingly steady beneath her, and she almost liked the rhythmic, constant movement of the mare's gait. There was something oddly comforting about being in the saddle, and she could almost understand why her sister and brothers were so horse-mad. *Almost.*

Angelina studied Logan as they rode, taking the time to really look at him. He still looked the same as she remembered, but now that she had time to study him, she could see the subtle differences. He was heavier now, more muscled and less lanky, but he was also older looking, as if he'd really lived. His eyes were bracketed with fine lines, his mouth kissed by smile creases that showed how much he liked to flash that trademark grin of his and erupt into belly-deep laughter. But what struck her most was the sadness that he seemed to be holding within him. When he was talking to her, his smile was there, his gaze warm, but when he was looking away like he was now, oblivious to the fact that she was watching him so intently, it was much easier to see his pain.

"When we get down here, we'll ride quietly through the young stock and check over them, and then I want to go check a fence down in the valley. I have some bulls down there, and they can make one hell of a mess when they want to."

"Bulls?" she echoed.

"You have heard of a bull, right?" he teased, even though his face was deadpan. "Male cattle beast, big horns, mean as a mother—"

"Yes," she interrupted. "I do know what a *bull* is, you idiot."

Logan took his hands off the reins and stretched, arms above his head and ankles flexing out. His horse kept walking, not looking fazed in the least, and when he finally picked up the reins again, he held them on the buckle with one hand.

"You do realize you could have done this with either of your brothers, right? I mean, I bet they would have loved to spend time with you."

Angelina's eyebrows shot up. "Seriously? First of all, they would have laughed so hard, they couldn't walk straight, just at the idea of me being on horseback, and secondly, getting away from my family was why I came to you."

"But you're here to see them, aren't you?" He frowned. "That is why you're home, isn't it?"

"Yeah," she said softly. "I am here to see my family. Well, mainly my dad."

"You haven't talked a lot about him," Logan said, slowing his horse so they were riding side by side instead of him leading. "I'm not gonna lie, I got a real surprise seeing him the other night. I mean, I knew he was unwell, but I didn't realize what a toll it had taken on him."

Ange felt a familiar prickle in her eyes, a burn that was almost impossible to blink away. She swallowed hard. "Yeah, he's not doing great. I mean, I don't know what I expected. I know he's terminal, but when I talk to him on the phone, it's so easy to just pretend he's the same as he's always been. In my mind, nothing's changed; it's like he'll always be here on the ranch. It's hard to come to terms with everything changing, with a future that might not, *won't*, include him."

"There's nothing easy about death," Logan said, so quietly she had to listen hard to make out his words. "It doesn't matter whether it's slow to come, or if it comes out of the blue, it's an impossible thing to get your head around."

"You must have seen a lot on your tour," she said, hoping she wasn't pushing too far by talking about where he'd been. "I can't imagine what you've seen the past few years."

"Sometimes I wonder how the hell I made it back, when so many others didn't," Logan said gruffly, before clearing his throat. "Anyway, you ready for a trot? Did you ever get taught how to post? You know, going up and down in time with the horse's stride?"

She grimaced. "I always preferred cantering. It seemed so much smoother."

"When was the last time you rode?"

Ange hesitated, trying to remember. "Ahh, I think when I was fifteen?"

His grin made her worry, but she didn't have time to back out as he clucked his horse on.

"Here goes. Hold your hat, darlin'."

She was about to call out that she didn't *have* a hat to hold, but the next thing she knew, her horse took off like a rocket, and she stifled a scream and held on for her life, fingers tightly clutching the pommel of the saddle, the other hand clasping the reins. Why hadn't she just agreed to a bumpy trot? She felt wildly out of control, and it was much faster than she remembered.

"How you doing back there?" Logan called out.

"Terrible!" she yelled back.

"Relax," he said, as if she were going for a casual walk instead of trying not to fall off a speeding horse.

"Easy for you to say," she muttered, surprised he'd heard her when he started to laugh. It took every inch of her willpower not to scream.

"Honestly, just feel the horse beneath you. Don't fight it, don't stiffen up, let your body move with the rhythm."

She *could* feel the damn horse, that was her problem! Why on earth had she thought going horseback riding with Logan was a good idea?

"Slow your breathing and try to soften your shoulders," he said. "She's not racing off anywhere, she's just keeping pace with me, so try to relax your body."

Angelina wanted to yell at him, but she knew that wasn't about to help and she'd only end up spooking the horse, so she tried to do what he said. She didn't let go of the pommel, her fingers digging in deep, but she did take a breath and force her shoulders down, feeling the breeze against her cheeks and the movement of the horse, trying to move in time with her gait.

They slowed a little, and she suddenly felt more in control, and eventually she eased up on her grip, letting her fingers soften as her bottom started to stay planted in the saddle instead of bouncing up and around rigidly. Why did everyone else seem to make cantering look so damn easy, as if it were no different than being on a rocking horse?

"Heels down," Logan commanded. "Push your weight into them and really sit up tall. It'll help with your balance."

She forgot all the anger she'd felt at him only moments earlier at being told what to do, and instead of panicking, she realized she actually kind of liked it, now that she didn't feel like she was about to tumble to the ground. She touched her legs a little more firmly to the horse's sides and felt her respond, increasing her speed a little. The ranch blurred past, and Ange had to stifle a scream, only this time it wasn't out of fear or frustration—it was because she felt free. Like she'd left everything behind, as if she could keep on riding forever, away from all her worries and problems. The exhilaration almost felt like it was setting her free.

She actually felt as if she could start over.

"Whoa now," Logan called, slowing down beside her as he reined back to a trot then a walk.

"Whoa," she repeated to her own mount, pleased when she responded and slowed, going through a brief teeth-chattering, bumpy trot to a walk. Ange was breathing heavily, but it was a good kind of exhausted, her body alive and her mind clear. She wished they could have kept going for longer.

"You okay?" Logan asked, riding so close that their knees bumped.

"I'm better than okay," she said, knowing how wide her eyes must be as she traded glances with him. "That was incredible! It was like nothing could stop us, as if nothing else in the world mattered."

"I know," he said, looking pleased with himself. "It's why I wanted you to ride with me. When you broke down last night, I knew you needed an outlet, and for me, it's always been riding it out. Once you feel comfortable in the saddle, it becomes a happy place, where nothing else matters except the animal beneath you and the air around you."

She looked around her, at the vast fields that seemed to stretch for as far as the eye could see, truly understanding why Logan liked being on the ranch. All around them was green—trees towering and waving their leaves in the breeze, grass for miles—it was beautiful in the most serene way possible. How had she never truly looked around her before? Why had she been so drawn to the concrete jungle of New York and then the competitive pavements of LA? She'd loved every minute of city living and working, but she should have been balancing that with Texas too. Maybe it had taken things going wrong for her to see what had been right in front of her all this time.

"Why does it take something bad happening to appreciate where we came from?" she asked.

"Because you don't know what you miss until it's almost taken from you," he replied, reaching out a hand and placing it on her thigh as they rode. Logan never looked at her, but his palm was warm and it sent shivers through her as he kept the contact. "Coming home has been my therapy. I might still be messed up about a lot of things, but it clears my head being here, on the land. I could do with a bit more company, but sometimes it's the simple things in life we don't know that we need. They're the things that get us through."

"Thanks, Logan," she said. "And you're right, maybe it's the simple things I've turned my back on. Maybe I don't dislike ranches as much as I thought I did."

"Sometimes, when I can't turn my memories off, I saddle up and go," Logan said, his fingers brushing her thigh as he withdrew his hand. "The faster I go, the faster they disappear, and even though I know it's not a permanent solution, it's worked for me."

Angelina didn't know what to say. Her worries, what she'd lost, they were financial. It was embarrassing, but it was also something she could possibly claw her way back from. But whatever Logan was suffering from, the memories and worries plaguing him, they were from losing people and seeing things he could never unsee, and she needed to remember that.

"If you ever need someone to talk to, Logan, you know I'm here for you," she said earnestly. "I'm not going to go blabbing what you tell me to anyone else, so you can trust me."

It was on the tip of her tongue to ask about the little girl on the phone, but seeing his shoulders drop and relax just now, his smile returning to his lips as the seriousness of their conversation faded away, it stopped her. If he wanted to tell her, wouldn't he have told her as soon as he'd finished the call? Instead, he'd pulled out a bottle of whiskey, which was evidence enough that whoever had been on the phone wasn't someone he wanted to discuss with her. Not yet, anyway.

"If you could do anything, start any business or move anywhere, what would you do?" she asked, surprising herself with the question. It had just fallen from her mouth—probably because it was one she'd been pondering a lot herself lately.

Logan didn't say anything for such a long time that she was starting to think he hadn't heard her, but then he finally looked in her direction, his eyes crystal clear. "I'd do something for service dogs," he said. "There's a lot of help still needed for returned soldiers, but I don't think enough resources go into the rehabilitation of our retired dogs."

Angelina looked at Ella, who'd managed to catch up with them. She was keeping an eye on Logan, and the loving look the dog was giving him made her think that Ella would do anything Logan ever asked of her. She was limping, but her tongue was lolling out and making it look like she was smiling up at them.

"But I'd want to be living here. I've travelled plenty of places overseas now, and here in America, but nothing rivals my home. This is where I belong."

They kept riding, until Logan turned the question back on her.

"What about you? Are you happy doing what you're doing, or do you have some other burning ambition?"

Ange kept her eyes trained ahead, not wanting to look at Logan. Not when she wasn't telling him the whole truth. "It's something I think about a lot, and I honestly don't know yet. I'm not happy, nothing's been going the way I expected lately, and I need to come up with something new to sink my teeth into."

"Any ideas?" he asked. "Is that why you're home? To explore new business opportunities? Your brother seems to be doing well now that he's moved back."

She laughed. "Cody is doing well here because he still spends half his time in New York. He'd go stir-crazy if he had to live and work here permanently."

"Look up there," Logan said, pointing. "That's where we're going. It's like a nursery field with so many weanlings in there."

She watched the young cattle beasts, some of them grazing, some of them fooling around and doing what looked to her like play-fighting. She had her money on the boys being the fools and the girls being the ones with their heads dipped to the grass ignoring them.

"What do we do now?" she asked, looking around as they both halted.

Logan's wink made her smile. "*We* don't do anything," he said. "You sit there and look pretty, and I'll check their water and give them all a once-over."

Angelina was happy to sit and watch, especially given it was Logan who was directly in her sights. She loved the soft touch he gave his horse on the neck after he dismounted, the big animal blinking its soulful eyes and watching after him as he patiently stood and waited, and the way his hand fell naturally to Ella's head as he walked with her alongside him. Logan was a good man. He was kind to animals, he was gentle, and he was intelligent. She only wished he'd talk to her about his troubles, because she hated seeing that cloud come over his gaze when he spoke sometimes, and she hoped the darkness didn't engulf him one day simply because he was trying to deal with his problems all on his own. Like I am.

He turned around, as if he knew she was thinking of him, and her body flushed at being the object of his attention, as if it remembered exactly what had happened when he'd looked at her like that the night before.

Logan gave her a slow smile, and she flashed him one back, happy when he turned and she got to see how well he filled out his faded-blue Wranglers.

An hour later, Logan and Angelina were riding back to the barn. The sun was high in the sky, and he liked the feel of it warming his back—it was the perfect time of year. He'd always thought he loved the heat—the hotter the better—until he'd been posted in the Middle East. And then he'd really found out what heat was about.

Since then, he'd preferred the warmth of a Texas spring or early fall when the leaves had started to turn.

"What are your plans tonight?" Logan asked, realizing how long they'd been riding along in silence. It had been comfortable, though, both lost in their own thoughts as they walked across the hard-packed earth toward home.

Angelina looked up as if his words had surprised her. She'd obviously been mulling something over. "I'm going to spend some time with my dad," she said, stroking her horse's neck as she spoke. "I came home to see him, but I almost feel like I've been avoiding him. Seeing him like that isn't easy."

"Soak up every minute you have with him, Ange. You'll always regret it if you don't."

He didn't ask her any more questions, and he certainly didn't ask what he'd been planning on saying. Having her over again had been a nice idea, and he'd have liked the company, but seeing her dad was more important than keeping him company.

They continued on in silence, and Logan forced himself to look around and take everything in, to remember what he had in life to be grateful for. But this was a hard time of year for him. In a handful of days, it was going to be the anniversary of Brett's death; a year since he'd seen his best friend killed beside him. He shut his eyes, steeling himself for the onslaught of pain, the memories that assaulted him over and over again. He could recall the smell in the air, the metallic aftertaste of the bomb going off mixed with dust; the pain that surged through him, his ears ringing as he tried to make his feet move. He remembered the feel of Ella in his arms, bloodied, her fur matted with not just her own blood, but someone else's. And he remembered the sight of Brett's boot, forlorn, blasted off him and ricocheted meters away, lying there. *And his friend.* Burned. Bloodied. Broken.

Coming home after all that, it had seemed like the easy part, except when he'd arrived, he'd realized that no one else knew what had happened to him. No one had seen what he'd seen, except for Ella, which is why he'd have walked over hot coals and fought to the death to have her by his side.

Everyone knew he'd lost his best friend. Everyone knew that he'd lost most of his small unit, with the rest injured. Everyone knew he'd received a medal for his supposed bravery.

What no one knew was how much he resented being told how brave he was, or how lucky he was, or that he needed to put it all behind him and move on. Because no amount of telling him how to deal with what he'd seen was going to stop the blinding assault of memories or the sleepless nights. The pain in his heart, a pain so deep that it cut through him every time he thought of his friend losing his life, and his miraculously being spared.

"Logan?"

He grit his teeth, pushing the wave of pain and anger away. His horse was agitated, spooking and jogging beneath him all of a sudden, sensing the change in him. He took a long, slow breath and placed his palm to his mount's neck, calming himself and the horse at the same time.

"Logan, are you okay?"

He found himself again, smiling at Angelina, her beautiful face creased in worry as she watched him.

"I will be."

She nodded, not asking any more, and for that he was grateful.

"It's been really nice seeing you again today, Ange," he said.

"Yeah, I feel the same. It's been, I don't know, just what I needed, I guess."

He nodded. "You feel like you're thinking clearer? Like some of that worry has lifted?"

Logan could see the change in her, her smile easier, her body much more relaxed than it had been.

"It sure has." Then she laughed. "Except for my butt. I doubt I'm going to be able to walk in the morning!"

Logan laughed along with her, tipping his hat as they left the sprawling acres of ranch behind them, the sun on their backs, and for once, a smile on his face that he didn't have to force.

Angelina brushed her hands on her jeans as she stood in the barn. Her legs were aching, her butt was sore, and her ankles were stiff, but despite it all, she felt great. Refreshed. Almost as if she'd had a massage or spa treatment, but instead, she'd done something she'd *never* have imagined doing in a million years, and it seemed there was something to be said about nature being as good as therapy.

"Thanks again for a great afternoon," she said as Logan emerged from the tack room, the saddles he'd been hefting safely put away.

"Want to lead the horses out with me?" he asked.

"Yeah, I'd like that," Ange said, not even thinking twice about helping.

She watched as he took off his hat, running his fingers through his hair and leaving his hat behind as he untied his horse. He was so handsome, so attractive in a rugged kind of way. There was something nice about spending time with a man who looked like he was physically capable of protecting her from anything, not to mention managing to keep her mind off her woes.

Angelina pulled the rope like Logan had, but she only seemed to make it tighter. "What am I doing wrong here?" she asked. "You make it all look so easy."

He grunted. "That's because it is easy."

Logan moved in behind her, leaning over and holding the long tail of the rope and pulling it. The knot was instantly gone, leaving only the rope lying through the twine.

"Well, you made that look *embarrassingly* easy," she muttered, turning around to glare at him. "You could have at least tried to make it look hard for my sake."

His eyes twinkled, clearly enjoying an excuse to tease her. "Honest to God, no one would believe you spent your entire childhood on a ranch."

Ange reached out to slap him on the arm, but he was too quick, grabbing her wrist and keeping a tight hold.

"Let go," she demanded.

Logan didn't, staring down at her instead, his eyes caught on hers. She was like a deer in headlights, only she liked being there. She wasn't frightened, even though her heart was beating at triple its usual pace.

Ange wanted to say something, *needed* to break the spell between them, but her body seemed to be back in charge again, thrumming with need, remembering how good it felt to be close to Logan. So much for willpower and deciding they shouldn't have a repeat of what had happened the night before.

"Logan," she started, pulling her wrist away. He let go this time, and when he did, she placed it to his chest, fingers splayed out.

She stood on tiptoes, one hand holding the horse rope,

the other still touching him. Angelina parted her lips, mesmerized by his mouth as she inched closer.

Logan dipped his head and suddenly their lips collided, brushing gently and then more intently, blood rushing through her as Logan's hand circled her back, warm and firm against her. But as quickly as it started, it was over.

His groan alerted her to the fact it was about to end, his hand falling away at the same time as his lips pulled away from hers.

"We can't do this." He ground out the words as if each one were painful. "You said you didn't want this to happen again, and I don't want to push you."

Angelina nodded, biting down on her lower lip as she pretended to agree. They were friends, they'd had one massive lapse of judgment in sleeping together, and she'd naively thought that one more slip would be okay. But from the look on Logan's face, it wasn't.

"Sorry," she murmured, passing him the rope she'd been holding.

"Ange, you don't have to go. I just—" Logan looked like he didn't know which way to run. "I don't want to hurt you. I don't want this to get complicated."

She nodded, wishing she could throw herself into his arms and stay buried there forever. But he was right, she'd told him their friendship was too important to risk, and she'd meant it.

"Thanks for today, Logan. I'll see you around."

Angelina blinked away tears, not succeeding as they started to trickle down her cheeks. The only consolation was that Logan hadn't seen them, because she didn't want him to think he'd hurt her.

Because she was the one inflicting the hurt, not him.

Chapter 9

"HEY, Daddy." Angelina's breath shuddered through her as she entered her father's library. To her surprise, he had the doors open, sitting in the fading sun with a drink in hand.

"Hello, darling," he said, clearing his throat. "Just in time for a pre-dinner drink with me."

She wasn't so sure about him drinking, but she wasn't going to say no. She opened his fridge and found a bottle of chardonnay, opening it and pouring herself a glass before joining him outside. She was surprised at how well he looked today, not as gaunt as the day before, or maybe she was getting used to it.

"How's your day been?" he asked.

She laughed. "Honestly, you won't believe it. I've been *horseback* riding."

"As opposed to, say, camel riding?" he asked, and she spluttered on her wine at his arched brow.

"Ha ha, I wasn't expecting such wit from you today." Angelina rolled her eyes and sat back in the chair, curling her legs up beneath herself. "You do recall that I was practically allergic to horses growing up? It's no mean feat that I went riding today."

"Of course I remember. I'm only teasing," he said, sipping on his drink. "It wouldn't be Logan who convinced you to find your inner cowgirl, would it?"

She could tell he was enjoying the conversation, but she didn't exactly want to talk too much about Logan with him. That was a slippery slope that she wanted to avoid at all costs—she needed to keep reminding herself about their friendship-only status. She was still cringing about kissing him earlier, practically throwing herself at him hours after declaring they shouldn't be intimate.

"Yes, it was Logan. I think he's the only person on the planet who could convince me to move so far out of my comfort zone." She sighed. "And how's your day been?"

"Just fine," he said. "Made nicer by an unexpected late afternoon drink with my eldest daughter."

They sat for a bit, both staring out at the sun setting, and Angelina thought again how magical the outlook was.

"Did you ever doubt yourself, in business?" she asked. "I mean, you had a very successful father and you followed in his footsteps in some ways, but you always made your own mark. Did you ever wonder if it'd all come crashing down around you?"

He chuckled, and she was surprised by his amusement. "Of course I doubted myself. In fact, I had this very conversation with your brother at Christmastime, and I'll tell you the same thing I told him." Her father paused, coughing a little before continuing. "Your grandfather thought I was the black sheep of the family, so I had to work hard to prove myself, and there were failures along the way. We don't talk about the bad times enough, we're all so aware of the successes around us, but no great success comes without some failure along the way. In fact, the more successful a person, the more failures they've probably had along the way. It's how we learn, it's how we develop strength, and it makes us stronger."

He knows. Angelina couldn't shake the persistent, overwhelming feeling that her father knew what had happened to her.

"We're defined by our successes, not our failures, my darling, but it doesn't make them any less significant." He reached out and touched her hand. "Without them, we wouldn't know how lucky we are in the good times. They make us resilient, not to mention wary of repeating them. They're not something to be embarrassed by."

She digested his words, looking into her father's bright blue eyes. They were so alive still, burning with life and love, with so much knowledge that she just wanted to soak up whatever time she had left with him.

"Daddy, I have—"

"Ange! I've been looking for you everywhere!" Mia's call stopped Angelina midsentence, on the verge of confessing everything to her father. She could see the look on his face, knew he was expecting her to say something important, but bless him, he simply sat back and nodded, understanding that she couldn't continue.

"Just having a drink with the old man," Ange said, holding up her glass. "Why don't you join us?"

Mia sighed. "Lexi would tell you off if she saw you drinking that."

Their father laughed. "Darling, who do you think poured this for me?"

Angelina smiled as she sat back, reaching out for Mia's hand when she sat beside her. It was good to be home. They were words she'd never thought before, but this time, the feeling was almost overwhelming.

Logan stared at his phone. It wasn't often he let himself get drawn so deeply back into the past, but tonight was different.

Tomorrow was the anniversary, and no matter how much he was trying to avoid thinking about it, his memories had an agenda of their own. And so here he was, staring at his phone, swiping through photos from the year before, when everything had been different. When they'd all been talking about coming home, about their tour almost being over, about all the things they'd do and the food they couldn't wait to eat.

Until there was no one left to talk to.

Logan stared at Brett. His smile was big, his arm curled around the back of Logan's head in the photo, the pair of them like brothers as they laughed at the camera. They were both wearing their green army T-shirts, and he recalled the day, how damn hot it had been as they'd kicked a ball back and forth, waiting for their orders but bored with sitting around.

Logan squeezed his phone, the memories too painful, the tremor of sadness as it pierced his body and shuddered through every inch of it too much to bear.

He threw the phone, using all his force as it slammed into the wall. And then the tears came, the first sob a wave of misery that he couldn't stop.

Ella leapt up beside him, her head against his chest, seeming to understand his pain. Logan wrapped his arms around her, holding her, crying into her fur.

She was all he had left and the pain of it was like a hand wrapped tightly around his throat, leaving him gasping for air and wondering if he'd ever he able to breathe easy again.

He needed to calm down. Take a shower, get dressed, and find some clean clothes to put on. It was almost show time, and he needed to get his shit together and focus. He'd made a promise to Brett that day, and he was damned if he wasn't going to keep it.

He'd selfishly wanted Angelina to spend the night again to distract him, to help forget what he was in for the following day. But what he needed to do was man up and deal with it, because like it or not, tomorrow was the anniversary, and there was nothing he could do about it other than face it.

"Logan!"

The little girl's scream cut through the air like a hot knife through butter. Logan smiled; he couldn't have reacted any other way, crouching low with his arms out-stretched as Lucy hurtled toward him. Her blond hair was pulled back into a fancy-looking braid, and when her little body collided with his, he wrapped his arms tight around her, kissing the top of her head as she clung onto him. The way she held him, the way she pulled back and smiled up at him, giggling as if he were the fun-niest thing around, it was almost as if she knew what a stone cold heart he had, or how much pain he was in. And funnily enough, as he stood with her little warm hand in his, he did feel better.

"How's my favorite girl?" he asked, swinging her around and then up into the air, hands on her waist as he lifted her and put her up on his shoulders.

Her skinny little legs were covered in tights, and he held on to her ankles as they walked over to her exasperated-looking mom.

"I'm good. Mommy's sad, though. She looks like you."

"Me?" he asked, hoping he sounded shocked. "I'm not sad, and Mommy looks pretty smiley to me."

"I heard her crying last night," Lucy said, wrapping her arms around his jaw as she leaned forward. He felt her chin rest on the top of his head, and her soft bunny toy bumped against his face, partly obscuring his vision.

Tears welled in his eyes as he thought about Brett; Lucy should be riding the shoulders of her dad, not him. He did his best, but he was no replacement for the dad she'd lost.

"We all cry sometimes. We loved your dad a lot, and your mom just misses him, that's all."

"Do you cry?" she asked.

Logan stopped beside Brett's widow, Kelly, smiling at her as she reached for his hand. He kept hold of Lucy, and Kelly held him, silently telling him everything he needed to know—that she was sad, that she hurt as much as he did, that this day wasn't going to be easy on either of them.

"Even soldiers cry, honey. Including this one."

"Really?" she asked, sounding like she didn't believe him for a second.

"Yeah, really," he replied, swinging her down so she was standing between him and Kelly.

Logan took the chance to lean forward and kiss Kelly on the cheek, giving her a big hug and holding her tight. There was so much he wanted to say, so much he still felt he had to apologize for, but right now, he didn't say a thing.

"You look beautiful today," he told her, squeezing her

hand before reaching down for Lucy, who was waiting impatiently. Her little palm slipped into his, and he noticed she took her mother's hand on the other side.

It was only a short walk to the veterans' cemetery, and they strolled together, Lucy swinging between them. He loved Kelly like a sister. They'd been close for years, but after Brett had passed, he'd found it almost impossible to look at her for the first few months after he'd returned. But she'd laid into him for shutting her out, and Logan had realized that the only way to make a crappy situation worse was to cut someone off when they needed the support, and so he'd vowed to be a better friend, and a better godfather too. From that day on, he'd showed up when he said he would, taken Lucy out for dates and even Kelly a few times, just to give her an excuse to get all dressed up and have a nice meal out, in a purely platonic way. And through it all, it had shown him that being there for Brett's girls was something he had to do, not only to honor his friend, but to help them all through a tough time.

"Can I ride on your shoulders again?" Lucy asked.

Logan glanced at Kelly, who looked like she was about to say no, but then shrugged, tears shining in her eyes.

"Why not?" she answered, flashing her daughter a smile. "If your dad were here, he'd have swung you straight on up and told me not to worry what anyone else thought, so go ahead."

Logan winked down at Lucy before bending to whisk her up onto his shoulders again, smiling to himself as she did something with his hair, her fingers dancing across his scalp. Hell, it was probably her soft toy having a party up there, but he didn't give a damn what she did so long as she was happy.

He reached out with his left hand and took Kelly's, not saying anything more to her for fear of choking on the rock-hard lump in his throat.

Some days were rough, but they were nothing compared to this day.

The rows and rows of white marble headstones, uniformly rounded on the top and straight on the sides, assaulted his eyes the moment they stepped into the field. The black outline of a cross was at the top of each one, and he walked resolutely beside Kelly, each footstep feeling like he was trying to move through sand. He silently counted the rows until they were there, turning right, and eventually stopping in front of the stone that marked Brett. He could have found it in his sleep, the route from the gate imbedded in his memory.

There was a red bow set among artificial greenery attached to each headstone, but only this one bore the name BRETT DANIELS. Kelly's hand slipped from his as she sunk to her knees in front of it, but Logan stayed standing, grinding his jaw and keeping hold of Lucy's warm little legs.

Kelly's sob cut through him, but he stared straight ahead. He was here to be strong for her, but as Lucy cupped her hands around his face, he felt tears slip down his cheeks. Like the soldier he'd once been, he refused to react, refused to break his stance or falter, no matter what, and he ignored the wet slide against his skin.

But Lucy had sensed it. Her small, soft hand reached down and brushed his cheeks, even though she never said a word, and it was so close to breaking him that it took every inch of willpower not to collapse alongside Brett's widow on the ground.

As Kelly rose, she reached out to him, arm sliding

around his waist, her head to his shoulder, as they both stood staring at the place Brett had been put to rest. It felt like only yesterday he'd arrived home, walking off the big military plane and knowing that Brett's remains were riding down below in the cargo hold. The military burial flag Kelly had received, the way she'd buckled as she received it, the willpower it took him not to break protocol and run to scoop her up. He steeled his jaw against the memories, wondering if it had been worth it. All the speeches about sacrifice and honor, some-times he found it hard to even get his head around the men they'd lost, even though he'd been a patriot his en-tire life.

"Logan, it's time to forgive yourself," Kelly said, her hold on him tightening. "I don't blame you for this, I never have, and it's time you listened to me say those words."

He swallowed, lifting his gaze, no longer staring at Brett's name. "I should have done something. I should have been the one. I should have . . ." His voice cracked and he cleared his throat. "It's bullshit that I'm here and he's not, and we both know it."

"But you couldn't have done anything, Logan, you must know that," she said, pushing back and walk-ing around to stand in front of him. She touched his cheek, her palm so soft and warm as she looked up at him. "Please, you need to find a way to forgive yourself, because *I forgive you*, Logan. You didn't do anything wrong in the first place, but if you need to hear me say it again, then there it is. *I forgive you*."

As her hand fell away, Logan caught it, holding it and staring into her eyes, forgetting about the little girl on his shoulders, she was so quiet.

"I should have swept the area again. I should have been the one going in first, not him. I should have tried harder to keep him safe, to get him back home to you."

Tears shone in Kelly's eyes, and it broke him, his chest tight as he tried hard not to visibly crack.

"Your life was, *is*, as important as Brett's. It's time you understood that, Logan. You deserved to live as much as he did, and he knew what the dangers were. He was prepared to sacrifice his life for his country, just like every other man in your unit was. Just like *you* were."

Lucy fidgeted on his shoulders and brought him back to the present, and he let go of Kelly's hand and placed both his hands on Lucy's knees instead.

"Uncle Logan, is Ella in your truck?"

Kelly smiled up at him, the warmth in her eyes softening him. "Yeah, she's in there."

"Can I ride with you? You *are* taking us out for lunch, right?"

Logan laughed though his tears, touching his hand to Kelly's back as they turned to walk back to the vehicles.

"Yes, sweetheart, of course I'm taking you out for lunch," he said, pushing away the image of Brett walking like this with his girls.

If you're up there, buddy, I'm doing my best. I'd put my life on the line for these two ladies.

"How is Ella? Still your shadow?" Kelly asked.

"She sure is, but if you ever decide you want her . . ." He hated the thought, she was his best friend, but she'd been Brett's dog, not his.

"Not a chance. That dog adores you," Kelly said. "Besides, we've been thinking about getting a Goldendoodle."

Logan cracked up. "Whoa, a doodle? You realize Brett would roll in his grave if he knew there was any kind of dog with *doodle* in the name living in his house, right?"

Kelly punched his arm at the same time as Lucy bopped him on the head with her soft toy.

"Ouch!"

"Logan! Brett would love to see me get Lucy a dog!"

He laughed. "A *doodle* is not a real dog."

Kelly folded her arms and stopped walking, glaring at him. "What is it with men sometimes? You're as bad as my husband."

Logan laughed, winking at Kelly and pretending he was about to drop Lucy as she squealed on his shoulders.

"You're serious about this?" he asked.

"Deadly."

"Okay then, I'd better get up to date on *doodles* so I can help you choose the right puppy. But trust me, Brett would never have let you get something that had doodle in it."

Kelly shook her head, and they walked back to his truck, Lucy excitedly leaping in to see an equally excited Ella. He watched as she licked Lucy's face, wriggling in happiness as she was lavished with pets.

"Logan?" Kelly asked, her voice low.

He turned to look back at her. "I know you don't go to church anymore, but Pastor Hanssen helped me a lot, and I know he'd love to listen if you ever feel like talking."

Logan nodded. "Thanks." He wasn't the talking type, and the last thing he was planning on doing was hunting down his childhood pastor.

"Come on, girls, time for lunch," he said.

He watched Lucy a moment while Kelly retrieved her car seat, taking it from her and fixing it in place when she returned. He waved goodbye to Kelly, then turned back to Lucy, strapping her in, amazed that his dog had such a bond with her. Ella was tucked up beside her in the back seat, head on her lap.

As he started to drive, checking in his rearview mirror that Kelly was following behind him, he thought about what she'd said to him. Maybe she was right, maybe he did need to forgive himself, but the nightmares, the memories that crashed back when he least expected them, made it almost impossible to escape the iron grip of pain that never seemed to let go of him.

"Clear!" Brett yelled.

Logan nodded to him. "What the hell would we do without that dog? We'd be dead men walking."

They both laughed, and the rest of their unit fell into step behind them.

"Damn, I can't stop thinking about Kelly's roast lamb. I can almost taste it."

"Only nine days to go, brother." Logan slapped him on the back, surveying the area, systematically checking the land around him, always alert. "And you'd better be inviting me over for—"

"Fall back!" Brett's scream cut through the air, his terrified eyes meeting Logan's as he spun around.

"Fall back!" Logan repeated, waving frantically to his men.

Brett moved up, calling Ella back, before Logan could take his place, before he could put himself closer to the danger.

"Brett!" he yelled, as dust erupted around them, the noise deafening, his body thrown back.

Logan gripped the steering wheel and forced the

wave of pain away. Ella had been Brett's dog. He was *supposed* to be the one closest to her. But it had been Logan's team and therefore his fault.

But Kelly was right, what point was there to living in the past, if she was prepared to forgive him and move on?

Angelina sat in the restaurant, staring out at the sun-drenched pavement as she waited for Mia to return to the table. She couldn't stop thinking about Logan, and it was starting to drive her crazy. Was she fixating on him because it was better than dealing with her business meltdown, or had her feelings genuinely changed about him? She'd never, ever thought of him as more than a friend before, but something about the way she'd felt when she was with him, it was making her wonder if they could have been more all those years ago.

"Sorry," Mia said, sitting back down and picking up the menu. "It's impossible to go anywhere without running into someone here."

She smiled. "That's the thing about leaving your hometown—everybody forgets you."

"Nobody has forgotten you," Mia said, taking a sip of water. "Everyone's just a little scared of you.'

"Scared of me?"

Mia laughed. But her smile faded fast. "Are you serious? Look at you! You look like a supermodel, and everyone's probably read about all the incredible things you've achieved. And then there's the ice queen look."

"*Ice queen?*" Angelina gasped. "Now that's plain mean."

"Hey, is that Logan?"

Angelina forgot all about her ice queen label as she stared out the window, following Mia's gaze. And she just about fell off her chair as she saw Logan holding the hand of the most beautiful little girl with long blond hair in a French braid. But it was the woman who appeared behind them, placing a hand on Logan's shoulder as they walked, that made her lose her breath.

"Who is that with him?" Mia asked.

Ange watched the way the woman looked at him, a familiarity there that made her feel sick to her stomach. Was this an ex of his? Was that his little girl? The girl who'd been on the phone the other night?

But they looked way too friendly to be exes, and the way Logan smiled at her . . . She groaned. Feeling betrayed and heartbroken was one thing, but she'd never forgive him if he'd slept with her when he was in a relationship with someone else. Surely he wouldn't have gone so far with her if there was someone else in his life?

"Ange?"

"I don't know," she whispered. "I—I can't believe it. Look at them; they're like a picture perfect family."

Mia's hand found hers. "Honey, we'd know if he had a family. There's no way we wouldn't have heard, and besides, he would have said something the other night when he came over. This is Logan we're talking about."

Ange wanted to believe that, but something about the look on Logan's face, it made her want to throw up. She'd thought he was her friend, that he was one of the few people she could trust not to lie to her. But then he'd probably have said the same about her, and she hadn't exactly been entirely truthful with him.

"They're coming in," Mia whispered. "You need to go say hi to him. It'd be weird not to."

"I'm not going over," she said. "What would I say?" Humiliation rippled through her body at the thought of what she'd done with Logan, and who this woman might be.

Their waiter came over, and Angelina relished the chance to study her menu, letting Mia order first. She eventually ordered a Caesar salad with chicken, and a glass of wine, before having to look up again.

And there they were. Why did they have to sit so close?

The woman was looking at her. She'd obviously caught Angelina watching Logan, and now the woman was curiously smiling over at her, as if she'd sensed something. Or maybe Logan had pointed her out. She felt queasy all over again.

"Mia, start talking to me. Quickly."

Mia went to look over her shoulder, but Ange kicked her underneath the table.

"Don't look!" she hissed. "Just talk."

But it was too late. When she glanced back up, she caught Logan's eye, and suddenly she was thrust straight into her worst nightmare.

"Ange?" he said loudly. She saw his mouth move around her name, even though the restaurant was so busy, she could barely hear him.

"Go," Mia urged, turning and waving at Logan before giving Ange a sharp stare. "Give him the benefit of the doubt and go over there."

Angelina knew she had no choice but to get up—if she didn't, she'd look rude, and the other woman looked very interested in her.

What was she supposed to say to her? *Is this your boyfriend, because we had great sex the other night, but I promise I wouldn't have gone there if I'd known he was taken?*

She stood, feet weighed down with lead as she forced

herself to stride the distance between them. The little girl was sitting on Logan's knee, tongue peeking out from the corner of her mouth as she colored in a picture, and it was looking at her that stole the words from Angelina's mouth. The woman seated with him didn't look anywhere near as intimidating as the child.

"Hey, Logan," she said, making herself smile, reminding herself to breathe.

"Hey," he said, shifting uncomfortably and clearing his throat. He was wearing a dress shirt and slim fitting jeans, looking polished and fresh—so damn handsome she couldn't take her eyes off him. She took in the freshly shaven cheeks, and when she stopped beside him, she got the faintest aroma of his cologne.

"I hope I'm not interrupting," she said, angling herself slightly so she didn't have her back to the other woman. "I tried calling you yesterday and this morning, but I . . ." Her voice trailed off. She was making a fool of herself. Why had she even said that?

"I'm Lucy," the little girl said, crayon poised as she blinked up at her. "What's your name?"

"Angelina," she stuttered, her eyes darting to Logan and wishing he'd help her out, but he didn't even seem to see the panic in her face. "I'm an old friend of Logan's."

The woman cleared her throat, and Logan seemed to realize how rude he was being. "Ange, this is Kelly. Kelly, Ange is my oldest friend from high school days."

Kelly held out her hand and Ange took it, trying not to cringe as she held her soft palm in hers. They were the most perfect-looking little family and guilt dropped around her like an incoming cloud.

"It was lovely to meet you, but I don't want to interrupt. Have a nice lunch."

Angelina tried not to run, but her first instinct was to flee the scene as fast as she could. And if she hadn't, she would have screamed at Logan for deceiving her.

She reached the restroom and quickly shut the door behind her, walking slowly over to the closest sink and turning on the tap, letting the cool water run over her wrists. If she hadn't been wearing makeup, she'd have splashed her face, but the last thing she was about to do was ruin the way she looked as well as let her heart break into a million shards.

She didn't look up as the restroom door swung open, staring down and trying to force the bile away so she didn't vomit.

"Angelina?"

The soft voice was unfamiliar to her, but when she looked up and into the warm brown eyes of Kelly, Angelina's breath shuddered through her. She slowly stood, turning the faucet off and shaking her hands dry.

She had no idea what to say, so instead, she stood frozen. Not saying a word.

"Back there, that felt really uncomfortable," Kelly said, moving closer, her hand falling to the sink when she stopped. "Sometimes men can be so clueless, can't they?"

Ange forced herself to open her mouth. "I'm sorry, I didn't know about you. I . . ." She shut her eyes for a beat. "Logan and I, we're just friends. I promise we're only friends."

Chapter 10

"WAIT, you thought I was Logan's . . ." Kelly's voice trailed off. "*Something*. You thought I was Logan's something, but I'm not. I mean, I am, but . . ."

Kelly burst out laughing, hand over her mouth. Angelina had no idea what was going on, but she was starting to think she'd missed a vital piece in the jigsaw puzzle she'd been trying to put together.

"I'm not his something either. I'm just Angelina," she said, wiping beneath her eyes and taking a long, deep breath. "Logan and I were best friends back in high school. We've seen a bit of each other since I got back, that's all."

Kelly nodded and came closer, holding out her hand and taking Ange's. Her small palm was warm and beautifully soft as she held it. "And I'm just Kelly. Wife, sorry, *widow*, of Logan's best friend Brett."

"Oh shit," Ange whispered, eyes growing wide as she stared back at Kelly.

"From that response, I'm guessing you know about Brett."

"His friend," Ange said, shaking her head and feeling like such a fool. "The one he lost, *Ella's* handler?"

Kelly nodded. "The one and only," she said. "And today just happens to be the anniversary of his death, the first one, so it's been a hell of a rough day. Although I'm guessing that Logan didn't tell you about the anniversary?"

Angelina's body ran hot at the same time as goose bumps moved like a wave across her skin. She let go of Kelly's hand and opened her arms, hesitating before enveloping this beautiful, brave woman in her arms. She wished Logan had told her. No wonder he'd been so lost in thought when they'd been out riding.

"I'm so sorry," she said, holding on to her for as long as felt right. "This must be such a hard day for you."

Kelly stepped back, tears shining in her eyes, but her hands lingered on Ange's shoulders. This woman, who was a stranger to her, was so warm and genuine, it made her feel like a fool for ever being jealous of who she might be to Logan.

"It's been a day like no other, but we're lucky to have Logan," she replied. "Lucy is smitten with him. I don't know how she'd have gotten through all this if it wasn't for him, to be honest."

"She was the little girl who called the other night," Ange said, relief coursing through her. She had no right to be jealous, but seeing him with Kelly and the girl she'd presumed was his had turned her into an emotional roller coaster inside. "When I heard her voice, and when Logan was so secretive, it made me wonder, and then seeing him today with you both . . ." It made her sound pathetic but it was true.

"Logan isn't the best at talking about what's happened," Kelly said, turning slightly and washing her hands as she spoke. "We all went through a lot after losing Brett, but he's fostered this deep remorse that it's somehow his fault my husband died. And I think we both know how ridiculous that is, because it was war and every single soldier there knew the risks."

"I wish he'd opened up to me," Ange said. "I asked him, but he seemed more intent on making his way through a bottle of whiskey, or tequila in the end, than talking about what he'd been through."

Kelly dried her hands, turning to look at her again. "He's a good man—Logan. One of the best. He'd do anything for me, and he'd sacrifice himself if it meant helping Lucy, but if he doesn't start talking soon, guilt or anger or whatever it is inside of him will start to get the better of him."

Ange watched Kelly for a moment, pleased she'd met her. This woman was so together, so strong and capable, even after what she'd lost, and it was the wake-up call to life she'd needed.

"How can you be so strong? Today of all days?" Angelina asked, the question falling from her mouth before she'd had a chance to curb it.

Kelly's laughter was as warm as her smile. "Hey, you didn't see me yesterday when I took the day off work to just lie about and cry in my PJs from morning till noon, wishing Brett were with me. And you won't see tonight when I eat an entire tub of ice cream after I put Lucy to bed. The truth is, I take it one day at a time, and some days are easier than others."

Kelly flashed her one last smile then left the restroom, and Ange took a moment to stare at herself in the mirror. "You've got this," she told herself, as she looked into her own bright eyes. She didn't see a failure standing there. She saw the same thing reflected she'd always seen—strong, manicured, determined. "It's time to start being honest," she said, before reapplying her lipstick and walking straight back out the door into the restaurant.

Logan might not have been honest with her, but neither had she been, and her web of lies had to stop. And it had to stop now.

"Logan, could I speak to you for a minute?" she said, touching his chair as she passed. "In private."

Angelina smiled at Kelly, who smiled straight back at her, but it was the little girl who truly melted her heart, now that she knew her story. Ange hadn't approached the table on her way back from the restroom, going back to her sister and eating their meal first, but she'd known that she only had a small window of time before they both left, and she wanted to talk to him.

"You want to join us?" Logan asked. "I lost my manners before."

No, you lost your best friend and today's the anniversary, she wanted to say, but instead, she pushed the thoughts away. "It's fine, we're about to go, so I wondered if we could talk for a moment?"

Logan nodded, and she watched as he excused himself from the table. He ruffled Lucy's hair as he stood, and she walked nervously with him to the front of the restaurant where no one could hear them. It was quiet, with not many people about on a Tuesday, and she was grateful for a few minutes alone with him.

"Sorry I didn't call you back. It's been a rough day," he said, and as he looked down at her, she wished she'd known so she could have been there for him. "And a pretty rough night last night if I'm honest."

"Kelly told me," she said quietly. "In the bathroom before. I thought she was, I mean, I thought they both were . . . something else to you."

His eyebrows shot up, and she wished she hadn't even said anything. "Yeah, well, like I said, it's been rough."

"I wish you'd told me, about her and about what this day meant for you," she said, reaching out to touch his arm. But Logan wasn't warm like he'd been to Lucy or to Kelly—she'd been watching him the entire time—he was cold as he pulled away, like she'd hit a sore spot. "I know things have become complicated between us, but I really wish you'd been honest with me—"

"Are you serious?" he said, his voice low. "You expect me to tell you everything when you're so clearly hiding the reason you're home? I think we're both good at hiding things, Ange, so don't make out like it's all on me."

She stared back at him, trying to stop her jaw from hitting the ground. "Logan," she started, but he was quick to cut her off.

"Why are you here, Ange? What are you hiding? Now you know my secrets, how about you tell me yours?" He shook his head. "Yeah, I didn't think so. I didn't push you because I didn't want to tell you what I was dealing with, but it looks like you found out anyway. What's the saying? Pot calling the kettle black?"

She wanted to tell him, was ready to open up and tell him everything—why she was home, what she'd done, what she'd lost—but Logan didn't give her the chance. He moved past her, walking away without another word, not caring that he'd left her standing there alone.

Ange watched as he opened his arms and scooped Lucy up, the little girl's face shining like he was the most incredible human being in the world. And maybe he was. To her. But to Ange? He'd called her out on her bullshit, just a like a best friend should. Only a best friend wouldn't have left her standing like that, alone, needing someone more than she'd ever needed someone in her life.

She quickly paid the bill and waved her sister over, hurrying to the car once she joined her so they didn't have to see Logan and Kelly as they made their way out.

"What happened there?" Mia asked.

"Nothing I want to talk about," Ange said, linking her arm through her sister's as they walked.

"Everything okay between you two?" Mia nudged her in the side and Ange took a deep breath.

"It will be," she said. "Logan and I used to tell each other everything, and in some ways we're closer than ever, but in others?" Ange sighed. "We've never been so far apart."

"Is there anything you want to do now?" Mia asked. "I have another hour without kids if you want to get our nails done or something."

Angelina wavered, liking the idea of spending more time with her sister and procrastinating about what she needed to do, but if she didn't do it now, she might never be brave enough to do it again later.

"I'd love to, but I really need to get home," she said. "There's something I really need to talk to Dad about."

Mia didn't seem to mind, and they walked together down the sidewalk to the car. She wanted to look over her shoulder so bad, to get a last glimpse of Logan and see if he felt bad for being so rude to her, but she didn't. Logan was her friend, not her *boy*friend, and that meant he didn't owe her anything. But as her friend? He'd called her out on her bullshit, and the only thing she could do to make that right was to start being honest. With herself, with her family.

And with her friend.

Logan walked beside Kelly, forcing himself to match her pace even though she was walking painstakingly slow. Up ahead, Lucy skipped, trailing her soft toy behind her and seeming to talk to imaginary friends. She was such a happy, bubbly girl, it was almost impossible to believe that she'd gone through the tragedy of losing her dad.

"You know, you might be able to turn your back on your friend, but I get to call you out on your crap," Kelly said. "You can hate me all you like, but I know you'll keep coming back because you feel sorry for us."

He grunted. "I don't feel sorry for you. I love you both. You're like a sister to me."

She bumped her shoulder into him. "Then as your sister, can I say that the way your friend Angelina looked at you? It's clear that you guys are way more than just *friends*, no matter what either of you says."

Heat rose within Logan, but he wasn't going to let Kelly know she'd hit a nerve. "I'm telling you, we're just friends."

"Yeah, well I don't believe you for a second. There's more going on there, and if you'd seen how crushed she looked in the bathroom, when she thought I was your *someone*, it would have told you that I'm right."

Logan kept walking, not sure what to say. But he decided to opt for the truth. "We got drunk the other night and things, well, things happened."

"*Things* being sex?" she asked.

Logan glanced at her, hating that she looked so damn amused. "Yeah, if you must know."

"And nothing like that had ever happened between you guys before?"

"No, Kelly, nothing like that has ever happened before!" He glared at her, starting to walk faster as he decided to catch up to Lucy instead.

"I'm simply saying that maybe you should open up to her a little. It wouldn't kill you to have someone other than me and Lucy in your life."

Logan stopped walking then. "That's what you think?"

Kelly's eyes softened, and he saw sadness there as she smiled up at him. "Logan, you have your whole life ahead of you. Don't let something that happened, something that was completely out of your control, stop you from opening up to someone and something that could be great."

He had no idea what to say.

"Logan, Brett was the love of my life. He was my soul mate and the father of my child, and I will never love anyone as deeply for as long as I live. But you?" Tears slipped down her cheeks as she took his hands into hers. "You haven't loved like I have. And what happened shouldn't stop you from being happy."

Logan pulled Kelly close, holding her as she cried. Seeing her pain almost broke him, but he tried his best to hold it together. It had been a tough day for both of them, and she'd held it together for her girl, but the cracks were finally showing.

"Promise me?" Kelly said as she extracted herself from his arms. "Promise me that you won't push her away?"

Logan sounded gruff, he couldn't help it, but with Lucy heading back in their direction, the last thing he was going to do was start crying all over again too. That was for later, with a bottle of Jack in his hand.

"Yeah, fine, I promise."

She stood on tiptoe and kissed his cheek. "Good, and keep me informed. I need to live vicariously through you."

Logan watched as she grabbed Lucy's hand and the two of them went running off toward the playground. But suddenly it wasn't them or even Brett he was thinking about, it was Ange.

Why had he been so damn hard on her? Why hadn't he been more friendly, more *welcoming* when he'd seen her at the restaurant? Just because he hadn't told her about what today meant, it didn't mean he'd needed to be so rude.

Or maybe Kelly was right. Maybe there was something deeper between them that scared the hell out of him. Because the way he'd felt with Ange in his arms, or the anger he'd felt when he'd watched her eyes flicker, knowing he was right about her keeping something from him, he'd never felt that way before.

He owed her an apology, but it was going to have to wait until tomorrow. Today was all about honoring Brett's memory, and tomorrow he could start to pick up all the pieces and make amends.

"Logan!" Lucy squealed. "Come push me. I want to go high!"

He jogged the distance between them, grabbing hold of the swing Lucy was sitting on and making her laugh as he pulled her all the way back before launching her with her little feet pointed toward the sky.

As Kelly swung more sedately beside her, he could see what he was missing out on. They were never going to be his family; they belonged to Brett. But without a family? Without people who loved him and had his back? He was nothing more than a lone soldier with no one to catch him when he fell.

"I wasn't expecting to find you in the kitchen," Ange said as she found her father sitting at the kitchen table, facing out toward the endless green acres of their ranch and bathed in sunshine. It was a perfect kind of Texas day, the kind she remembered so vividly from her childhood, and seeing him sitting there took her back years too.

"I don't always live in the library," he said, and she liked the familiar twinkle in his eye as he looked up at her.

She smiled to Lexi, who was leaning on the counter, eating something with one hand and wiping the bench with the other.

"Don't mind me, I'm leaving," she said. "Harry's being dropped home from a play date soon, so I need to get back."

Ange nodded, anxiously making herself a coffee before passing by Lexi again.

"You okay?" Lexi asked.

Ange gave her a tight smile. "I will be soon."

Lexi had grown on her. They hadn't exactly had the best start, and she hadn't really spent a lot of time with her, but seeing the way she cared for her dad and the easy relationship she'd developed with Mia and the rest of the family, it told her everything she needed to know. She was caring and loving toward her brother, and to everyone else at River Ranch, and she admired how she'd single-handedly raised her son and was now back studying to follow her dreams. Cody might have given her the financial freedom to be able to do it, but she was the one putting in all the hard work.

"Mind if I sit with you?" she asked her dad.

His smile greeted her. "Do you even have to ask?" He chuckled. "Although this is reminiscent of when you were a little girl, wanting to butter me up for extra pocket money."

She sighed. "I haven't wanted your money for a very long time, Dad."

His face creased. "Darling, I know that. Of course I know that! I was only teasing." He reached for her, and she hated to see the shake in his hand. Her only hope was that it wasn't from pain, but she was too scared to ask him if it was. "I'm so proud of you and what you've achieved."

It was almost impossible to hold it back then, to not give in to the overwhelming waves of emotion that threatened to steal the words from her. But this wasn't a time for tears, this was a time for honesty. And bravery.

Angelina blinked the tears back and took a deep, shuddering breath. "You're wrong," she whispered, clearing her throat and forcing her voice to be louder. "I'm not who you think I am."

He kept hold of her hand even when she tried to pull away. "You're exactly who I think you are, darling. And I've never been more proud of you."

A few tears escaped, dropping from her lashes, and she raised her head, ignoring them. "I had to walk away from my company, Daddy. I lost everything," she admitted. "I've gone from being successful beyond my wildest dreams to a complete failure, and it's the reason I'm home." She gulped. "And why I haven't left."

Walter's smile had faded, but it hadn't disappeared

entirely. And when he finally spoke, she'd never been so shocked.

"I'm pleased you finally confided in me," he said. "But failing doesn't make you a failure, Ange. Failures don't ever succeed, they don't take risks, they don't think big. I thought I'd made that clear to you the other night."

His words were kind, but they didn't help. He was her father, of course he was going to say nice things to her. It was what he thought deep down that she was scared of, what he was secretly thinking but not saying.

"I thought you'd be more shocked," she admitted, taking a sip of her coffee and finding it was her hand that was shaking now.

"Sweetheart, I've been waiting all this time for you to tell me," he said gently.

Ange spluttered on her coffee, staring at him over her mug. "You knew something was wrong?"

"I knew what happened."

She froze. "All this time you've known? Why didn't you say anything?"

Her father had once been a force to be reckoned with, a businessman so ruthless, more successful than she could ever have dreamed of being herself. But now, he was softer, calmer, as if his illness and perhaps his age had changed him.

"I keep an eye on all my children's investments. Why wouldn't I? I follow each of you with interest, wanting to know what's happening, and I follow the markets in LA and New York as closely as I do here."

"So you've known since before I arrived?"

He nodded. "I have. I read about the company's demise but chose not to say anything until you were ready to come to me." His laughter surprised her. "Although I was starting to think I'd die before you confided in me!"

Ange took another sip of coffee, more to stall and give herself longer to think than because she really wanted to drink it.

"How much do you know, and how much do you want me to tell you?" she asked, sitting back in her chair and watching her father.

"I want you to tell me everything," he said. "But before you start, I want to say how proud I am of you. Because if you've done it once, you can damn well rise up and do it again. Don't let this slip define you, Ange. You take the time you need to lick your wounds, and when you're ready to launch again, don't doubt yourself. Be fearless when it's time to start over."

This time, when the tears pricked her eyes, she didn't bother to hide them. All this time she'd been keeping her secret, terrified of admitting to her father what had happened, and he'd known all along. He patted the seat beside him, and she rose, back to being that little girl in her memories again, curling up beside him, head to his shoulder as he scooped his arm around her.

"Thank you," she whispered.

"Don't thank me," he said with a chuckle. "I'm going to give you about ten minutes to feel sorry for yourself, and then we're going to dissect what went wrong so you never have to feel this way again."

She hugged him, inhaling the strong woodsy notes of his cologne as she started to let herself think big again. He was right—there was no reason she couldn't rise up from this. She'd paid all her bills and her employees to make sure no one went down with her. She still had her house to sell, and if she'd started with nothing more than tenacity and a huge work ethic before, she could sure as hell do it again.

Chapter 11

LOGAN startled when he heard a knock at the door followed by Ella's loud *woof*. He turned the television down and stood, padding down the hallway and giving her the command to stop barking. She quietly came to stand by his side, but her hackles were up and she was sure as hell on guard.

Who on earth would be knocking on his door this late?

He swung the heavy oak door open, surprised to find Angelina standing there. Her hair was pulled up into a big messy knot on top of her head, she was barely wearing any makeup, and she was dressed as casual as he'd ever seen her. In fact, if he hadn't known her so well, he might not have even recognized her on first glance.

Ella leapt forward, wiggling around the legs of their guest as Logan just stood there.

"Hey," he finally said.

"Hey," Ange replied, patting Ella before straightening. She looked nervous when she opened her mouth to speak again. "Can I come in?"

He swung the door open fully and stood back, gesturing for her to walk in and wishing things didn't feel so awkward between them.

Ange kept walking, eventually stopping and standing in the open area between his kitchen and the living room. "I was going to call first, but I figured you probably wouldn't answer and . . ."

Her voice trailed off and he cringed. She was right to think that—he'd have pretended not to hear it ringing, just like he had when she'd been calling the day before.

"I wanted to talk to you about earlier today, at the restaurant."

He cringed again, shoving his hands in his pockets as he stared at her. This was beyond awkward.

"Look, I should never have been so rude. Today's a shit day on the calendar for me, and I took it out on you. I'm sorry."

She shook her head. "No, Logan, you were right. I did come home for a reason, and I've been lying to everyone I care about because I've been scared. Of what everyone will think, how you'll all look at me." She paused. "But if you hadn't pushed me, I still wouldn't have told anyone. So thank you."

He watched her, as she stood so bravely before him with her shoulders squared and her chin jutted up a little. Even without her fancy clothes, she was still the same fierce girl he knew.

"Why did you come home?" he asked, his voice raspy as he watched her, scanning her face to see if she was going to tell him the truth or not.

Her chest rose as she took a deep breath. "Because my business was a failure, and I've been left with nothing," she said quietly. "All I have left is my house, but within a month, I won't even be able to afford to pay my household bills. I lost everything, and I came home to hide, lick my wounds, and figure out what the hell to do next. I didn't want anyone to know."

Logan stared, the shock of what he was hearing leaving him lost for words. "But you were flying, you were doing so well. I mean, we'd all read about how you were the businesswoman to watch . . ."

She sighed. "I know. Trust me, I know. I've gone around and around it all in my head, and I wish I could go back and make different decisions, but I can't."

They were still standing, and Logan knew he should invite her to sit, but she started to talk again and he didn't want to interrupt her.

"Everyone's always thought I was given money, and that assumption always hurt me so much when I've done virtually everything on my own. So the only silver lining to all this is that my failure has proven there's no one standing behind me, waiting to catch me when I fall." Her laughter when it came was shallow. "And so here I am, the prodigal daughter returned home with a few suitcases of designer clothes and a failed business behind her."

"You're not a failure, Ange. I promise you, you're not." Logan finally stepped forward, moving closer to her and holding out his arms, but she didn't come toward him. Instead, she looked into his eyes, and in that second he knew she expected honesty from him now too. That she'd given him what he'd pushed for, and now she wanted the same in return.

"Now I've told you," she said, side-stepping away from him and dropping into his sofa. "So it's your turn to tell me."

He followed her lead and sat on the sofa opposite her, leaning back with his arms spread out, wondering where the hell he was supposed to start. "What do you want to know?"

"I want to know why you feel guilty about your friend's death when there's no way you could have known what was going to happen," she said, her voice low as she appeared to study him. "And then I want you to tell me about Kelly and her little girl."

"Pass," he said. "Next question. Let's go back to talking about what happened to you."

But Angelina wasn't giving up. "The property market was cooling, and I started to make the wrong decisions. I stopped listening to my gut and tried my hand at too many different things," she said. "Now back to you, and don't give me the same bullshit response this time."

Logan leaned forward, forearms to his knees. "What happened to me over there, how I ended up all fucked up and full of guilt?"

She nodded, her eyes wide as she leaned forward too.

"It's my business and no one else's."

She looked like he'd just slapped her—her face was red, and she was glaring at him as if she wanted to kill him.

"I opened up to you, and that's what you give me?" she said, her eyes wide as she fumed at him. "I can't believe you. Who's the hypocrite now?"

"It was your choice to tell me," he said, shrugging as he sat back again. "But I don't want to reopen old wounds."

"Fuck you," she spat, standing and marching off, before spinning around at the door, tears clearly shining in her eyes as she watched him. "You were my best friend, Logan, and seeing you has been one of the best parts of coming home. Or at least it was. Until you showed me what a cold-hearted bastard you've become. You're not even the same person I spent the night with."

Logan stared after her, listening to the door slam and her angry footfalls echoing out on the timber veranda.

He glanced at Ella, who was giving him a disapproving look, her graying eyebrows raised. "Don't look at me like that," he muttered.

Ella whined and tilted her head to the side. *Even the goddamn dog knows what a jerk I'm being!*

But as soon as he heard the sound of a car door slam, he sprang into action, leaping up and sprinting down the hall. Logan ran across the veranda and leapt down the steps in his bare feet, ignoring the stab of gravel against his bare feet as he ran toward the vehicle she was driving and grabbed the passenger door just as she started to accelerate.

"Shit!" Angelina swore, slamming on the brakes as he lurched with the door and managed to swing himself inside.

They both sat there, her breathing as loud as his as he sat back, eyes shut, the cool of the leather seat against the skin of his arms bringing him to his senses.

"I promised Brett," he ground out, his voice so low he didn't even know if Ange would be able to hear him. "As I stood over what was left of his body, I promised Brett that I'd take care of his girls. He loved them more than life itself, and being here for them, it's the only thing that brought me home. They're all I have."

Tears started to slide down his cheeks then, and he fought them, not ready to give in to his emotions twice in one day. His body started to shake, and he dropped down, head in his hands as the pain of it all rocked him. And as warm arms draped over him, holding him tight, everything he'd kept bottled up for so long poured out of him, like a faucet that no one, no matter how strong, could ever have a hope of turning off.

Angelina had never seen Logan cry before—never seen that strong façade of his crack, let alone break open completely, and all the anger she'd been holding on to disappeared. She'd wanted to strangle him moments earlier, but now, all she wanted to do was hold him through his pain.

"What the hell happened to us, Logan?" she whispered, head against his as she held him.

He didn't answer for a moment, his breathing shallow, but when he finally looked up, and she stared into his damp eyes, she felt a change between them. They might have been friends for years, and those feelings still ran deep, but there was so much more to them now. A primal kind of attraction that had been ignited and was almost impossible to stamp out.

They were deluded if either of them thought they could change that. She knew it, and from the look on his face, she was almost certain he knew it too.

"Logan, we . . ." She took a breath, searching for the right words.

But Logan didn't give her words in reply. Instead, his mouth found its way to hers, seeking her out, brushing against hers in a touch so gentle, it made her ache for more. When he pulled away, she wanted to say something, wanted to put words to whatever the hell was going on between them, but the need to touch him was too intense.

Angelina gripped the front of his shirt, fingers balled against the fabric as she drew him closer to her. Logan groaned, but he didn't pull away, hungrily claiming her mouth again, tongue colliding with hers as she pressed against him. His hands were at the front of her shirt, fumbling, and she did the same to his, wanting to feel his skin. She dragged her fingernails across his chest once she'd undone all his buttons, not caring what was unsaid between them when she had Logan's body to explore, to make her feel good. No, better than good, Logan made her feel great.

Logan pushed up, suddenly rising higher than her as he stripped off his shirt, leaning over her and flattening her against the steering wheel, mouth still on hers.

Honk!

Ange squealed, the horn frightening the life out of her as she pressed into it. The spell broken, Logan looked down at her, and she blinked back at him, chest rising and falling rapidly, the desire in his eyes impossible to ignore.

But as he opened his mouth, about to say something, he clearly changed his mind, pressing the automatic buttons on her driver's door to move her seat, tilting back as far as it would go.

Then he leaned down and started to kiss her again, taking it slow this time, trailing his lips over hers before moving down her body. His mouth was wet and warm over her collarbones, his fingers grazing the skin on her stomach as he trailed lower and lower.

Angelina squirmed, struggling to lie still and let him tease her when what she wanted was to grab hold of him and put *him* in the chair so she could climb on top and take charge. But she forced herself not to move, lapping up the attention, switching her mind off and letting herself enjoy every second of it.

"Dammit!" Logan swore as his head slammed into the sunroof.

She laughed, dragging him down by his shirt again

for one more slow kiss. "How about we take this inside?" she asked. "I think car sex is only fun when you're a teenager."

"I disagree. This is plenty of fun," he murmured, still kissing her.

Logan kissed her again, then again, until she pushed at his chest, and he slowly rose, moving back into his seat. His fingers skimmed hers and he squeezed her hand.

"You want to come inside?"

She grinned. "I thought you'd never ask."

Logan grinned and grabbed his shirt, and she followed his lead, holding her shirt together as she stepped out of the car. He was waiting, holding out his hand, and she took it, leaning into him and dropping her head to his shoulder as they walked. The energy was so different between them now, and her body was thrumming with anticipation as he hugged her to his side.

"You sure you don't want to talk?" she asked. "If there's anything you want to tell me, I mean, after what you've been through today?"

Logan's grunt didn't surprise her, and neither did his words. "Talking is overrated."

She was about to disagree with him when he turned and swept her up into his arms, barging through the front door and kicking it closed behind him as he stormed down the hallway to his bedroom. She should have told him that she wasn't falling for it, that he needed to open up to her, but as soon as his lips found their way back to hers and he dropped her onto the bed, she'd forgotten all about what she was going to say.

Logan looked down at her. He stood at the foot of the bed, bare-chested, his jeans riding low on his hips. She watched as he undid his belt buckle, grinning at him staring straight back at her, his eyes never leaving hers as she watched him strip out of his clothes. Her breath caught when he dropped to his knees, moving over her before slowly inching lower. Soon his chest was against hers, breasts crushing between them, his knee parting her legs.

"Where were we?" he said.

Angelina hooked a leg around his waist, smiling against his mouth.

Talking could wait until tomorrow. Logan was right—it was definitely overrated.

Chapter 12

THE first thing Angelina saw when she opened her eyes was Logan. He was still asleep, giving her time to study his face and look at him in a way she'd never have been brave enough to do if he was awake. His black lashes brushed his cheeks, skin tanned golden from all the hours he spent outside, and she wondered if he'd looked the same when he'd been serving. She could imagine him in his uniform, how handsome he would have been in army fatigues.

Last night had been a nice distraction, but today she was starting over. And as she turned and looked out the window, with the sun rising in the sky and starting to cast a warm glow into the room, she knew it was time to go.

She rose as quietly as she could and put the covers back, so tempted to curl back up into bed with Logan, but knowing it was the wrong thing to do. All she'd be doing was delaying the inevitable, and if she didn't follow through with her plans now, she probably never would.

Angelina dressed, silently padding around to find her

underwear and then her jeans and shirt. She crept from the room as she was doing her buttons up, almost tripping over Ella as she tiptoed down the hall.

"Hey, girl," she whispered, dropping a pat to her head. "You look after him, okay?"

Ella turned her head, eyes bright as she watched her, and Angelina actually felt like the animal understood her. She walked into the kitchen, looking for a pen and finding an envelope to write on. She leaned on the counter for a few minutes, trying to figure out what to say.

Logan, thank you for everything. If you ever want to talk, just pick up the phone and I'll be there. Until next time. Angelina.

She reread her words three times, knowing that nothing she wrote was ever going to be enough. Then she quickly scribbled her mobile number down and let herself out the front door. Walking out on him without saying a proper goodbye felt immature in a way, but it also seemed like the right thing to do when they were so bad at talking to each other.

They'd had their chance at opening up and it hadn't gone well, other than the part where their *bodies* got to talk, which seemed to be the only communication they had down pat. But she'd said everything she needed to say, to Logan at least, and he'd had every opportunity to talk.

She fumbled for her phone, noticing there were a couple of texts from Mia and one from Cody, but she ignored them, knowing she'd been seeing them all soon enough. The last thing she needed was to explain that she'd spent the night with Logan again—hopefully she was home early enough to sneak in and reemerge as if she'd been there all night.

Angelina dialed and put her phone on hands-free, slowly driving away from Logan and his ranch. She glanced in her rearview mirror, half expecting to see him standing there, but all she saw was Ella standing in the window, watching her go.

She would have rather stayed, to hide away with Logan and pretend she was happy in the little bubble that was him and his ranch, but she knew it wasn't her. That life wasn't her—all she'd be doing was hiding from her real life. And that life was in LA, it wasn't in Texas. It never had been.

When her call was finally answered, she took a deep breath, hesitating before speaking.

"It's Angelina Ford. I need to have the jet ready for two o'clock this afternoon, travelling to Santa Monica Municipal Airport please."

The attendant confirmed and she clicked off the call, both hands on the wheel as she turned out onto the road and sped toward home.

It was time to stop hiding and get her ass back to LA.

An hour later, Angelina finished packing her suitcases, hair freshly washed and her makeup perfectly in place. She checked her reflection in the mirror, touching the diamond solitaire earrings hanging from her lobes, her diamond pendant *A* chain hanging loosely from her neck, black silk shirt unbuttoned just low enough to show some skin without any cleavage.

She was back in her work uniform, and despite not having a business to go to, she felt like her old self again. What was the saying? *Clothes maketh the man*? Well, she believed that clothes made the woman too, because right now she felt like a million dollars from simply dressing as if she were still successful.

A soft knock echoed on the door.

"Come in," Angelina called out.

Lexi's head appeared, and Angelina smiled. "Sorry to disturb you, but your father wanted me to pass a message on."

Ange hauled her largest suitcase up to standing. "Don't tell me, he's invited everyone over?"

Lexi laughed. "I'm not sure if you remembered, but it's Father's Day today. He wanted me to let you know that he took care of it for you and organized brunch. He's happy for you to take full credit for it, though."

Ange groaned. "Oh my God, I did forget! I'm the worst daughter in the world."

"He also said you'd say that," Lexi said. "But he said the present you can give him is downstairs. I'll give you guys some privacy if you like."

"Thanks," Ange muttered, feeling so stupid for forgetting. It had been her excuse for coming home, and she'd hardly given it any thought since she'd arrived. "Is today rough for you, I mean, being Father's Day?" she asked just before Lexi backed out of the room. "It must be tough when your little guy doesn't have his dad around."

She knew from Cody that Lexi had a rough time with her ex, and that her son often waited for his dad to call or show up, only to be left disappointed. But if Lexi's smile was anything to go by, it wasn't an issue today.

"Harrison actually did a card and made a gift for Cody," she said, shaking her head as she spoke. "I had nothing to do with it, but it was the sweetest thing ever."

Angelina shared her happiness, smiling straight back. "Cody must have been thrilled."

"He was," Lexi said. "Honestly, your brother's been a better father figure to Harrison than his biological dad ever has. He deserves all the love Harry showers him with."

Lexi took one of the cases, and Ange took the other one with her carry bag, and they bumped down the stairs with them.

"You sure you can't stay a little longer?" Lexi asked.

Angelina looked at her cases. "I wish I could, but I can't. I've been hiding from reality here, and while it's been a nice interlude, I need to go back to my real home." Or not, since her home had a buyer going back for a second look. But either way, she needed to return to the city she worked in.

Lexi disappeared then, and Ange found her way to her father's library. She looked around when she stepped in, expecting to find him resting, but instead, she found him with a pile of papers strewn around him and his glasses perched on the end of his nose.

"Happy Father's Day," she said, opening her arms.

He just laughed, looking up at her and shaking his head. "Darling, I know you forgot. But come here. I have a Father's Day gift for you."

She frowned. "I'm supposed to be giving *you* a gift, Dad."

"Well, here it is," he said, pushing a handful of papers toward her. "All this money, it's yours. You've been leaving your trust fund money to accumulate all this time, and it's time you accepted it for what it is."

She balked at the digits on the page. "I'm not a charity case, Dad. There's a reason I never took this money."

"Stop being so arrogant. This is your birthright. It's yours whether you want it or not, so I'd suggest not looking a gift horse in the mouth and taking it." He sighed. "Sometimes you're so like your mother, it infuriates me."

"Being like Mom is a bad thing?" she asked.

"No," he said, shaking his head and smiling sadly at her. "It's a great thing, except for when I'm trying to do something for you."

"I can find my way back to my own two feet, Dad. I need to do it on my own."

He gestured for her to come closer. "Think of this as seed money. You can take it and use it for a new venture, and if you must, you can pay it back to the trust. Hell, give it to charity once you've made it back if you want. Or start a new venture with a charity arm that gives back right from the start." He studied her, long and hard, and she felt her defenses start to break down. "Why make life hard when you're so fortunate to have this opportunity? You're a fool if you don't take it."

"Take the money, Ange," came a deep voice from behind her.

When she turned, she saw Cody standing there, and within minutes Tanner and Mia had filed into the room too.

"What is this, an intervention?" she asked, hating how fake her trill of laughter sounded, even to her own ears.

"No, this is Father's Day brunch," Tanner muttered. "But if we don't eat soon, then I'm happy to intervene in any way I need to."

"He told you?" she asked, turning around to face her army of siblings.

"Told us what?" Cody asked.

Angelina took a shuddering breath and then slowly let it out. "I came home because my company collapsed and my bank account is virtually at zero," she admitted. "It's a long story, but the short of it is that I've been hiding from the world here, and I didn't want you all to know what an epic failure I am."

They were all silent, but it was Cody who broke the spell first, coming up to her and enveloping her in a big bear hug.

"Hey, I've been close to the edge," he said. "Every successful person has scars, and I have plenty of them."

She held him back, surprised at how sweet he was being. And as he stood with his arm around her, it was her father who spoke again.

"You've all made me proud, each and every one of you in your own way, and I trust you all to manage my legacy once I'm gone."

A shiver trawled up and down Angelina's body, and she held on tighter to her brother. "Dad, don't talk like that."

He fobbed her off, waving his hand. "I'm transferring the money into your account tomorrow," he said. "You don't need to sell your house, not yet. I don't want you making any knee-jerk reactions when you're fortunate enough to have other options."

Angelina nodded, laughing when Tanner's stomach growled loudly.

"Come on, can we eat now? I'm starving," her brother asked.

They all walked off, and Angelina held out her hand to her father, wanting to walk with him into the dining room.

"Thank you," she said. "For believing in me, and for giving me this."

"I'm your father, it's what I'm supposed to do." He chuckled. "I'm just pleased you decided to take some help for once. Some young entrepreneurs would kill to be given a hand up."

She nodded. He was right, she did need to stop looking this particular gift horse in the mouth.

Something else he'd said had resonated with her too. She'd always given generously to charity, and she'd been known in certain circles for her philanthropy over the years, but she'd never attempted to turn it into a business. Her mind started racing as she thought about the incredible things she could do with her inheritance, the money her mom had ensured each of her children had before she'd passed, which up until now, Angelina hadn't wanted to touch.

But up until now, she hadn't had a business idea that needed it.

Her brain started to whir, and she grinned over at her father.

"Should that look scare me?" he asked.

She smacked a loud kiss to his cheeks. "Yes," she said. "It should *definitely* scare you."

And just like that, she was excited about work again. If she could feel passionately about a project, then she was sure she'd be able to convince other people to do the same. Why had she never thought about a business that gave back to the community before?

"Daddy," she said when they'd reached the kitchen. "Would you mind if I made a quick call first?"

She didn't wait to hear his response, pulling her phone from her pocket and dialing a number she knew by heart.

"Angelina!" the voice on the other end answered.

"Hi, Penny. How are you?"

"Missing you," Penny replied with a sigh.

"Does that mean you'll come back to work for me?" Angelina asked. "I know it's a lot to ask, and to start with, it'll just be you and me working from my place, but I have the beginnings of a new idea and you're the person I want to grow it with me."

Penny's laughter was like music to her ears. "When do I start?"

Angelina grinned into the phone. "I'm on a flight back to LA this afternoon. How does tomorrow sound?"

"Perfect. But you do realize I'll be expecting a raise."

"Done," she replied. "But don't forget my double-shot cappuccino."

Penny laughed. "Yes, boss."

Angelina hung up, making one more call to her realtor. She had to leave a message, but she knew it was the right thing to do. If she had to sell her house, she would, but she needed to stop making knee-jerk reactions and give herself a chance to get her life back on track without giving up the one thing she was so proud of.

She wasn't going to use her trust fund to pay her mortgage, but she was going to use it to build a business, and after this one, she was going to move on to the next.

"Ange, you coming?" Tanner hollered.

She slipped her phone back into her pocket, marching straight back into the kitchen and finding her family engaged in a lively conversation. Her father sat at the head of the table, as always, and she slipped into place beside Mia, smiling as Sam arrived with his daughter holding his hand. Lauren was already there at the table beside Tanner, her head on his shoulder as the others talked, and Cody was joking around with Harry, the pair of them laughing and having fun. It was so good to have their entire family together again.

"Aunt Angie!" Sophia squealed, and she opened her arms, hugging her little niece as Mia piled pancakes on a plate for her.

Coming home had been the right thing to do, and for the first time, leaving was going to be hard. An image of Logan came into her head, imagining him reading her note, remembering the warmth of his body and the whisper of his kisses against her skin.

But Logan didn't want a relationship. He didn't even want to talk, let alone have something bigger develop between them. He was a friend and nothing more, and she needed to remember that. It would have been so much harder to leave if he wasn't.

Logan hadn't bothered to saddle his horse today, deciding to go out on the quad bike instead, given his foul mood. The last thing he wanted was to let his horse feel his anger and tension, and he'd never forgive himself if he took his frustrations out on an animal.

His phone rang for the third time that day, and when he pulled it out of his pocket, he saw it was same caller again too. *Kelly.* He was being an ass not answering, and he knew he couldn't ignore her again. He'd promised himself he was going to call her back as soon as he finished his work for the morning, but morning had turned into lunchtime, and now it was early afternoon.

"Hey," he said, clearing his throat and leaning against the quad. Ella was curled up asleep on the back of it, and he reached out to stroke her ear.

"Hey, stranger, thought you were never going to answer."

He had no comeback to that, and he wasn't going to lie to her. "Sorry. Rough morning."

"Everything okay?" she asked. "You know you promised me that if things ever got too tough, you'd call, right? I can't lose you too, Logan."

Logan smiled into the phone. "I know. I'm not going anywhere," he said. "I, uh, had some personal things going on, that's all."

"Personal, as in Angelina?" she asked.

He didn't want to get drawn into talking about her, but he knew Kelly wouldn't give up if he didn't give her something.

"Hey, how's Lucy holding up? Do you have any special plans for Father's Day?"

"She's holding up just fine, and we're planning on pancakes and a movie, thanks for asking. But back to you, Logan. What's going on?"

"Look, she came over last night and she ended up staying, but now she's gone, so that chapter is over."

The silence between them was so loud, he cringed, expecting to receive an earful from Kelly. But instead, she spoke quietly, which made it almost worse than being yelled at.

"What exactly do you mean when you say *gone*?" she asked.

He stared out at the field in front of him, taking in the trees and the cattle grazing. "I think she's already gone back to LA. Her note sounded pretty final."

There was silence again, but the response when it came wasn't so quiet this time.

"Hold up, she left you a note, and you *think* she's gone, and instead of going after her and admitting how you really feel, you've just moped around all day feeling sorry for yourself?"

He grunted. "Pretty much."

"For fuck's sake, Logan, excuse my language, but do you love this girl? Because I've never seen you look at someone the way you looked at her, even if you were being a jerk at the time."

Logan swallowed, kicking at the dirt and covering the end of his boot in muck. "We're friends who happened to fool around. We both agreed that's all it was."

"I obviously have to spell this out for you, you big

idiot, but if you think there's something there, if you think you might be in love with her, then go get the damn girl before it's too late."

"It's not as easy as that. There's so much other stuff going on between us and—"

She cut him off. "You can work all that stuff out later. Just don't let her go without telling her how you truly feel."

Logan listened to her words, knowing Kelly was right, but also knowing how impossible it would be for anything to ever develop between him and Angelina. She lived in another state, and he wasn't about to walk away from his legacy, or from Brett's girls for that matter. But . . .

"I gotta go. I'll call you later," he said, hanging up the phone as soon as Kelly had said goodbye.

He looked at Ella, seeing her raise her eyebrows as if to tell him that she would have told him the same thing if she could have.

"Sit tight," he muttered as he jumped on the quad and fired up the engine. He drove carefully down the incline he was on and then hit the accelerator, going fast across the field and back to the barn. He had no idea what time she'd be leaving, or if she was even still here, but Kelly was right, he needed to go. He already had enough regrets to last him a lifetime, and this didn't need to be one of them.

Once he was back at the house, he ran inside and showered, drying off and dressing in clean jeans and a shirt before heading for the door again.

"Ella, come," he commanded as he skidded in his socks down the hallway, almost tripping as he reached for his boots and stumbled into them. She was hot on his heels, and he slammed the front door shut and ran to his truck, opening the door and letting his dog jump up before he got in and gunned the engine, sending gravel flying up behind him as he headed down the drive. His father would have slayed him for going that fast, but there was no one else around, and if he didn't hurry, he might miss her.

Or lose the confidence to follow through on what he was about to do.

Logan was surprised by how quiet River Ranch was. He pulled up outside, having forced himself to drive painfully slowly up the mile-long driveway, and got out of his truck. The garage door was up, displaying a fleet of luxury vehicles, but he could see that there was one space empty.

"Logan?"

He looked up and saw Mia standing at the front door, and he jogged up the steps toward her.

"Hey, Mia, I need to see Ange. Is she here?"

But her face fell, and he knew. He was too late.

"Logan, you missed her. She's already gone to the airport." Mia reached out and touched his arm, her face falling from happy to sad.

He ran a hand through his hair. "How long ago? Can I still catch her?"

Mia shook her head. "It's no use. She left an hour ago and they'll be—" He watched as she checked her watch. "I'm so sorry, but they would have been wheels up a few minutes ago."

He nodded, keeping his anger in check, refusing to let Mia see how upset he was.

There was movement behind Mia and suddenly her husband appeared. Logan recognized Sam straight away.

"Hey, Logan."

Sam held out his hand and Logan clasped it. "Nice to see you again."

"Do you want to catch up for a beer on Friday night?" Sam asked, leaning in the doorway. "There's a few of us going, and it'd be nice to have a fellow vet there."

Logan was going to say no, but saying no to everything was starting to wear thin. And he'd missed his one opportunity to be real with Angelina.

"Yeah, that'd be great," he said.

"We'll be at the Tavern from six, just swing past whenever."

Sam dropped a kiss into Mia's hair before disappearing again, and Logan started to back up. But Mia wasn't letting him get away so easily.

"Logan, she really likes you. I know I shouldn't be saying this, but I've never seen her like this over anyone before."

He swallowed, shaking his head. "No, I was a good distraction, that's all."

"Don't go discounting her like that," Mia said. "She had a lot of stuff to work through, and I know how much easier it would have been for her to stay here and keep hiding from the world."

He knew Mia was right, only he didn't want to admit it.

"She'll be back. I promise," Mia said.

"Mia, we both know that's not true." He actually found a smile just thinking about Angelina's face when he'd first asked her to go horseback riding. "Texas isn't where she belongs. She ain't coming back."

Logan turned and got into his truck, smiling as Ella leaned into him, putting all her weight against him as if she knew he needed some love. "I was too late," he muttered to her as he put his arm around her. "She's gone."

What would he have said if she were here? Had he even thought that through properly? Or was he just going to say what came into his head?

He tipped his head back and shut his eyes. *Stay.* That's what he was going to say. *Just stay.* It was as simple as that. But she was gone now, so it didn't matter what he'd thought about saying. It was over.

"Logan!"

A bang against his driver's side window sent him flying, eyes popping open and finding Mia standing in the driveway beside his car. Ella responded with a loud *woof*, but he silenced her with his hand held high.

Logan put his window down.

"Call her," Mia said. "Whatever you came here to say, you need to tell her."

Logan nodded.

Because it was easier to nod than admit the truth. Angelina was gone, on a jet plane back to LA, and he wasn't going to mess with her head now she'd made the decision to go.

Chapter 13

ANGELINA looked around her house, wondering how she'd ever left it behind. She loved everything about it; the dark polished wood floors, the chrome-legged furniture, and neutral color scheme—it was her dream house that she'd spent years saving for.

And she wasn't letting it go without a fight.

"Knock knock," came a familiar voice at the front door.

"Welcome to your new office!" Ange called out, laughing when she saw her faithful assistant coming through the kitchen, a box balanced in one hand and coffees in the other.

Penny set everything down, then hurried toward her, throwing her arms around Ange in a big hug. "It's so good to see you again. I told everyone that you're like a phoenix, that you'd rise up from the ashes."

"And here I am," Ange said. "I'm not sure about being a phoenix, but I'm sure as hell not going to go down without a fight, now that I've had time to lick my wounds."

She collected her coffee and groaned when Penny opened the box to reveal macaroons.

"Hey, it's worth celebrating our first day back working together."

Ange picked one up and popped it in her mouth as she walked, gesturing toward what had been her dining room. Now the big table had her laptop at one end and another laptop at the other—one she'd ordered and had sent over that morning. Plus she had paper, pens, and other office supplies neatly stacked. There were only two chairs now, the rest stacked away in another room.

"I know this isn't like our old office, but it's only temporary," she said. "I wanted us working in the same space so we could bounce ideas back and forth."

Penny's smile was bright. "Sounds good to me. Now, are you going to tell me what you're working on?" she asked.

Angelina didn't reply.

"Please tell me you know what we're working on here?" Penny's eyebrows shot up and made Angelina laugh.

"Just drink your coffee and come sit with me," Ange said, linking her arm through Penny's. "I've been up all night scribbling ideas, and I want this launched within the next few weeks, so it's going to be a big task."

"Okay, boss, whatever you say."

Angelina was on cloud nine. She knew she should be tired and falling into an exhausted heap, but her entire body was thrumming with excitement, loving the chase of something new. She'd be lying if she didn't admit to staying awake thinking about Logan for part of the night, especially when her new project was so intrinsically linked to him, but she wasn't going to contact him. Not yet. What was the point? He was dealing with his own stuff—stuff he sure as hell didn't want to talk to her about—and they were just friends.

She sighed as she settled down in front of her laptop. But if they were only friends, then she should have been able to pick up the phone to talk to him without being so anxious about hearing his voice.

Or remembering what his mouth had felt like on hers, or his skin as it skimmed her body.

Work, she reminded herself. She was here to work, and if she wanted to keep the house she loved so much, there was no time to waste.

"This is going to be very different for us, because it's going to be charity based, but this is my stepping stone back into the business world," Ange told Penny. "I want this project to find its feet and to find great people to manage it once we're up and running, and then I'm going to put on my big girl panties and rise like that phoenix you mentioned."

Penny's smile told her everything she needed to know. She was back on the horse, and no one was going to deter her from what she needed to do.

Logan entered the bar and soon spotted Sam tucked away in the corner. He was standing with Tanner, and someone else that Logan hadn't seen in a long while—Nate King.

"Hey, guys," Logan said, raising his hand.

They all called out, full of smiles, and Logan ordered a beer as he passed the bartender. He was tempted to have something stronger after the week he'd had, but the others were nursing beers, and he didn't want to be the first to move to top shelf.

"Long time no see," Nate said, holding out his hand and clasping Logan's. "Good to see you back here."

"Hey, I couldn't stay away. Where else was I going to go?"

The others chuckled, but Sam's face was more serious. He nodded, like he understood, and Logan knew that for once, someone actually did get what he was going through.

"It's a strange thing, how much we crave home when we're serving, and then how easily we can feel like a fish out of water when we get back," Sam said quietly. "Don't you think?"

Logan took a long pull of his beer. "Yeah," he replied. "It's exactly like that."

Nate and Tanner picked up the conversation they'd been having when he arrived, and Logan ended up standing at the bar, elbow braced on the counter as Sam mimicked his stance and ordered another beer.

"How're you actually doing?" Sam asked. "No bullshit, tell me straight."

Logan laughed. "Finally someone who talks my language."

Sam chuckled. "Yeah, well, I know how easy it is to bullshit and pretend like everything's fine when it sure as shit ain't."

"It's been rough," he admitted, draining half his beer to bide himself some time. "I lost my buddy over there, and I think about him 24/7." The words seemed to flow much easier talking to another returned soldier.

Sam nodded. "You keep playing it over and over, second-guessing yourself and figuring out all the different things you could have done?"

Logan stared at Sam, seeing the truth in his gaze. "Yeah, I do."

"Well, you need to stop," he said. "I know, easier said than goddamn done, but it'll keep eating at you. You need to run it through one last time, then let it go. Trust me, there's a lot to live for in this life, but regrets aren't one of them."

"You really think that?" Logan asked.

"I'm living proof of that," Sam said. "I spent way too long alone with my horses, trying to figure shit out, but the truth is, I just dug myself in deeper and deeper. And then went to counseling and eventually I met Mia, and everything changed."

Logan held up his hand and gestured for another beer. "So the darkness lifted? Like that?"

"No. I decided I deserved to be happy." Sam stared at him, long and hard. "Every year on Memorial Day, I go to ground. Mia knows to leave me, and I do my own thing, grieve for what we lost and what I went through over there. But the next day, I force myself to join the land of the living again and hold my head high."

His words made sense, of *course* they made sense, but he still knew it was easier said than done.

"So, what do you say?" Sam asked.

"I know you're right, logically," Logan said.

"So, what's holding you back?"

Nate interrupted them then, and Logan slowly turned to follow his gesture. All the color had drained from Tanner's face, phone pressed to his ear, and when he finally lowered it, Logan knew it was bad.

They could all see Tanner's hand shaking as he gripped his phone, eyes wide and filled with tears.

"He's gone," Tanner said, his voice more of a choke than his usual deep baritone.

Nate leaned past Logan and ordered whiskey, thrusting one at Tanner as he stood, shaking his head.

"Christ, you mean *Walter*?" Sam asked. "Walter's gone?"

Tanner cleared his throat. "We thought we had months left with him, but he just . . ." He never finished his sentence.

Sam moved forward and gave Tanner a big hug. "I'm so sorry, Tan, you know how much I loved the old man." He paused, knocking back the whiskey Nate passed him. "I need to get to Mia. I want to be there when she hears."

Sam disappeared and suddenly it was just Logan standing there with Tanner and Nate.

"I need to get home. I need to see Cody. I need . . ."

"I'll take you home," Nate said.

Logan knew he needed to say something to Tanner, to say how sorry he was, to offer proper commiserations, but his head was full of only one thing, and that thing was Angelina.

"Tanner, does Angelina know yet?" he asked.

Her brother shook his head. "I need to call her," he said gruffly.

"Where's your jet? If it's here and it needs to get to her in California—"

"It is," Tanner interrupted. "Christ, I had it back here for a business trip Dad wanted me to take this week."

"Tanner," Logan said, needing to be heard.

Tanner's gaze finally met his.

"Angelina's gonna be hurting real bad, and if you don't mind me riding in the plane, I'd like to be there for her."

Tanner opened his arms up and gave Logan a big hug, slapping him on the back. "Yeah, I bet she'd like that. Can you be wheels up as soon as the plane's ready?"

Logan nodded. "I'll be at the airport in less than an hour. But, Tanner?"

"Yeah?"

"Don't tell her I'm coming. I'd rather not make a big deal out of it."

Tanner nodded, already pulling his phone out and calling to get the plane on standby.

Logan was probably making a mistake, but he didn't care. He'd taken too long to act last time and missed her, and now she really needed him. In the past, when he'd really needed someone, it had been Ange who'd been there, and this time, he was going to be the one there for her.

Whether she felt the same way about him as he felt about her or not.

Angelina put the phone down, her hand shaking so hard that it landed with a clatter on the table.

"You okay?" Penny asked, looking up over her glasses, concern etched on her face.

She was numb. She knew the tears would come later, that one day or hour or minute they'd be a torrent that she wouldn't have a hope of turning off, but right now, she was frozen.

She needed to get home.

"Penny, I . . ." She stared at what she'd been working on, trying to figure out what to ask for, what she needed to do, what she should say.

But Penny seemed to sense it, rising and moving to sit on the back of the chair in front of her.

"Ange, tell me what you need me to do."

"I have to go," she whispered. "I don't know how long but . . ."

"You need me to handle all this while you're not here," Penny finished for her, taking hold of her hand and gently squeezing it. "I'm not going anywhere, so all this work here and all these emails that need to be sent? Consider it done. We've been working together so closely this week, so I know what you need me to do."

Ange took a deep, shuddering breath. "My dad, he's . . ." She gulped down air, wondering why her lungs felt like they were completely depleted of oxygen.

Penny's hold on her hand tightened.

"My dad passed away," she murmured, wondering how the words could even be true. "The jet's going to land in less than two hours, so I need to pack and head straight to the airport."

Penny nodded. "Of course."

They stared at each other for a moment, before Penny slowly rose and wrapped her arms around her, holding her tight. "I'm so sorry, Ange. I know how much you loved him."

Angelina numbly hugged her back, her breath calming as Penny slowly stroked her back in big, comforting circles. When she finally released her, Ange headed for the bedroom, pulling out the suitcase she'd only unpacked days earlier. It hadn't even been a week, and she was heading home again. Only this time, nothing was going to feel the same.

She hurriedly packed, fumbling for her cosmetics and grabbing an oversize cashmere cardigan to snuggle into on the flight. A wave of emotion shuddered through her, then, but she clamped her jaw and fought it, not wanting to lose her composure just yet. She needed to get to the airport, board the plane, and then she could fall apart.

He's gone.

She gasped, her breath shuddering out of her as she doubled over, the pain in her stomach, in her heart, so severe, it was like someone had actually knifed her. Ange's hand slapped the wall, her palm flat against it as she tried to steady herself.

"Hey, come on, I'm here," came Penny's soothing voice. "Let's get you in the car and to the airport."

Ange was incapable of speaking, following along after Penny, gripping her hand tight, and letting her assistant and friend bundle her into the car. She stared at the houses blurring past, rain starting to fall in irregular streaks down the glass as they drove.

Eventually they arrived, and Penny ran around to open the door for her, taking out her duffel bag and case, and holding out her cardigan so she could shrug into it.

Penny hugged her again, kissing her cheek, and even though Ange could see her lips moving, she couldn't hear what she was saying.

She mumbled "thank you," walking into the airport, trying to focus on her surroundings even though everyone was blurring into nothing, tears starting to fill her vision as she stumbled on.

But as she finally stepped outside onto the tarmac, a voice calling her name had her spinning around.

"Ange!" he called. "Ange!"

She was dreaming. Why was she hearing her name? Who on earth would be calling her?

"Ange!"

Then she saw him.

She opened her mouth to say something, hardly believing he was even there, but all that came out was a gasp.

"Ange," he said again, but this time it was softer and she heard it properly, the way his voice seemed to echo around her.

Logan. She wanted to say his name in reply but nothing came out.

Then his big arms engulfed her, holding her up as her legs started to buckle. He caught her as she shuddered, as sobs so guttural erupted from deep within her that she couldn't say anything or even move.

"I got you," he whispered, catching her and scooping her into his arms. Her head fell to his chest as he carried her, as he murmured to her even though she couldn't hear him.

Angelina found herself on the plane, being put into her seat, Logan's strong hands moving her and buckling her into her seat as if she were a child. She shut her eyes, the pain too intense, the emotion bubbling inside her impossible to swallow down. She was aware he'd disappeared, but then she felt him back beside her again and she reached out.

"I'm here," Logan said, his voice making its way to her as his hands clamped tight around hers. "I promise, I've got you."

He sat beside her, his thigh pressed to hers, his hand on her lap as she held him.

Logan was her best friend, and no matter what had happened between them, she knew then and there that no one was ever going to come close to being as real to her as he was.

And always had been.

Logan stared down at the woman in his arms. He could see the irony in what he was doing, looking after someone deep in the throes of grief when he himself couldn't deal with his own grief. But he hadn't been lying to Angelina; he was there for her, and he did have her.

All he'd been able to think about was her doing it alone. Finding out so far from home, getting to the airport, the plane ride and the emotional drive to her family's ranch. Helping her with part of her journey was the least he could do.

Ange had been resting her head on his shoulder, but as he stretched out his legs, the weight against him lifted.

"Sorry, you must be so uncomfortable."

"I'm fine," he insisted. "You rest on me all you want."

He was about to touch his hand to her thigh but thought better of it, not wanting to blur the lines between them or make her think he wanted something other than friendship.

"How did you find out?" she asked. "How did you get here so fast?"

Her eyes were so wide when she looked at him that she reminded him of a small, terrified child.

"I was with Tanner and Sam when they found out," he said. "When I heard the jet was in Texas, I knew that someone needed to be on it for you."

She smiled through her tears. "I think that's the sweetest thing anyone's ever done for me."

Logan stared at her, hating that she was in so much pain. "I was an asshole last week to you, and you deserved way better," he said. "This is my way of showing you that I actually give a damn. A *big* damn."

Angelina nestled back into him again. "Thank you," she whispered. "I won't ever forget this."

They stayed silent until she broke it again.

"Are we just friends, Logan?" she whispered.

He put his arm around her and held her tight. "Yeah, Ange, we're just friends. Damn good friends."

The words came so easily. They'd fallen out of his mouth as if they were fact. But the truth was, he didn't think of Ange as only a friend anymore; what he did know were all the reasons they couldn't be together. He'd lost the confidence he'd had the day she'd left, the words he'd wanted to say to her, because he'd had time to think about it. To really mull it over and see how futile it all was.

She lived in another state. It would ruin their friendship. She was a high-flying businesswoman and he was a rancher.

Logan gulped and stared out the small round window at the dark night outside.

And I'm too broken to ever be more than just a friend to her.

Angelina was the most accomplished, beautiful, together person he'd ever known, and he knew without a doubt, even if she didn't, that she'd recover from her business collapse. There were some people in the world built to succeed, and she was one of them.

"What do I do?" she asked. "When I land?"

"Your family will all be at the house. I understand your father left very specific instructions so it's a matter of . . ." Logan paused as he saw tears start to stream down her cheeks again.

"Keep going," she murmured, jutting her chin high, her jaw clamped so tight, it looked as if it were made of steel.

"I called Tanner on my way to the airport, and he said Mia and Lexi were following your father's wishes, and that they were all going to spend some time together tonight before organizing the service tomorrow."

She nodded, her grip on his hand ironclad.

The rest of the flight passed in silence, with Angelina's hand in his. So many emotions were running through him, including the desire to run for the exit the second the door opened and hole up at his house with only whiskey for company. But he knew that him being there was what she needed, and as her friend, it was what he was going to give her, no matter how hard it was seeing her pain.

He nodded to the attendant as she motioned that it was safe to leave, collecting Ange's bags and gesturing for her to pass him. She walked slowly, robotically down the stairs, and he jogged behind her, taking the lead on the ground so she didn't have to think about anything. They went through the terminal and out into the lot, and he walked them to the car, opening her door for her.

Angelina sat, staring straight ahead, and when she didn't move to do anything, he reached over her and clicked her seat belt into place. He guessed she was in shock, that the effect of finding out, rushing to the airport, and flying across state like that was only just registering.

Logan gently closed her door and put her bags in the back, going around to the driver's side and starting up the engine.

"I'll get you there as quickly as I can," he said, foot on the accelerator as they left the airport behind and headed for River Ranch.

Angelina opened her mouth, but it was dry and the words she wanted to say seemed to be stuck in her throat. She cleared it, but as she stared at Logan beside her, she suddenly didn't know what to say anyway.

She was thankful it was nighttime, otherwise the sight of the fences, the manicured drive, the big house sitting proudly at the end of the driveway—it would all have been too much. Because it was her first time going home, going *into* her home, and knowing that she no longer had a parent waiting for her.

Losing her mom had been crippling, but losing her dad and knowing that she was an orphan now? Tears stung her eyes, and she tried futilely to blink them away. That was the worst feeling in the world, even though she was an adult who'd long ago flown the nest.

When the car stopped, she took a moment to breathe, to ready herself for what she was about to experience, and it was Logan opening the door for her that jolted her into action. He held out his hand and she grasped it, happy to draw on his strength and so grateful that he'd been there for her.

"I don't know how to thank you," she managed, surprised at how croaky her voice sounded.

He squeezed her hand tighter, not saying anything in reply. Within seconds, they were at her front door, and she hesitated, hand over the doorknob as she took a big, shuddering kind of breath.

But when she couldn't do it, it was Logan who reached around her and pushed it open, his hand to her back as he nudged her forward.

"You can do this. Just one step at a time, okay?"

She glanced at him and followed his advice, taking that first step into the house. But she turned back around when she sensed he wasn't following her.

"You're not coming in?" she asked.

Logan shook his head. "No, I'll leave you to it," he said. "I just . . ."

She smiled through her tears, seeing his pain, the almost panicked look on his face about having to go in with her. It had been so easy to lean on him, but she could see how hard it was for him. Death wasn't easy for anyone, especially not for someone who'd experienced loss like he had, and when she had her voice back, she would thank him for his bravery.

"I'll see you soon, I guess," she whispered.

Logan leaned in, his hand to her shoulder as his lips grazed her cheeks. "If there's anything I can do, anything at all, you know where to find me."

Angelina breathed in the familiar scent of him, eyes opening as he pulled away, an acute sense of loneliness wrapping its cool tentacles around her. She was about to step into a room filled with her family, but for some reason, without Logan, she'd never felt so alone.

Ange watched as he turned and jogged back down the veranda steps to his car, the outdoor lights illuminating his truck as he got in and started it up. He braked right in her line of vision, window down, his hand raised as his eyes met hers, and then he was gone. She tracked the red taillights until she couldn't see them any longer, and then she bravely shut the door and prepared to enter a new world that didn't include her father.

"Ange?"

Mia's voice cut through her, the very sound of it sending tears sliding back down her cheeks again.

"Hey," she whispered, colliding with her sister in a hug so fierce, she didn't ever want to let go.

Then Tanner and Cody were with them, their big arms circling, holding both their sisters tight as emotion shook each and every one of them.

When they finally let go of one another, Angelina wiped her cheeks and looked at her siblings.

"Where is he?" she ground out.

"In his library," Tanner said, clearing his throat. As an adult, she'd never seen her brother's eyes red-rimmed from crying or his voice catching with emotion. "Lexi put him into a comfortable, uh, position."

She nodded. "Do you all mind if I have a private moment with him?"

"Honey, we've all had our time with him. You take whatever time you need," Mia said, slipping her arm around her for another cuddle. "We'll all be in the kitchen having a drink when you're ready to join us, but just so you know, the funeral home is coming to get him tonight."

Angelina felt like her shoes were full of lead, but she made herself walk the short distance down the hall to his library, stepping through the open door and bracing herself for what she was about to see.

She expected it to be hard, to be shocked by the way he looked, but she wasn't. Angelina stopped a few steps away from him and smiled, grateful to Lexi for making him look so comfortable and normal the way he was lying on the sofa.

"Goodbye, Dad," she whispered, forcing herself to take another step and then another, before reaching out to touch his hand. "I'm going to make you proud. I promise."

She took one last, long look at him. Only twenty-four hours earlier she'd called and told him what she was working on. She'd asked him how he was, but he'd brushed her off and insisted she tell him everything about her new venture. His voice had been strained, but he'd refused to talk about his illness or how he was feeling.

Angelina smiled and blew him a kiss before turning to go and find her siblings. He should have told her how bad he was, but that was her dad, protecting her and caring for her until the very end. And that call she'd made, it was the best thing she could have done. It would have been so easy to wait until the next day or just shoot him an email, and she would forever be grateful for the decision she'd made.

The low hum of voices echoed faintly out into the

hallway, and she followed the sound into the kitchen, taking the glass of whiskey Cody offered her, not hesitating to take her first sip.

"To Dad," she said, holding up her glass.

"To Dad," they all called out with her.

They talked and drank together for the next hour, but it was late and one by one, everyone left. First, it was her sister when Sam arrived to pick her up, the children asleep in the back of the car, and then Tanner left with Lauren tucked to his side, and then eventually Cody left too. Lexi had stayed in the guest house with Harry, so by the time he went, it was only her.

"You sure you're okay here on your own?" Cody had asked as he left. "You can come stay with us."

"Don't be silly. I'm fine," she'd insisted.

But as she listened to the patter of rain on the roof and heard every creak and groan of the house, she couldn't stop thinking how alone she was.

You're fine, just go to bed and get some sleep. This is home.

Angelina hesitated at the foot of the staircase, her fingers thrumming rhythmically along the bannister as she breathed deeply and looked up at all the treads she had to step to get to the top.

Just go.

She turned slowly, her eyes catching the keys sitting forlornly on the table near the entrance to the house.

Then she ran, grabbing the keys and running to the garage. She couldn't stay here alone, not even for one night.

And there was only one place she wanted to be.

Chapter 14

ANGELINA got out of the car and pushed the door shut behind her. Most of the house was dark except for two of the rooms, so she knew he was in there. But still, even knowing he was home, she wasn't sure she'd done the right thing.

The rain was starting to pelt down, soaking her hair and plastering it to her face, but for some reason she couldn't move. And then something touched her hand, nudged her, and she looked down to find Ella standing quietly beside her.

"Hey, girl," she said, drawn from her trance and dropping to her knees. "Hey."

Angelina wrapped her arms around the dog, holding her as she cried, needing to feel her fur between her fingers even if it was wet, to have the warm body of another creature against her.

She'd come for Logan, but instead, she'd ended up with her arms around his dog. It was like the animal had sensed she needed to be comforted, and she hadn't moved an inch.

"Ella!"

She heard the call and slowly let go of the dog, her fingers unclenching as she pushed back, but Ella only moved closer to her as she stood, not leaving her side as she whimpered.

"Ella!" The outdoor lights came on then, and as Angelina blinked through blurry, tear-filled eyes, she saw Logan appear on the veranda. "What the hell?"

His call cut through the air, audible over the rain as he cursed and ran toward them, barefoot across the gravel.

"Ange? What the hell are you doing out here in this?"

She shook her head as Ella nudged her hand, her nose insistent like she was trying to tell her something.

Logan looked fierce, but as he stopped in front of her, his face softened and he seemed to take in the sight of her standing there with Ella.

"Come on," he said. "We need to get you out of this rain."

His arm scooped around her, half walking with her, half carrying her to the house, bustling them in out of the elements. Ella shook the second she was inside, sending water spraying everywhere down the hall, but if Logan noticed, he didn't say a word.

"Shit, your teeth are chattering," he swore, tugging at her top.

Angelina lifted her arms, letting him take off her sweater and T-shirt beneath that, then her shoes and pants, as if she were a child that needed to be looked after. Soon she was standing in only her underwear, arms wrapped around herself as Logan quickly stripped out of his wet top.

"Come on," he said, holding out a hand and guiding her with him.

She found herself sitting on the edge of his bed as he turned the shower on, letting him walk her in.

"You need to have a long, hot shower, warm up, and I'll put dry clothes on the bed for you," he said.

When she didn't move, he frowned.

"Ange, you need to help yourself here," he said.

But when she looked up at him, knowing he was right, all she wanted was to be in his arms. She stepped forward, studying his face, remembering the feel of his lips on hers, and she stood on tiptoe, pressing her mouth to his.

Logan stood still, his mouth moving slowly beneath hers for all of two seconds, before his palms covered her shoulders.

"No," he muttered.

She saw the look on his face, knew how wrong she'd been to kiss him, but her emotions were all out of whack.

"Sorry," she whispered, her voice cracking as tears threatened again. "I'm so sorry, I don't . . ."

Logan didn't say anything, he just pulled her against his big, firm chest, his skin so warm against her cool cheek, and held her.

"Have a shower," he said, before letting her go. "And then we can talk."

With that, he turned and left the bathroom, leaving her to stare at her bedraggled appearance in the mirror and wish she hadn't just made a fool out of herself by kissing the man who was supposed to be nothing more than a friend to her.

Logan listened out for Angelina. He'd heard the shower turn off a few minutes earlier, but he had no idea whether she'd stay in the bathroom a while or venture out to find him.

He finished toweling Ella off, giving her a pat on his way to the laundry. He had Ange's jeans in the dryer, but he'd hung her sweater and T-shirt out, not knowing whether they might shrink if he tried to dry them.

When he walked back through to the living room, he saw her, and his breath caught in his throat. Never before, even after all the years of knowing her, had he ever seen Angelina look so vulnerable. Or so beautiful.

Her hair was wet still and falling over her shoulders, her face scrubbed free of makeup, but it was what she was wearing that really got him. He'd left his softest cashmere jersey for her, not realizing quite how enormous it would be on her, and she was wearing it with bare legs, his wooly socks the only other item of clothing he could see on her body. Her tanned legs were so long and smooth, and she looked so soft in the cashmere.

"Better?" he asked, almost choking on the lump in his throat.

"Better," she replied. "But I'm sorry, you know, about before."

He shrugged. "It's fine. Although Ella was pretty wet from being out in the rain. I can't believe she found you out there."

Ange smiled, faintly, but it was still there. "I meant about before in the bathroom."

Logan grinned. "I know."

He watched as her cheeks ignited into a much deeper shade of pink than usual. "I was going to offer you a stiff drink, but I'm thinking hot chocolate would be a better option."

She nodded, curling her fists into the long sleeves of his sweater at the same time.

Logan headed for the kitchen, knowing she'd follow, and by the time he'd opened the fridge to get the milk out, she was sitting at one of the upholstered bar stools on the other side of the counter.

"Why are you being so nice to me?" she asked.

"Well, you kind of turned up on my doorstep in the rain, so I didn't get much choice."

When she didn't answer, he set the milk down, palms on the counter as he stared at her.

"Ange," he said softly, wishing her eyes weren't so beautiful, wishing that he didn't care about her so damn much. "We've been friends for longer than I can remember, and you've just lost your dad. Is it so hard to believe that I actually give a damn about you? I like the fact that you came here."

The way she was looking at him, blinking, her eyes so big and wide, it made it almost impossible to hold himself back. What he wanted was to crush her body against his and kiss the breath out of her, to tell her it was the worst goddamn decision of his life to push her away in the bathroom before.

But he didn't. *He wouldn't.* She was grieving, and she'd be gone again within days, a week at best. And he already knew how that story ended between them.

"You're always there for me," she said. "When I was called a slut by those girls in senior year, when I came home broken, and now."

He shrugged like it was no big deal and turned back around to make the hot chocolate. "Hey, that's what friends do, right?"

"Why?" she asked. "Why do you do so much for me when I don't do shit for you?"

Logan broke chocolate into the pot and started to stir it. Was it really that hard for her to see? He took a deep breath, feeling her behind him, knowing she was staring at him.

When he finally turned, his head started to pound. With frustration, anger and a passion that could have ignited the room.

"The hot chocolate's almost done. Why don't you go curl up by the fire," he said, trying to keep his voice even, to not sound like he was grinding out every goddamn word. "You must still be cold."

"No, I'm good," she said, but she did slip off the seat.

Logan's heart was pounding as he stared at her and she stared straight back.

"Please," he said, pointing to the adjoining room. "Just go."

He refused to keep watching her, needed some distance between them. What he didn't need was her looking all gorgeous and vulnerable in his clothes, in his house, with eyes as big as saucers staring at him.

Logan took out two mugs and filled them with hot chocolate, every fiber in his body acutely aware of the woman behind him.

"Logan." Her whisper slayed him. It broke down every inch of his willpower, of what he'd been trying so damn hard to keep in check.

"No," he said, refusing to turn. "Go into the other room, Ange. Please."

Her hand slid down his arm, trailing from above his elbow to his fingertips as it hung at his side.

"Logan," she murmured again.

He swallowed and turned, shaking his head as he looked down at Angelina, at her full mouth, lips parted, as her eyes so open and full of question met his.

"No," he said.

She didn't move.

"Goddamn it, Ange!" he swore, flinging the wooden spoon he was holding across the room.

Her eyes widened, and he saw the panic in her gaze as she backed up.

"I'm sorry," he said, hands hovering as she kept moving out of his reach.

"It's fine, I just, maybe I should go. I should never have come, I . . ."

"No," he shouted, cursing himself as she blinked back at him. "No," he said more softly this time.

He took a deep breath and wished he could say everything he was swallowing down, so good at keeping every single damn thing locked away inside of him.

"Can't you see, Ange?" he whispered, having to force the words out like his life depended on it.

"Can't I see what?" she asked.

"That I love you," he said, opening his arms, palms facing up, as he ground out the words. "I goddamn love you, and it's taken every inch of my willpower not to do anything about it."

Her silence was like a slap in the face.

"I'll get that hot chocolate," he finally muttered. *Why the hell did I say anything? What the hell was going through my head?*

"Logan," she said as he passed.

But Logan didn't stop. He didn't want to hear whatever bullshit she'd thought to say to him, to make him feel less stupid for admitting his feelings to her.

"Logan, please," she said, her hand sliding past his arm as he ducked out of reach.

"Sit," he said, putting the cups down with a bang and dropping onto a sofa.

"Logan, I don't know what to say," she said, looking embarrassed.

"Then don't say anything. You've just lost your dad and you need to rest."

She stared at him, but he shook his head.

And that look on her face, that look that told him how pathetic he was for thinking for a second that she might feel the same way? That's why he didn't talk about his feelings.

Tonight was a mistake. Emotions were running high, feelings were heightened. But he wasn't going to make the same mistake twice.

Angelina sipped her hot chocolate, savoring the thick milky chocolate as she tried not to look at Logan. *He loved her?* His words had hit her hard, jolting through her, and they were so unexpected, she'd had trouble processing them. And instead of managing to say something, *anything*, she'd ended up staring at him like he'd just told her he wanted to travel to the moon.

Her instincts were telling her to leave, but she didn't want to go. She wanted to be with Logan, to be right here in this room with him, sipping her hot drink and reminiscing with him. But instead, she'd never felt so awkward and she had no idea what to say.

"Logan, about what you said before," she finally said.

"Please," he replied, eyeing her cautiously from the other sofa. "Forget it, would you? I shouldn't have said it."

"But you did." There was no changing the fact that he'd said it, and the words weren't going to go away.

"I'm not going to pretend like I didn't mean it," he said, leaning forward and setting his mug down. "You know me too well, and I don't say anything I don't mean."

"I just," she started, feeling overwhelmed, not even knowing where to start.

She blew out a breath she hadn't even known she was holding, staring at Logan's face. At the familiar features she'd been so comforted by seeing earlier in the day, at the eyes she wanted trained on hers, the hands she wanted skimming against her skin.

But love? That was something else entirely.

"Ange, you've just lost your dad. I'm here for you," he said, sounding like he was on autopilot now instead of speaking from the heart. "You take my room; it's already warm and the sheets are clean."

"I don't care about clean sheets and . . ."

"What?" he asked as her voice trailed off. "What else don't you care about?"

"Nothing," she said. "I, well, where are you going to sleep?"

"Don't you worry about me," he said as he rose.

Ange sat there, eyes down as she watched his feet track across the carpet to her. When he stopped, he bent and dropped a kiss into her hair, on top of her head, and she froze, waiting for something to happen.

"Good night," he said.

Angelina sat there, staring at the roaring fire, listening to the pad of Ella's paws across the timber floor in the hall. The dog whined, and she turned to look at her.

"You don't have to stay with me. Go," she said, smiling as Ella seemed to understand, walking off after her master.

The events of the day weighed heavy on her shoulders, her head pounding as she thought about her dad. About seeing him. About losing him.

Had she lost Logan now too?

She took her final gulp of chocolate and stood, collecting the cups and walking them into the kitchen.

She rinsed and put them in the dishwasher before turning off all the lights and walking to the bedroom.

The house was warm, and Logan's sweater was soft and snuggly against her skin. She paused as she passed one of the guest rooms, seeing the puddle of light beneath the door.

Most of her wanted to knock softly; it was like there was a little voice in her head chanting: *do it, do it, do it*. But she didn't, because what would she say when he opened it? What could she even give to him if she walked in there?

So she kept walking.

She didn't bother undressing, climbing beneath the steel-gray bedcovers that smelled like him and tucking her bare legs up close to her body as she curled into a ball.

As she prayed for sleep to find her, to take away the memories and the pain, and the worry of what she was going to have to face in the morning, there was a slight creak of a door behind her.

Angelina stayed still, breathing as quietly as she could as a weight settled behind her. Logan's arm wound around her, drawing her back slightly, cupping her against his warm, firm chest, his legs tucked into the back of hers.

She felt his mouth against the back of her head, breath hot, his other arm above her head on the pillow. He never said a word, because he didn't need to, and she gratefully took the comfort he offered.

Sleep had felt like an impossible-to-achieve luxury before, but now she could feel her heartbeat slow, her eyelids no longer fighting to open as she tucked back into him.

Into Logan, the man that kept on rescuing her, no matter how many times she ran away from him.

Tomorrow, she was going to be brave and thank him for everything he'd done for her. She was going to stop taking from him, stop expecting him to comfort her when she had nothing to give him in return.

As his arm tightened around her, Ange finally succumbed to sleep, drifting off as she wondered whether this was what love felt like. Because it wasn't something she'd ever truly felt before.

Chapter 15

WHEN Logan woke up, he was surprised to find Angelina curled against him. She'd gone to sleep in his arms, and he'd meant to sneak out before morning, but instead, he'd fallen asleep too. Now, he was lying on his back and she was cocooned against him, her cheek to his chest, her arm splayed across him.

He stared down at her, at the puddle of her blond hair as it covered his chest and the side of her face. This was dangerous. He did not need to be waking up with her in this bed, when the last time they'd been in it together, they'd . . . He steeled his jaw and slowly extracted himself. The best thing for both of them was for him to get up now before things got even more complicated between them.

Logan glanced back at her, but she was still asleep, no doubt exhausted from everything that had happened the day before, so he quietly went into his closet, took out what he needed, and padded down the hallway to the kitchen. He hadn't been up fifteen minutes when there was a knock at his door, and he followed Ella down the hallway, swinging it open to find Cody Ford standing there.

"Sorry to come knocking so early."

Logan glanced at his watch. "It's after eight, so definitely not too early." He stood back and waved him in. "Come in for a coffee."

He shut the door behind Cody as he kicked off his boots, before showing him the way.

"I'm real sorry about your dad," Logan said as he pulled out two cups and set about making them both a coffee. "He was a good man."

Cody nodded. "Yeah, he was." Cody rubbed at his face, palms into his eyes, as Logan nudged a coffee in his direction across the counter. "He was sick a long time, but it's still hard to get my head around the fact that he's gone."

Logan nodded. He knew a lot about that feeling. "I'd say it gets easier, but in some ways it never really does."

They both stood in silence, sipping their coffee, until Cody looked up at him.

"You know, I was a real asshole to you when we were kids."

Logan laughed. "If you were, I don't remember it that way."

Now it was Cody laughing. "You don't remember when Tanner and I threatened to string you up by your feet outside of school if you dared touch our sister?"

Logan grimaced. "Well yeah, I sure as hell remember that! But you were only looking out for her."

Cody's expression turned more serious, and Logan studied him over his coffee cup.

"Seeing the way you've been there for Ange, through all of this, and when she came home all broken, before any of us even knew what was going on," Cody said, "it makes me realize how out of line I was back then. She'd have been lucky to end up with someone like you."

Logan looked up as Angelina entered the room, stretching in the doorway and looking surprised to find her brother sitting there.

"You were right to protect her back then," Logan said in a low voice. "It was for the best."

"What was for the best?" Angelina asked. "And what are you doing here?"

Cody stood and greeted his sister with a hug and a kiss to the cheek. Logan saw the love there, could see how close the two siblings were.

"I was worried about you," Cody said. "You and me, we spent our whole lives wanting to show Dad what we could do, that the apples hadn't fallen far from the tree. I just wanted to make sure you were all right."

Logan cleared his throat. "I'm going to make you coffee," he said to Angelina, "and then head off to do my rounds of the ranch. You're both welcome to stay as long as you like."

"Logan, can we talk for a moment?" Angelina said, and he saw the look she flashed her brother.

"You want me to go?" Cody asked.

"No," Logan answered, at the same time as Ange replied "*Yes.*"

"I just wanted to thank you, Logan," she said, turning her back to her brother. "For everything. You've been the most incredible friend to me, and I guess I want you to know how much I value our friendship."

Logan kept his distance, not wanting to disrespect Cody by touching his sister, but it was Ange who opened her arms and pulled him close for a hug.

"I love you too, Logan," she whispered in his ear, so

softly that there was no way Cody could have heard, as he held her in his arms.

When she stepped back, he had no idea what to say or where to look, but the emptiness that ran through him when he looked at her, knowing that somehow, even though she'd told him what he'd wanted to hear, that it was still goodbye . . . it hurt.

"Let me know the details for the service," he said, looking between Ange and Cody. "I'd really like to be there."

With that, he said his goodbyes and patted his leg for Ella to follow him. He had animals to feed, fences to check, and enough jobs to keep him busy for days on end. Which was exactly what he needed to get Angelina Ford the hell out of his head, because all they ever seemed to be doing was saying goodbye to each other.

"That man's in love with you," Cody said, and Angelina shot him a look that she hoped told him he was the last person on earth she wanted to talk to about her love life with. Or lack of.

"Please can we not?" she said. "I . . ."

"What? You won't talk to your brother about your love life? I've gone from being a cold-hearted bastard to a soft-hearted God only knows what, so I reckon I'm well qualified to talk to."

Angelina groaned. "Cody, can we, I don't know, talk about funeral arrangements or something?"

He shook his head. "Nope. Dad had everything planned, so all we had to do was notify the funeral director he'd specified and show up three days from now at the service."

"God, that's so Dad, isn't it? All the i's dotted and the t's crossed."

Cody pulled her in for a hug, and she went willingly. "I'm sorry for ever telling Logan to back off. He's a good guy, Ange. He'd be good for you."

She pushed him back. "What are you talking about? When did you tell him to back off?"

Cody looked guilty; it was written all over his face.

"Cody?" she cautioned. "Tell me right now what the hell you're talking about."

"When you were kids, back when the two of you used to be joined at the hip. Surely you knew he was in love with you, then?"

Angelina knew her jaw was dropping open, and she fought to shut it. With everything that had happened in the past twenty-four hours, her emotions already at boiling point, it was too much to hear.

"Cody, seriously, we were only friends. Logan never thought of me that way then, and now we're just . . ." She tried to figure out how to finish that sentence. "We're complicated, that's what we are. But the one thing I do know is that he's got his own stuff to deal with, and we live in different states for Pete's sake and . . ."

"And what?" he said. "In case you've forgotten, Lexi and I lived in different states too, and now look at us."

Angelina stared back at him. What the hell was he saying, that she *should* be thinking about Logan like that? "I don't want to be having this conversation with you right now."

Cody just smiled at her. "Hey, it beats talking about why you're home and what we've got to deal with right now. It's a nice, how can I put this . . . interlude?"

"Ha ha, very funny. I like that my complicated love life is a welcome *interlude* to you. Let's go."

Cody laughed. "I'll go, but I recommend finding some pants before you head out to the car."

Angelina's cheeks ignited as she looked down at her bare legs. No wonder Cody was giving her hell—she looked like she'd just rolled out of Logan's bed.

Which she kind of had, only not in the way her brother might have thought.

Logan looked at his phone, surprised to see a message from Angelina waiting for him. He'd been out riding most of the morning, keeping himself busy and checking on his ranch hands, but there was nothing left to do and he'd ended up back inside.

Logan, thanks so much for all your support. The service to celebrate my dad's life will be held two days from now at 2pm. Hope to see you there. A x

He stared at the little *x* mark, wondering if she did that with all her messages, before deciding he didn't really care if she did or not.

We're just friends. But for some reason, he couldn't get the sight of her, all tousled and barefoot, out of his head. He'd had plenty of girlfriends over the years, the recent drought excluded, but he'd never been serious about any of them. He'd liked them, some of them a lot, but it had never been love. Women had come and gone out of his life, and the longest relationship he'd ever had . . . He scratched his head as he looked out the window. He actually had no idea, but it was months not years.

In some ways, his friendship with Angelina had felt like his longest relationship with a woman, before they'd both parted ways to pursue their careers. And the only other one was . . . He chuckled to himself. *Kelly.* Which was ironic, given it was a platonic relationship with his best friend's girl.

He made himself a coffee and sat down at the table,

Ella by his side as he watched some young weanling horses having fun in the near distance.

Have I been waiting for Angelina all this time? Logan actually laughed out loud at that. They hadn't even been in touch properly for so long, so it wasn't that, but maybe he'd subconsciously been comparing every woman he'd ever met to her all these years. He had no other reason to be a commitment-phobe. He was so messed up right now, in that limbo of battling what had happened and what he'd seen, but before Brett's death, he'd had nothing to make him afraid. His parents were in a loving, long marriage, he had a sister who'd been happily married for years, albeit in a different state, and he loved women. And yet he'd never had a long-term relationship.

His phone buzzed again, and he glanced down, expecting it to be Angelina again, but it wasn't. And it wasn't a text either. It was a video call. From Kelly.

Logan cleared his throat before he answered. He was notoriously terrible at answering his phone, but he very rarely let Kelly go to voicemail, and given it was a video call, he was almost certain that it was Lucy, not her mom.

"Hey!" he said when he saw Lucy's little face appear on his screen.

"Logan, where are you?" she asked, her lower lip pushed out in a pout. "I can't order ice cream without you."

"Ice cream?" he repeated, before seeing her eyes widen as her face took on a horror-stricken look. "Ice cream!" he said again, frantically running to his bedroom to throw on some clean clothes. "Of course, I'm on my way. I just got a little held up on the ranch. See you soon!"

"Hurry, Logan," she said. "I'm hungry!"

Goddamn it! How the hell had he forgotten his ice cream date with the girls?

Logan slipped a clean T-shirt on, sprayed on some cologne since he didn't have time to shower, and gestured for Ella to follow him. She jumped in through his driver's door, and he drove down the drive, praying that his best little buddy was going to forgive him for being so late.

"Logan!" Lucy squealed when he finally arrived.

He mouthed "sorry" over Lucy's shoulder as he scooped her up, her little body hurtling toward him at full speed, expecting to be swung up and into the air.

"Logan, where were you?" she asked, arms looped around his neck as she studied his face. "Did you forget?"

"Forget? No!" he said, half expecting her to call him out on his lie. "I had a lot of ranch work to do. Have you already had your ice cream?" he asked, studying the chocolate around her mouth.

Lucy nodded.

"Well, maybe Mom will let me buy you a drink or something too."

He set her down and made his way over to Kelly. She was sitting at a little stainless steel table, sipping a milkshake.

"Can I get you anything else?" he asked. "I'm so sorry I kept you waiting."

"It's fine, don't worry. If it weren't for this little munchkin, I'd never expect to see so much of you anyway."

Logan frowned, but he knew she was right. Lucy was the glue that bound them together, and she was a good excuse for him to keep an eye on Kelly.

He took Lucy up to the counter and ordered himself a chocolate milkshake and a small one for the kid, watching as she wandered off to see another little girl.

"She's one of her best friends at school," Kelly explained, waving past him at the other mom. But when Kelly glanced back at him, he could see something wasn't right. She averted her gaze almost instantly and stared into her drink.

"Kelly?" he asked. "What's up? If it's about me being late, I'm sorry, I just—"

"It's not that," she said quickly, finally looking up again. "Logan, this is really hard for me to tell you, and I want you to know that before Brett died, it had been ten months since I'd seen him, so for me it feels like closer to two years since he's been gone."

Logan listened, his brows pulling down as he watched her. "I'm not sure I'm following."

"I love him so much still, and not a day goes by that I don't think about him, but . . ."

Logan leaned forward. "But?"

"I'm seeing someone."

He gulped. "*Seeing* someone?" he repeated, as his entire body started to heat up.

"I don't want you to go all crazy protective soldier on me, but he's really nice, and when I say that I'm seeing him, we've only been out twice. But I'm really looking forward to seeing him again."

Lucy came bounding back to their table, then, and he froze, trying to digest the words. Brett's wife was *seeing someone*? He tried to slow his breathing, knowing that the last thing she needed was for him to freak out.

"Say something," she said, looking worried.

"I don't have anything to say," Logan said, shaking his head, not sure *what* to say. "But if he—"

"Hurts me you'll break his legs, blah blah, yeah, I get all that," she said with a laugh. "I don't mind all that. I like that you're here to protect me. But I don't want you to flip out at the idea of me being with someone new."

Logan frowned at her, doing his best *not* to flip out. "Well, when do I get to meet him?"

Kelly reached out and took his hand, squeezing it. "That's the thing, Logan, you don't. You're the best friend of my husband, and as much as I appreciate all the love and support we get from you, I don't want you scaring him off. And he's a nice guy." She smiled. "A really nice guy."

Logan wanted to bare his teeth and growl, but with Lucy blinking at him from her mother's knee now, he could hardly get all worked up.

"It doesn't mean I don't love him, but he'd want me to keep living my life."

Logan got that, he did. He just hadn't expected to be hearing this so soon.

"And you know what?" she asked.

"What?" he replied.

"He'd want you to be living your life too."

Logan looked up at her, meeting her gaze head-on. Her eyes were bright now, burning into him. "I am living, Kelly. I'm drinking a milkshake and having fun with you guys."

"*Really* living, Logan. Not just being some shell of who you once were and hanging out with us every now and again."

He studied her, knowing she was right even as he wanted to protest it.

"You need to really live, Logan. Don't waste your life living alone, wondering what could have been," she said. "We only get one life, and if we're lucky enough to be living, we need to make the most of it."

He laughed. "Why do I feel like you're breaking up with me?"

Kelly laughed along with him. "In a way, I kind of am. Because we're never going to be enough for you."

Lucy slurped the last of her milkshake and ran around to give him a hug, climbing onto his knee as he embraced her. He loved this little girl more than life itself, and part of him had always expected to be a dad one day, but all those hopes and dreams, they'd died along with Brett. But Kelly was right, they didn't have to. Just like she didn't have to stop living because she was a widow.

"If things go well with this, uh, *date* of yours," he said, "I'd like to meet him. Not to size him up, but just to know who he is. I'm happy for you, Kel. Truly, I am."

Her smile lit up her face. "Thanks, Logan. It means a lot to hear that from you."

Lucy started chatting away, then, telling him about her day and her friends, and he sat back and listened, pleased he'd come to see them. His friendship with Kelly might have started because she'd needed him, just like he'd needed her, but they'd come a long way since then. She'd become a true friend to him, not just someone he saw out of duty, and one day he hoped he could figure out the words to tell her that.

Chapter 16

ANGELINA found herself looking over her shoulder at the church, trying to spot Logan. Every time she did, though, someone else would make eye contact with her, and she'd end up turning back around without finding him. She knew he'd be there, but she also guessed that funerals might be harder for him, given what he'd been through.

As far as funerals went, it had been beautiful. Her heart felt like it had been ripped from her body and broken into a million fragments, but she was still able to appreciate the beauty of it all. It had been a celebration rather than something morose, and her admiration for her father had been invigorated all over again hearing the stories of his life and how he'd come to be such a success in his own right.

As heiress to a quarter of his billion-dollar fortune, she knew she technically didn't ever have to work again, but it'd had the opposite effect on her. It had put an even stronger fire in her belly, to prove herself in her father's memory, and to put her inheritance to good use.

She couldn't wait to tell Logan what she was doing.

As of this morning, everything was running to plan for her new venture, and now that she was able to privately fund the start-up costs from her own personal wealth, she was going to be able to hit the ground running. Fast. She only wished she'd been able to tell him the other morning before Cody had arrived out of the blue and surprised her.

Mia patted her hand and brought her back to the present, and they all rose. It had been a long day, and they still had the post-service gathering to go to with all their guests, but they'd gotten through it.

Logan.

She saw him, then, at the back of the church, ducking his head and disappearing from sight. If it had been anywhere else, she would have excused herself and quickly gone after him, but seeking him out was going to have to wait. Surely he'd stay to talk to everyone as they filed out?

But once they'd watched their father being taken away in the black hearse, and hugged and kissed more people than she'd ever expected to even see at the service, Logan was nowhere to be seen.

"Who are you looking for?" Tanner asked, coming up beside her and putting his arm around her shoulders.

"Logan," she said, still scanning the rapidly dispersing crowd. They would all be back at the ranch soon, and she knew the rest of her siblings would be anxious to get going.

"'Fraid to break it to you, but he left already," Tanner said. "I saw him heading down the road when we carried the coffin out."

She ducked her head to her brother's shoulder, giving him a sideways hug and trying to hide her disappointment. "Thanks. You doing okay?"

"Yeah, I'm doing okay. I think Dad would have been proud of how today went."

The others joined them, including Lauren, who came straight up and gave her a big hug.

"Come on," Lauren said. "Let's try to get back before the masses descend on the ranch."

Angelina couldn't help but look around one last time, expecting to see Logan waiting for her, leaning against his truck or something, but Tanner was right, he'd gone.

She wondered, then, if she'd lost him, and the thought carved an empty space inside of her that hurt more than she could have imagined. It was like they'd played this game of back and forth so many times, and now the game was over.

Two hours later, she was nursing the same glass of wine she'd started the afternoon with, talking to yet another well-wisher who wanted to reminisce about her father. It had been a lovely afternoon, but she was ready for the house to empty out and to simply crash for the rest of the day with her family.

Her phone buzzed in her pocket, and she ignored it. But when it started to buzz again, she decided to check it. Someone obviously wanted to get in touch with her.

"Excuse me, I'm so sorry but whoever this is, they seem insistent," she said.

Ange stared at the screen, not expecting to see Logan's name. "Hey, Logan," she answered, smiling at the people around her as she extracted herself and headed for the kitchen.

"Angelina, it's not Logan, it's Kelly. Remember we met the other day at the restaurant?"

"Oh," Ange said, not expecting to hear a female voice. "Of course I remember, how are you?"

"I'm fine, and I'm sorry to call you because I know it was your father's service today, but—"

"Is everything okay? Is *Logan* okay?" Ange asked, panic rising inside of her.

"He's fine, or at least he will be." She heard Kelly sigh. "I'm with him right now. I stole his phone to call you. He's at that dive bar on the main road, and he's pretty drunk."

"Ahhh," she said. "And you think it has something to do with him attending my dad's service today?"

Kelly's pause was longer than Ange expected, and she was about to say something when Kelly finally spoke.

"I think it has something to do you with you, period."

Angelina digested the words. "Can you stay with him until I get there?"

"Of course."

"Okay, I'll get there as soon as I can."

She hung up and took a minute, catching her breath and drumming her fingers across the counter. Mia came in, then, looking as exhausted as she felt, and she pushed her phone into her pocket and took a deep breath.

"Mia, can you tell the others I've gone out for a bit? There's something I need to do."

Mia's eyebrows shot up in question. "Everything all right?" she asked.

"It will be," she said, not giving her sister any more information as she found the keys to the Range Rover and hurried to the garage. She glanced down at her outfit, knowing her silk shirt, blazer, and slim-fitting black dress pants were way too over the top for the bar Logan was holed up in, but she didn't care. Logan had always been there for her, no matter what, which meant the one time he needed her, she wasn't going to start worrying about the clothes she was wearing.

I've always loved you. They were the words she'd been trying to pretend she hadn't heard, too scared of digesting them, of trying to figure out what Logan meant to her and her to him. But if anything, the past few days had shown her that she needed to be brave.

Nothing in this world was forever, but it was time she started letting her heart have a voice.

And the first thing she needed to do was tell Logan how she felt about him, really tell him, instead of whispering the words in his ear then disappearing.

The bar was dim, and it took a moment for Angelina's eyes to adjust to her surroundings. But when they did, she could see why Logan was in trouble. The bar was host to only a handful of patrons, and other than a few friends in one corner laughing and sharing a beer, she had a feeling the others slumped over the bar were in need of help. Afternoon drinking solo was never a recipe for success.

"Hey," she said when she found Kelly. "Thanks for calling me."

Kelly gave her a quick hug. "I left Lucy with a sitter, so I'd better go, but . . ." She sighed. "Good luck."

She waited for Kelly to leave before slowly making her way over to Logan. He was hunched forward, one hand curled around a glass of ice with a small amount of amber liquid filling it. Her guess was whiskey.

She leaned in and tried to pry it from his fingers, but it was useless.

"Logan, I think you've had enough."

He looked up then, slowly, his eyes bloodshot as he stared at her. "Ange?" he said, clearing his throat and sitting up straighter. "I thought you were Kelly."

"Nope, it's me," she said, reaching for the glass again.

This time, he let her take it, but he lifted a finger and motioned to the bartender.

"Noooo," she said, shaking her head. "No more for this one."

"I need more," he said. "Got to keep going 'til I can't feel it anymore."

Tears pooled in her eyes as she watched him, as she saw him unclench one hand and saw the silver glint of a dog tag attached to a silver chain sitting in his palm.

"Today must have been really hard for you," she said, sitting beside him, her hand on his back as she started to stroke it in big circles. "I should have told you that I didn't expect you to be there."

He reached for the glass she'd taken away, and she didn't bother stopping him. His pain was so visceral, and seeing him like that, it showed her how much he'd suffered, what he'd endured to come home and start over again.

Logan turned to her, then. "We fucked it up, didn't we? All these years, and we screwed it all up by sleeping together."

She shifted uncomfortably in her seat, shooting the bartender a sharp look and hoping he wasn't listening.

"I'm still here," she said, taking his hand and stroking her thumb across his skin. "We're still friends. Look how you cared for me the day I found out. It doesn't get any more epic than that."

The way he shook his head told her he disagreed.

"I've been thinking, Logan, and I know this is messed up but I . . ."

He dropped lower, his forehead colliding with the bar. Shit! Was he out cold?

"Logan?" she whispered, bending low. "Logan!"

Just when she was about to scream for help, he turned

his head to the side, laughing as he stared up at her. He was just drunk. It was as pure and simple as that.

"Come on," she said, grabbing him around the arm and hauling him off the seat. "It's time we got you home."

To her surprise, Logan barely fought her, stumbling beside her as she marched him outside and to her car. Once she had him buckled in, she went around and got in the driver's side, pausing for a breath before starting the engine.

She looked over at him, handsome even when he was drunk and snoring.

"I think I've always loved you too," she whispered.

Logan woke up to the smell of food. He went to sit up and realized he was fully clothed still, and he smelt like a distillery.

Then he cradled his head. It was pounding like someone was operating a jackhammer inside of it.

What the hell had happened? He tried to piece together how he'd ended up in his bed, and as he swung his legs over and his feet scraped the carpet, he spied a big glass of water with two white pills beside it. He recognized them as ibuprofen straight away and quickly reached for them, dropping them into his mouth and greedily gulping down the entire glass of water.

Then his nose caught the scent of food again, and he realized what had woken him. His stomach was growling like he hadn't eaten in days.

Angelina. That was how he'd gotten home. He had no idea how she'd found him, but he remembered being bundled into her car. A noise from the other end of the house alerted him to the fact she was most likely still in the house, so he stood and decided to get cleaned up first.

Motherfucker. He groaned, his head pounding with every step, and gingerly crossed the room, turning the shower on, and stripping down. Once he was in, he stood under the burning hot spray of water, head tipped forward so it ran over his entire body, waiting for the medication to work its magic.

What the hell had he been thinking, drinking like that? Before deployment, he'd been a few-beers-on-the-weekend kind of guy, whiskey on special occasions only. But since he'd been home, he'd been drinking way too much, and he decided then and there to put an end to it.

He slowly straightened, scrubbing at his face and then reaching for the soap to lather up and get rid of the stench of alcohol from his skin.

Giving up alcohol wasn't the only thing he needed to do. When he was dressed, he was going to thank Angelina and then put an end to this, whatever it was, between them, before things got out of hand.

It didn't matter what feelings he might or might not have for her. He wasn't capable of being anything more than a friend to her, and he needed to make it clear that whatever he'd said the other night was bullshit. There could be no love, no more falling into bed because they were lonely or sad.

Friends. That was all they were and ever could be. Because he was way too broken to give anyone any more of him, especially her.

"Hey, sleepy head," Angelina called out, smiling when Logan appeared. She'd been up for hours, although technically she'd never actually gone to bed. She'd curled up on the sofa with Ella after she'd manhandled Logan into his bed, watching Netflix until she'd fallen asleep.

Then she'd woken and tidied up, keeping herself busy as she listened for him.

She hadn't known whether to leave and go home, or stay and wait for him. Neither had seemed like the right decision, but she had nothing to go back to the house for, so she'd decided to stay. In a way, it had been nice keeping her distance, creating a little bubble so she didn't have to think about how empty the ranch was without her dad in residence.

"Hey," Logan mumbled back, his hair wet from his shower as he stood in the middle of the room. His shirt was undone, showing off his muscled torso and a fine sprinkling of hair that trailed down into his jeans.

Angelina swallowed, wishing she didn't look at him that way. It was like a switch had been flicked and she couldn't look at him anymore without imagining his hands on her.

"I thought you'd be hungry, so I made some breakfast," she said. "You want it now?"

He nodded, but she could see from his expression that he was cautious. She kept talking, deciding to fill the silence instead of letting it stretch on uncomfortably.

"I'll heat it up and fry the eggs," she said. "Coffee?"

"Ange," Logan said, his voice gruff and cutting straight through her babble. His fingers closed around her wrist, surprising her from behind.

She wanted to pull away, but his grip was firm enough to tell her that she wasn't getting away so easily.

"I need to get breakfast," she said.

"Ange." His words were as insistent as his touch. "We need to talk."

She slowly turned, her eyes dragging up his body until they reached his. "No," she whispered. "We don't. I'll just get breakfast and then . . ." The look he was giving her told her she wasn't getting off the hook so easily.

"Ange, what are you doing here?"

"Cooking you breakfast," she said, as if it was the most simple explanation in the world. "I just wanted to do something nice for you."

He stared at her, and she sighed, managing to extract her arm from his ironclad grip.

"I saw you, at the service yesterday, but you were gone before I could find you."

She saw the tick in his jaw as he steeled it. "I don't do well at funerals," he ground out. "But I wanted to be there."

For me? She gulped. "For me? Or because you knew my dad?"

"For you," he muttered. "Of course I was there for you, Ange. Just like I came for you the second I heard he'd passed away."

She stared up at him, hating that he had such a height advantage. "Why are we arguing? Is this a battle of who gives a damn more than the other? Because I'm well aware that you're the one who's been there for me lately, and this is *me* being there for you."

He stared back at her, and she felt her chest rising and falling as her heart started to pound and her breathing became almost rapid-fire.

"When Kelly called me last night—"

"Wait, *Kelly* called you?" he blurted.

"How the hell else would I have known you were there? I don't exactly frequent dive bars in the afternoon, Logan. And why the hell are you so angry with me?"

She could see the anger seeping from him, the tick in his jaw becoming more prominent.

"You need to go, Ange. I really—" He shook his head at her. "I really think it's best if you just went."

"Go?" she spluttered. "You're kicking me out? After I dragged your ass home drunk and looked after you?"

"I would have made it home fine on my own."

His words were so cold, so blunt, as if he truly did just want her the hell out of his house.

"Logan, you can't mean it," she said, tears welling as she saw an unfamiliar hardness cross his face.

"You were perfectly happy to leave me last time without any encouragement, so I don't see why this is any different."

He may as well have slapped her across the cheek, his words stung so bad.

"Logan, we both knew that what happened between us was a mistake," she said. " And I had to go."

"Yeah, I know, you don't have to tell me," he said, backing away and moving to stare out the window away from her. "It was okay to come crawling home when it suited you, but the second you had a chance to leave, you were gone faster than you arrived."

Tears spilled from her lashes, and she furiously wiped them away. She was not crying over a boy, not for a second. She was stronger than this, and she wasn't going to let Logan get to her.

"Logan," she said, moving toward him, not about to blow her chance to make things right between them. "I went to that bar last night because I care about you," she said. "And because I had something to tell you."

He didn't turn around, and she lifted a hand to touch his back, hovering before she connected with him. But he was stiff beneath her touch, his body never softening even as she kept her palm there.

"Logan, please turn around," she asked.

He didn't do it straight away, and just when she was about to ask him again, he finally, slowly, turned.

"What?" he asked, shaking his head. "What is it that you're so desperate to tell me?"

"You told me the other day that you'd always loved me," she whispered. "You hurled those words at me, and I didn't know what to say."

He raised a brow, and she reached for his arm when he went to turn away from her again.

"I should never have said it," he muttered.

"But I feel the same, Logan," she said, staring up into his eyes, silently pleading with him to look back at her instead of straight through her. "I, I—"

"Don't say it," he said, pulling away from her. "Don't say it, Ange. I should never have said it the other day, and neither should you."

"I love you," she said, almost laughing over the word, it sounded so foreign to her. "I love you, Logan, so much it hurts. I always have."

"No, you don't," he said, succeeding in pulling away from her this time.

"I thought you'd be happy!" she said, throwing her hands in the air. "You told me, you were the one who started this, who . . ." Angelina didn't even know what to say. How had she misread this so badly?

"So, you don't love me?" she asked. "Was that just a line the other night? Because if it was, you did an Oscar-award winning performance."

"Come on, Ange, how did you think this was going to work out?" he asked. "You thought you'd tell me you loved me, and we'd somehow live happily ever after? Because reality check, darlin', that's bullshit. It doesn't matter how I feel about you, this can't ever work between us."

"Excuse me?" Anger was pulsing so rapidly through her, she could barely breathe.

"You know you'd never be happy back here. You'd be gone the second something bigger and better comes up, back on a plane to California to start a new company or join some big firm." He laughed, and it was the cruelest sound she'd ever heard.

"You're a real bastard, you know that?" she said, trying to swallow the lump in her throat, instead of giving in to the pain of his words. "And for the record, you're wrong about me. You're acting like I'm shallow and don't give a damn about anything or anyone other than myself, and you couldn't be further from the goddamn truth if you tried."

Her fingers itched to hurl something at him, to smash something at his head and launch at him. She wanted to beat at his chest and scream and hate him, but as she looked at him standing there, all she saw was someone broken. Someone reacting out of pain, someone lashing out just for the hell of it. This wasn't the Logan she knew. The Logan she knew would never treat her like this.

"I love you," she said, jutting her chin higher, drawing on a strength she didn't even know she had left in her. "And you can hurl insults at me all you like, but I'm being brave and I give a shit, and I'm not going to let you treat me like I'm a heartless bitch. Because I'm not."

He stared back at her, his mouth curling into what she thought was going to be words but ended up being more silence as he shook his head.

"Logan!" she demanded. "We are not ending like this."

"There's nothing to end," he said.

"What the hell is wrong with you?" she asked, grabbing his hand and wanting to shake him. "It's like someone sucked all the compassion, all the love out of you, and . . ." She stepped back, laughing. Because if she wasn't laughing, she'd have been bawling her eyes out.

"Can't you see, Ange? I'm broken," he said, turning again and staring out, away from her. "I'm so fucking broken. I'm so messed up from all the shit I've seen and what happened."

She stepped into him, her chest to his back, holding him, feeling the way his body shuddered and hating the pain he was in. They stood like that for what felt like forever, her cheek to his back, listening to his breathing slow again.

"You're not broken, Logan," she whispered, just loud enough for him to hear. "I promise you, you're not. But I think you're afraid of letting me in."

He never turned, and she never asked him to. Instead, she slowly pulled away from him, picking up her bag, glancing at the food in the pan that she'd so lovingly cooked for them to share. She'd sure expected this morning to go differently than it had.

"I went after you," he said, and when she turned, his back was still facing her. She stared at his silhouette, at the fit of his jeans, the looseness of his shirt as he stood. "When you left, I went after you, but your plane had already left."

She looked at the ceiling, waiting, wanting him to say the words she so desperately wanted to hear. "Are you going to come after me this time?"

He was silent so long that she turned, about to go again.

"No," he rasped. "I think it's better for both of us if I don't."

Angelina wasn't going to tell him he was wrong, because this wasn't her fight. She'd told him how she felt, and it was Logan who had to decide if he could deal with his demons.

"Just so you know, I'm going to be travelling back and forth between Texas and California for the next month, so I can spend as much time with my family as possible. My phone's always on if you ever need to talk," she said, proud of herself as she held her head high and walked straight down his hall and out the door.

It had been the most emotional week of her life, but she'd survived it. And for that alone, she was proud.

Logan listened to her go. He knew he'd behaved like an ass, that he should have stopped her, that it wasn't too late to apologize. But maybe it was. Maybe he'd already blown it, and there was no going back. He'd wanted to end their romantic relationship and salvage their friendship, and in the end he'd managed to sabotage both.

He touched his head to the cool window pane, eyes shut as his head filled with noise, the pain of everything slamming through his body and threatening to fell him.

Angelina Ford is walking out of my life, and if I don't do something about it, I'm going to lose her forever.

The worst thing was that she'd been right. He *was* afraid. It was the only reason he'd been able to listen to her pour her heart out, and then turn his back on her as if her words meant nothing to him.

She was the girl he'd always wanted, one of the last good things in his life, and he'd let her go.

Tears spilled down his cheeks as his shoulders heaved, hating what he'd become. Because the one thing he *had* been right about? Was that he was broken. It was like every part of him had broken and someone had tried to patch him back together, except that none of the pieces fit anymore.

He knew what he'd wanted, only he didn't seem able to find his way back to the man he'd once been.

For the first time in his life, he knew he needed help. Logan's hands started to shake as he dropped his face into his hands, unable to stop the sobs wracking his body as he slumped over the kitchen table. Alone.

Chapter 17

TWO weeks later, Angelina smiled to herself as she sat at her father's desk. It was a surreal feeling, sitting at the big man's desk, and although she'd worried about even being in the library again after seeing him in there that last time, it felt fine.

Well, fine was an understatement. She felt like her heart had been ripped out and trampled over multiple times, but she was a survivor, and nothing was going to bring her down. *Nothing.*

So similar to her, her dad had left everything perfectly in order. He'd obviously shown her the information on his currency trading for a reason, and she'd cried happy tears when his attorney had messaged over documents that morning for her, outlining her father's intention for her to continue his work in that sector.

"Thank you, Daddy," she said, tipping her head back and looking up. "Thank you, thank you, thank you."

A noise in the hallway startled her, and she stood to investigate. Her sister was at her own home, Cody was out with Lexi, and Tanner was out on the ranch. She wasn't expecting anyone back for hours.

"Hello?" she called out.

A dark, black nose poked into the room, followed by an excited scrambling of paws.

"Ella!" Angelina laughed and dropped to cuddle her, loving the way she wiggled with happiness at the attention. "What are you doing here?" And as she slowly rose, she felt someone else in the room.

"Hey," Logan said, his hands shoved in his pockets as he watched her.

"Hey, yourself," she replied. "Smart move sending the dog in first."

He laughed. "Yeah, I know. I think it's the only smart thing I've done in a long time."

"Hey, at least you're admitting it." They both laughed, but it felt forced, and Angelina folded her arms. "What are you doing here, Logan? How did you even know I was here?"

"I spoke to Cody this morning, and he told me you were home and that you might be here alone this afternoon," he said. "And the reason I'm here is to apologize," he said. "I don't even know what to say or where to start, but I am sorry. I'm so, so sorry, and that's what I should have said to you weeks ago instead of pushing you away."

She nodded, not ready to face him yet. He'd hurt her the last time they'd seen each other, and she didn't want to just forgive him, even though she appreciated the apology. Not yet.

"This suits you," he said, looking around the office. "It's a beautiful room."

"Thanks," she said, studying his face, wondering what was going through his head. "Logan, last time—"

"Stop,' he said, holding up a hand. "I have so much

to explain, and I just, I handled myself badly that day, and there's so much I need to tell you."

Angelina gestured for him to sit, and dropped into the leather sofa opposite him as she studied his face.

"Kelly has been telling me to talk to someone for a long time now, but it wasn't until I treated you so badly that I realized she was right. That I did need help." Logan leaned back into the cushions, and she knew how hard it must be for him to open up to her. "It's been a long time since I've been to church." He laughed. "In fact, I used to joke that I'd probably burst into flames if I ever went back after all my years of sinning. But I reached out to my old pastor a few hours after we last spoke, when I was at rock bottom, and he's really helped me to forgive and leave some painful memories in the past, where they belong."

Angelina leaned forward and took Logan's hand in hers, clasping his palm. "I'm so pleased you reached out to him." She took a breath, not sure whether to ask him more, but knowing she had to if she wanted to understand him better. "I'm guessing your bad memories are linked to Brett? You must miss him so much," she said.

"Every damn day," Logan replied, the words seeming to catch in his throat. "And I know there are going to be plenty of dark days still, but I'm coming to terms with it now. On his anniversary, when all those memories come flooding back, I'll probably lose my way every year for a bit, but I feel like I can deal with it all better now, without swallowing my feelings instead of asking for help."

She held his hand even tighter, tears burning in her eyes as she watched him—she'd never seen Logan so raw before. "I'll never understand what you went through over there, Logan, but I'm good at listening. You know you can always talk to me if you want to, but you also don't need to tell me anything you don't want to. I want you to be okay."

Logan was staring at their hands, but when he spoke again, he met her eyes.

"Everything is heightened over there," he said, his voice low. Logan shut his eyes, and she wondered if he was seeing it all in his mind again.

"The dust is dry in your throat, and the heat is next level. But what I remember most is the extreme boredom some days, followed by extreme exhilaration the next. I mean, we went days sometimes just throwing a ball around, talking shit, and then we'd have days of being hyperfocused, clearing an area and setting up so our sniper was in position."

Angelina didn't say anything, because she didn't know *what* to say, but she stroked his hand with her thumb so he knew she was right there with him. His voice was husky now, the memories obviously so hard to talk about, but it was the first time he'd truly bared his soul to her, and she couldn't stop thinking how brave he was being.

"Brett and I were already friends, but serving together, well, we were like brothers after our first tour," he told her. "And I suppose I always thought that if it came to it, I'd put myself in danger first. I guess I never considered that he might not go home to his girls, because I was the one without a wife and kid of my own. His life always seemed more important than mine."

"And you blame yourself, still?" Angelina whispered.

Logan didn't answer, not right away. But when he did, his eyes stared straight into hers. "Logically, I know his death had nothing to do with me. I understand that."

He paused. "But deep down, in my heart, I will always believe that I could have done something, that I should have seen something, that somehow I could have prevented it. That's what I needed to talk about, to work through."

Logan was silent, then, and she squeezed his hand before standing, pulling him up with her.

"Come over here," she said, walking back around to the desk. "There's something I'd really like to show you."

Logan followed her, and she clicked on a link then turned her laptop around to face him, waiting for him to read it.

"Four Paws Foundation," Logan read out loud. "Giving ex-service dogs the second chance they deserve." He looked up at her. "What is this, something you found online?"

"No," she said. "It's why I left in such a hurry after Father's Day a few weeks ago, and if you'd given me half a chance, I'd have told you all about it last time we were together."

"Hold up, you're *involved* in this charity?" he asked.

Angelina grinned. "Maybe I'm not as much of a corporate bitch as you thought, huh?"

His face softened, and it only made her laugh more. And it felt *damn* good to laugh.

"I never thought you were a corporate bitch," he said.

"Really? Not even a little?" she asked. "I mean, when I came riding back into town looking like I was too good for the place?"

It was him laughing now as he looked her up and down. "You kind of still look like that."

She touched her chest then, hand over her heart as her laughter turned into just a smile. "I might look the same on the outside, but I feel different in here now," she said. "I really listened to you, Logan. I heard what you were saying, about your struggles and what so many veterans go through, the emotions at stake over being parted from their dogs, and I decided to do something about it."

"You're seriously doing this?" he asked, taking a step closer. "You're actually starting this business?"

"Yeah," she said, not able to hide her grin. "I am, *I have,* and it feels damn good."

"It should." The softness in his gaze, the way he was watching her, it was making her squirm, making her feel out of control in a way she wasn't used to.

"Want me to tell you all about it?" She was hesitant, not sure about sharing it for the first time with someone like this, but she wanted Logan's approval. If she was honest with herself, she'd probably been waiting all this time for this exact moment, showing him what he meant to her, what his struggles meant to her, and that was before he'd poured his heart out. Now, she loved that she was about to show him she'd truly seen him and listened to what he'd been through.

"I don't think I've ever wanted to hear anything as much as I want to hear this," he said, taking her hand when she outstretched hers to him.

Angelina grinned, leading him back to the big leather sofa, the one she'd sat on so many times talking through business deals and ideas with her dad, and she sat with him. Her dad might be gone, but she felt like he was still there, that his presence in the room was enough. If she was telling him about this, she knew he'd have been so proud, and in a way, being in his library, opening up for the first time about what she was doing there, it felt right.

"Shoot," Logan said. "I want to know everything."

Angelina tucked her legs up beneath her, leaning against the arm of the sofa as she smiled at Logan. "Well, it all started with you. I wanted a new business to sink my teeth into, and I was trying so hard to figure out how to reposition myself and what to start with, and then I couldn't stop thinking about you and Ella."

Logan stared at Ange, hardly able to believe what she was telling him. How the hell had he managed to inspire her new business venture? He'd been so nervous coming over to see her, wondering if he was doing the right thing, but now he was so pleased he'd been brave enough to do it.

"So," she said, her excitement obvious as her eyes lit up, "I didn't want to limit this to only military dogs. When I saw the way you talked about Ella, and the way you treated her, I realized it was more of a universal issue. There are police dogs and other working dogs in enforcement and border patrol that all deserved a financial package on retirement or injury. There's some funding there and other programs in place, but I wanted to take it one step further and provide full support."

"How did you even know where to start?"

She laughed. "Starting a business is what I do best, and I've actually seen that it's the start-up I thrive on." He watched her shrug, like it was no big deal. "Besides, I had you in my head, seeing you with Ella and . . ."

When her voice trailed off, he raised a brow, watching the way she suddenly sucked in her bottom lip and chewed on it. He was not used to seeing so much as a flicker of Angelina looking uncertain or vulnerable.

"What? What is it?" he asked.

"I would love to use Ella as the face of the company, if you're okay with that," she said.

"You're going to have to be a bit more forceful if you want people to give you money." He hesitated, watching her face, seeing how genuinely uncertain she was about his response. "But of course you can use Ella," he said. "I'd be a jerk if I said no."

Her smile was so sweet, he wanted to bundle her up close to him and kiss her, but he pushed the thoughts away. This was about her sharing something with him, not about how he was feeling.

"I could have used any photogenic dog, but I want this to be real. I want to merchandize and really be able to stand behind the brand and be genuine in every aspect, and with Ella as my ambassador, that's how I'll feel. It's really important to me that we show the real face of these dogs and the people who care about them." He watched her light up as she told him about her business and her plans, and he couldn't help but be drawn in to her excitement.

"So, where is all the money coming from, or do you have a wealthy benefactor?"

Her cheeks flushed then as she opened her mouth to answer. "I'm the benefactor," she admitted. "To get it off the ground to start with, anyway. I have huge merchandizing plans to roll out, to raise ongoing money, but I'm putting up the seed money. I have a trust fund I've never used, and I've realized that not using it at all is disrespectful. I've never wanted to gain personally from it, but I feel like this is a pretty good compromise."

Logan couldn't believe it. This woman, this incredible, brave, successful woman, had listened to him and somehow turned his pain into the most beautiful gift.

"You're amazing, Angelina Ford, you know that?"

She frowned—the complete opposite reaction to what he'd expected. "I'm not amazing, Logan. *You* are, and so are the other people who fight for the dogs they love every single day. I just saw a way to ensure they received the veterinary care they need to recover for a civilian life, the training they might need or ongoing therapies, and the travel and assistance to ensure they're reunited with someone who loves them."

Logan shook his head. "I could have done this," he said. "God knows I have the money to help out and . . ." Why the hell hadn't he done something like this? "I moaned to you, and I thought I'd done something good by making sure Ella made it home, but in the end, all I did was save one dog. What you're proposing will mean so much to so many people and so many animals."

"It starts with one," she said. "And if you hadn't saved Ella, then I would never have seen what could be done. But, talking about all your money . . ." Her smile made him groan.

"What about my money?"

"If you're feeling so guilty, then why not make a donation? The more money we have—"

"You don't need to justify it, just tell me where to mail the check."

She smiled and he smiled straight back at her.

"You did good, Angelina. I'm so proud of you."

Her smile was shy this time, and he could see how much she had changed. She was wrong; it wasn't just the inside of her that was different, he could see it on the outside too.

They were silent for too long, and Logan decided

to break it. They'd been tiptoeing around each other, doing some kind of weird dance ever since they'd reconnected, and he wanted to change it.

"Ange, I said something to you last time, and I've been an ass to you ever since I said it."

He could see her swallow, like she was nervous.

"I told you that I'd always loved you, and I meant it." Logan could see the way her eyes widened, wished he knew what she was thinking. "But I threw the words at you like it was somehow your fault, and it's not. I'm the one who was too scared to ever say anything, and then when you told me that you might feel the same way, I pushed you away as quickly as I'd opened up."

"So, how *do* you feel?" she asked, her voice barely a whisper now. "Did you mean it? Do you still feel that way?"

"Yes," he said quickly. "Yes, of course I do. I just don't know what to do with it. All these years I've buried it, along with almost everything else I've been feeling. But yeah"—he reached for her hand, turning her palm over in his—"I have always loved you, Ange. You're one of the most incredible women I've ever met, and that scares the hell out of me."

Her smile was so sweet as she stared back at him. "We were such good friends, it always seemed sacrilegious to even think of you that way."

"Until we both came home all screwed up and in need of some comfort," Logan said wryly. "And then managed to stuff up our friendship in the course of a couple of weeks."

"Yeah, something like that."

Logan kept hold of her hand. "So, what do you say that we go out on a real date tonight? I don't want to blow our friendship either, but I feel like we've crossed a line already, and we can't take back what's happened between us anyway."

"I'd really like that," she said, leaning toward him.

Logan moved too, waiting for her to come to him, eyes on her lips as she hovered before closing the distance. Their kiss was sweet, tentative even, and he lifted his hand to cup the back of Angelina's head.

When she finally pulled away, he let her go, happy for her to set the pace.

"Shall I pick you up at seven?"

She nodded. "I'd like that. But, Logan?"

He waited.

"I want you to know that I'm scheduled to go back to California in three days. I want to be upfront with you this time instead of . . ."

"Disappearing on me?" he asked.

"Yeah, something like that."

He nodded. "Thanks for telling me. I'll see you tonight."

Logan tapped his thigh, and Ella jumped up and trotted beside him. He turned at the door and smiled at Angelina. If he'd ever had a chance to make things right between them, to see if they could be something more than friends, it was now. And he was not going to blow it, not this time.

Which meant he had to pull all the punches and work out how to make the night the most memorable date of her life without sabotaging it.

Chapter 18

ANGELINA startled when she heard a noise downstairs. She'd been expecting Tanner to come over at some point, but it sounded like a lot more than just her brother coming in the door.

"Hello?" she called out.

No one answered, but she heard laughter and recognized the high-pitched laugh that belonged to her sister.

When she looked into the kitchen, she saw two bottles of wine open on the counter, and a few more steps in she saw Mia, Lexi, and Lauren sitting around the table.

"What are you guys doing here?" she asked.

Mia's eyebrows shot up when she spun around and stared back at her. "Where are you going in that dress?"

Angelina looked down at her dress. "What, is it too much?" she asked. "I'm going out with Logan."

"On a date?" Mia asked.

Angelina didn't answer.

"Honey, this is Texas, not—"

"She looks fantastic," Lexi said, jumping up and throwing an arm around her neck. Angelina shot her a desperate look, needing to know if her sister was right or not. *Was* she too overdressed?

"Honestly, honey, you look fantastic. And it's *you*," Lexi said. "You're brave and real, and you *should* dress however the hell you want, no matter where you are. Isn't that right, girls?"

Mia nodded, but Angelina noticed her sister had downed her wine in record time.

"What is this, anyway? I didn't know you girls were all coming over."

She took in the platter of food and the wine glasses, the other women all in jeans and sweaters, and she realized how overdone she looked in her silk dress and stilettos. She'd dressed as if she were going on a date in LA.

"We were worried about you rattling around in this big house on your own," Mia said. "So we thought we'd surprise you with an impromptu girls' night."

"Oh." Angelina felt bad for not thinking of her sister and the other girls, but in her defense, she'd expected them all to be busy with their own lives. "I can cancel," she said, pulling out her phone from her bag.

"No!" Lexi cried, and Lauren was shaking her head at the same time.

"Honestly, it's fine, I'll just text Logan and . . ."

Mia stood, her hand closing over Angelina's phone and pushing it back into her bag. "Are you going on an actual date with Logan?"

Ange nodded. "Yeah, I am."

"Does that mean you two have finally come to your senses and figured out how freaking amazing you'd be together?"

Ange reached around her sister and collected her

wine glass, filling it and taking a long sip. When she looked back up, Mia was still watching her.

"Am I the *only* person who couldn't see this whole Logan thing?" she asked.

Lexi and Lauren laughed at the same time her sister did, and Angelina hung her head. It seemed like she and Logan were late to their own party when it came to figuring their feelings out.

"I need more wine," she said. "Someone, quick, get me wine before he gets here."

"Ahh, Ange?" Lauren said, pointing out the window. "I, um, I think your date's already here."

Angelina looked out the window, her breath catching in her throat as she saw Logan leaning against his truck, dressed in his usual jeans and shirt, but this time holding a guitar.

"Oh Lord," Angelina whispered, shooting her sister what she hoped was a plea for help.

But Mia wasn't helping her. "Go on," her sister murmured, giving her a push from behind. "Your man's waiting for you, and I wouldn't miss this show for the world."

She only moved because Mia's hand was at her back, and as she pushed open the door and was thrust outside onto the veranda, she quickly glanced back and saw that all three women were gathered behind her.

"Go," Mia whispered. "You've got this."

Ange's feet were glued to the spot now, and her hand flew to her mouth as Logan began strumming the guitar. She didn't even know he could play the damn guitar!

"Oh my God, he's *serenading* her!" she heard Lexi hiss.

But when he started to sing, everything else faded away. All she could see was Logan's face, all she could hear was his song, and she'd moved well past mortified at what he was doing to absolutely gobsmacked.

Logan sang as he leaned against his truck.

Angelina sucked in a breath, listening to his soft melody as he edged closer to the chorus of "Free Falling," one of her all-time favorite songs.

He started to walk, but as he opened his mouth to sing again, Ella let out a long, low howl that had Logan's face falling, clearly mortified, and Angelina erupting into laughter.

"Well, that ruined my grand entrance," he said, taking the strap of his guitar from around his neck and carrying it in one hand as he walked toward her.

"How did you know I loved John Mayer so much?" she asked.

"Honey, that song was by Tom Petty. Mayer just did a cover of it."

"Oh." She wrapped her arms around herself, watching, not sure whether she should go closer to him or stay where she was. And suddenly she was acutely aware of the women behind her. She knew they'd be rooting for her, urging her on, but there was so much history with her and Logan, it just wasn't as simple as him being a great guy and them needing a push in the right direction.

"Logan—"

"Ange—"

They both grinned.

"Ladies first," he said, moving closer until he was only a few feet from her. She was still higher, though, on the veranda with him on the step below.

"No one's ever done anything like that for me before," she admitted.

"It was corny, I know, but I couldn't come up with another big gesture, and Kelly insisted it was a good idea."

Angelina bit her lip to stop from laughing. "I have Kelly to thank for this?"

He grimaced. "Technically it was my idea, but she was just the backup to make sure I didn't skip out on the whole thing."

They stood and stared at each other, and Angelina's stomach erupted into butterflies when Logan reached for her hand.

"Ange, we have so much water under the bridge between us," Logan said softly. "We've both been so worried about not ruining our friendship, but in the end we've ruined what we had anyway, so I figure the only thing left to do is give this a chance, whatever it is."

She sighed. "I know. We can't ever go back to the way we were."

"But if you're prepared to be brave and give us a chance, a real chance . . ."

"Baby steps?" Angelina asked, swallowing emotion as he looked back at her so earnestly, with so much truth in his gaze that she knew without a doubt she could trust him.

"Baby steps," he repeated, his fingers tightening around hers. She looked down at his touch, at their connection. "Starting right now. And if everything falls apart, if we ruin everything, then at least we know we tried."

"Am I too overdressed for dinner?" she asked.

He shrugged. "Kind of. But you know what? I don't give a damn. You look beautiful, and I want you to be . . ." He stepped up, his feet beside hers now, his mouth hovering over hers as he dipped his head. "You," he whispered.

Angelina didn't move a muscle as his lips found hers in a kiss so sweet it left her aching for more. His mouth only grazed hers, so gently, just a taste, his lips so soft she wanted to cry for him to keep going.

Instead, he touched his forehead to hers, looking into her eyes as one hand cupped the back of her head, the other around her waist.

Clapping erupted behind them, and Angelina laughed along with Logan as he took her hand and spun her out before doing a deep bow.

"Thank you, ladies, I'm glad you enjoyed the show."

Angelina caught Mia's wink, saw the genuine happiness in her smile. "Have a good night, kids," she called out, before ushering the other two inside with her and shutting the door.

"Who's she calling kids?" Logan asked, wrapping his arm around her. "I thought you were the older one?"

Ange smiled. "She's enjoying her new role as mother and matriarch of the family, and I'm not about to argue with the mighty Mia."

They walked to the car, arms looped around each other. It was the strangest feeling, being so physical with someone who'd always been her friend, but at the same time, nothing had ever felt so right.

Logan pushed open the door to the restaurant and suppressed his laughter as Angelina stepped in and looked around. Almost everyone was dressed down in jeans and plaid, like they'd just come off the ranch, and the few that didn't were wearing T-shirts. It made Angelina look like royalty as she stepped in, more dressed up for a dinner out than any of the other patrons had probably ever been in their lives.

Angelina groaned, but he shook his head. "Don't say it," he said.

"Why didn't you tell me we were going here? I'd have changed!"

"You like dressing up and you look beautiful. Don't worry so much about what other people think."

"That's real easy for the guy wearing jeans and fitting in with the crowd to say."

He laughed and pulled her close, kissing the top of her head. "Come on, beautiful, let's find our table. And I wouldn't worry because no one's going to be watching us where we're sitting anyway."

He saw her open her mouth, but he grabbed her hand and tugged her along with him, winking at the waiter who approached them.

"Evening," he said, and she didn't miss the wink he gave the waiter.

"Come this way," the waiter said, grinning as he marched into the kitchen.

Logan pulled Angelina with him as she protested.

"Where are we going?" she whispered.

But when they stopped, her questions stopped too. The table was set up at the far end of the kitchen, out of sight of anyone, just like he'd promised.

"How did you do this?" she asked. "This is insane!"

The waiter pulled out her chair and she sat, shaking her head as she watched him, and he sat across from her, happy to see how surprised she was.

"It's not only fancy restaurants in LA that have chef's tables," he said.

Angelina laughed and leaned back, her long hair

falling over her shoulders as she tipped her head back. Logan admired her soft, creamy skin, waiting for the moment that she straightened and fixed that beautiful blue gaze on him. And when she did, it was worth the wait.

"So, do we get to see a menu or is the chef deciding?" Angelina asked.

"Let's just say that you'll need a plastic bib to eat what I've ordered."

"Oh really?" Her brows arched, laughter in her eyes.

"Yes, really."

They sat for a moment, the only movement the rise and fall of both their chests as they eyed each other over the table.

"This is fun," Angelina said, but she broke their gaze for a second.

"I hear a *but* coming," he said, nodding to the waiter when he came back with their champagne. He let him open it but then took the bottle from him, pouring a glass for Angelina.

"There is a but, Logan," she said softly. "No matter how I feel about you or how beautiful tonight is, there are still big hurdles in our way. I mean, we live in different states and . . ."

"And what else? As far as I see, we live in different states, and that's it," he said. "We've wasted too long because we're both scared of change, or what could happen, of taking that leap and just letting ourselves be happy for once. I for one am not going to sabotage this before we even give it a chance."

She held her champagne glass by the stem and he clinked his glass to hers.

"To happiness," he said. "Because God only knows we both deserve some."

They sipped and he watched her, saw the way her shoulders dropped a little as she relaxed.

"Ange, we can travel. We both have money, and I don't care where I am." He reached across the table and she grasped his hand, holding on to him as he spoke. "So long as I have you, so long as I know we've tried to make this work, I say we simply do our best."

"You're sure? I mean . . ."

"No second-guessing, okay? We need to take this one day at a time. Baby steps, remember?"

She nodded. "Okay."

"But there is one thing that's nonnegotiable."

Angelina looked worried until he smiled.

"You have to be stepmom to Ella, so we can't be anywhere that she can't be with us."

Angelina leaned in to kiss him, her eyes lowered and clearly focused on his mouth.

"If that's the only rule, then we might just make this work."

Just before their lips collided, their waiter came back with two overflowing plates.

"BBQ ribs, duck fat potatoes, and our famous slaw."

Angelina's laughter echoed around them as she stared down at her plate. "You've got to be kidding me."

"Darlin', if you don't eat ribs, are you even in Texas?"

She held up her champagne glass and took one more sip before pushing up imaginary sleeves and reaching for her first rib.

"You eat that entire plate with your fingers, and you might just be my dream girl."

Angelina waggled her eyebrows. "I'd better start eating, then."

Chapter 19

ANGELINA watched Logan across the table as he chatted so easily to the waiter, tipping him and thanking him for the table. She'd always known how generous he was, that he was the kind of guy who'd stop and talk to anyone without any pretenses, but until now, she hadn't realized how important that was to her. Logan was a man who looked like he could tackle an intruder and complete a citizen's arrest without breaking a sweat, but he was also a decent human being. And no matter how screwed up he might be about what had happened to him when he was serving, and his fear that he somehow hadn't done enough to protect someone he cared about, she knew better.

He stood and pulled out her chair, holding out his arm as if they were in a formal restaurant instead of a glorified diner.

"Thanks for a great night," he said. "I think it was pretty good as far as first dates go."

She leaned into him, craving him, not wanting their night to end. "Aside from the sticky fingers from all that sauce, it was pretty good."

They walked through the kitchen, Logan calling out thanks to the chefs as they passed, and she was happy for the delays. Because it let her hold on to Logan a little bit longer. It might have been a first date, but to her it felt bittersweet, as if their time were limited.

"Hey, why the sad face?" he asked as he held open the door for her.

"I just . . ." She didn't know what to say without sounding silly. "I've had a really great night, that's all. It's one of the best dates I've ever been on."

He ducked his head, grinning. "And that's bad because?"

"Because this, *us*, it just seems too good to be true," she admitted. "I don't want to be negative but I also—"

"Don't want your heart to get broken?" he asked softly.

She looked up at him. "Yeah."

"I'm already broken, Ange. I've barely had all my pieces put back together again, so trust me when I say that I can't handle any more *broken* in any shape or form."

"So you're scared too?" she asked. "I mean, it's not just about not wanting to ruin our friendship, it's about me being so used to putting up walls and protecting myself. If I'm not in control, then I usually won't do something."

Logan drew her into his arms, cocooning her and making her feel so warm and safe that she never wanted to step out of his embrace.

"We owe it to ourselves to be brave," he whispered. "I can see that now more clearly than I've ever seen anything in my life before."

She held on to him, not caring who was watching them as they stood outside the restaurant.

"Now I don't want to be presumptuous, because I know this is technically a first date, but if you want to come home with me . . ."

Angelina tucked tighter against him, tipping back to look up. "So you just said all that sweet stuff before to get me into bed?" she asked.

Logan dipped his head and kissed her, slowly, exploring her mouth and making her melt in his arms, his tongue finding hers as he deepened the kiss. "Hell yeah," he whispered when he came up for air. "If we're gonna be trying long distance, it's all about the physical contact when we get to be together."

Angelina laughed and swatted at him. "How about I spend the night, but no contact?"

Logan groaned. "Can we compromise and at least make out?"

"Just because you serenaded me with a guitar doesn't mean I'm putting out."

She held out her hand and he took it, raising it and pressing a kiss to her skin before walking her the rest of the way to his truck.

It had been a beautiful night, the best, but she still had that pit in her stomach. Whenever they were connected, the fears disappeared, but the second he left her side, in the seconds that she was sitting alone in his truck, the fears started to gnaw at her that whatever was happening between them was too good to be true.

But when Logan got in beside her, reaching for her hand after he'd reversed out of the parking spot, she knew she was being stupid.

Give it a chance, not everything you're not in control of is destined to fail.

Logan could tell how nervous Angelina was. She was jittery, in a way he wasn't used to seeing, and he could feel the change in himself too, the way he wasn't as natural as usual around her. When they'd fooled around and it felt like a mistake, he'd still been himself, but there was a change between them now, a heightened awareness that was more first date than friendship. It wasn't that he didn't like it, he just wasn't used to it being that way with Ange.

"Hey, what do you say we enjoy this beautiful night?" he said, looking up at the glistening stars in the inky-black sky. "We could throw some blankets in the back of the pick-up and just hang out. No pressure."

Her smile told him it was a good idea. "I'd really like that."

"Give me a sec and I'll be right back."

He quickly opened the door, tripping over Ella, who'd been locked inside while they were out. Logan jogged down the hallway into his room and pulled out a couple of sweaters, and then rummaged around for spare pillows and blankets. When he came back down the hall, he heard a noise and backtracked, finding Angelina in the kitchen.

"What're you looking for?" he asked.

"Just some beer," she replied, appearing with two bottles in each hand. "I figured we might need it."

Logan grinned, and they went back outside. He whistled to Ella and she followed, eager to come with them. He passed Angelina his cashmere sweater when they got into the pick-up, and she shrugged it on, snuggling into it as he slowly drove.

"There's a real nice spot up here," he said. "I think you'll like it."

It only took a few minutes to get there, and when he stopped the truck, he turned the ignition off and looked over at Angelina. She stared back at him expectantly, and he leaned in, palm to her cheek, listening to her breathing, before kissing her. Her lips were hungry against his, but he kept the kiss sweet, not wanting to push for more. But he couldn't not kiss her, not with her lips looking so plump and pillowy, her eyes so hungry when he pulled back.

"Come on," he said. "We've got stars to gaze at."

He got out and heard her door open, and he quickly climbed up into the back and spread the blankets out, offering Angelina a hand to help her up. Ella was off exploring in the dark, and he lay back with Angelina, tucking the blankets around them, loving seeing her in his sweater. There was something primal about knowing she was wearing his clothes, that she'd smell like him because of it.

Logan reached for her hand and stared up at the night sky. "You know, when I was in the Middle East, we often just lay outside, Brett and I, imagining what the sky looked like at home. This kind of reminds me of that."

"It's really nice to hear you talk about him," she said, her fingers tucking tighter around his. "I know it's hard for you."

"It is. But it's starting to get easier now. The fog has definitely lifted."

"You know, you're the bravest person I know, Logan. I'm so proud to be your friend."

"Friend?" He chuckled, hauling her up a little as he stared down at her. "I don't want to be your friend, Ange. Every time I ever said it, I was lying."

He saw her eyes widen. "What exactly do you want, then?"

Logan kissed her, brushing his lips over hers, needing to connect with her. "I want *you*," he said. "As something more than my friend. For as long as I can have you."

"I think I want that too," Angelina whispered.

"So we have a great night tonight, then we both figure out what we truly want," he said. "If we both want this to work, it'll work."

"You sound so confident," she said with a laugh.

"It's because I am."

Angelina pushed up, hands to his chest, and straddled him, staring down as she slowly moved her body, and mouth, closer to his. Her hair fell around them, skimming his shoulders and then his face as she lowered herself.

"Sorry about blocking your view of the stars," she murmured.

"Hey, I'm happy with the change in view," he said back, arms around her, feeling her body, wanting her pressed against him rather than teasing him from above.

"I love you, Logan," she whispered, her lips finally connecting with his.

I love you too. He didn't get a chance to say the words, because Angelina was hungry, her hands already fumbling against his buttons. He slipped his palms beneath the sweater, wishing she didn't have so many clothes on beneath it as she started to grind against him, her intentions for the bed of his pick-up blatantly obvious.

This time felt different. This time there was nothing hurried and frenzied about sex with Logan; it was slow and passionate and beautiful. *She* felt beautiful, as Logan slowed them down, his hands gliding against her skin, his mouth almost lazy against hers, as if they had all night. And she supposed they did.

Logan's mouth slipped down her neck, his fingers shedding her of her dress as he pushed the straps down. The night air chilled her skin, but Logan warmed it faster than she could shiver, stroking her breasts until his mouth took the place of his hands, his fingers making their way down her body.

She moaned as he pleasured her, as he took his time touching her, tasting her, as he smiled up at her with such hunger is his gaze.

"How did I get so lucky?" he asked, his words a throaty whisper that made her dip her head to kiss him again.

Angelina pushed at his jeans, fumbling with them, not wanting to wait. She was impatient, knowing what she wanted, not wanting to take things slow any longer.

But Logan wasn't going to be hurried, laughing at her impatience.

"Slow down, tiger," he muttered.

He flipped her then, his arms holding her safe and tight as he moved her beneath him. Logan pulled the blankets up higher, no doubt feeling the goose pimples that were coursing across her skin.

"Logan," she whispered, as he lowered, moving down her body as he pushed her dress up, the dress that was now scrunched up at her waist, and then expertly tugged at her panties, wriggling them down as she groaned and leaned back.

"I want you," she said, trying to tug at his hair. "*Now.*"

He grinned up at her, his eyes twinkling in the moonlight. "Well, you'll just have to wait."

She was about to protest, to insist he move back up, but then his mouth closed over her most delicate parts, his breath hot, his tongue . . . She moaned, fingers digging into his hair now for an entirely different reason.

Angelina lay back, giving in to the pleasure, wrapping her legs around him as he stroked her, as he kissed her intimately, making her pulse race faster as wave after wave of pleasure powered her body.

Logan didn't stop, not until she tensed, until her body shuddered with climax, not until she went limp and her fingers fell away from his hair. But he wasn't done with her.

His smile reminded her of a satisfied predator as he moved back up her body, as he kissed her inner thighs, and then finally made his way back up to her mouth. And then he was inside of her, rocking into her as she tensed around him. Her body was supple as marshmallow, she was so relaxed and satiated, but as he moved inside her, she could feel her pleasure building again.

Angelina looked up into his eyes, trusting him, loving him, and she dug her fingernails into his back as she arched up to him. He wasn't giving in, though, slowing her down again, refusing to move faster, sliding in and out of her so slowly.

"What's the hurry?" he asked, kissing her, his lips plucking at hers over and over again.

He was right, there was no hurry, only she wasn't used to taking it slow, wasn't used to a man looking into her eyes with so much unsaid between them as he took his time to love her.

"I want to remember this night forever," he murmured against her skin, kissing her neck now, in the hollow just above her collarbone. "This is going to get me through the darkness when you're gone."

His words were true for her too. She needed this. She needed to know that she was loved, wanted to remember what it felt like to just be her, not having to pretend to be more confident or more successful than she was. Logan knew the real her, he'd known her before anyone else in her new life had, and he still wanted her.

Angelina cried out his name as he lifted her, his hands to her back as he finally started to move faster. She clenched around him as her body started to lose control again, as she started to ride the exquisite waves of pleasure.

This was truly a night she'd never forget.

Chapter 20

THEY lay together under the stars, and Angelina stroked Logan's chest, shivering despite the blankets they had pulled over them. She wanted to reach for the sweater she'd been wearing and shrug into it, but she also didn't want to move. It had been one of the most memorable nights of her life, and she didn't want it to end.

"I have to meet lawyers tomorrow and sort through some business affairs, and the day after that I fly out," she told him, strumming her fingers against his skin. "I'd get out of it if I could, but I can't."

"I understand. Besides, you need to spend time with you family while you're home too," he said, his lips to her hair as he spoke. "I know firsthand why it's wrong to distract yourself with something. You need to cry all your tears, talk to your siblings, grieve together instead of trying to keep going like you haven't just lost the centerpiece to your family. Just because some time has passed now doesn't mean it's going to get easier."

"So, what do we do now?" she asked.

"We just trust that if this is meant to be, we'll make it happen."

She laughed. "You do realize I'm a type A personality with serious control issues, right? I'm not exactly the type to wait and see. I need plans and action and—"

"Hey, I have no problem with the action side of things," Logan whispered, kissing her neck when she angled herself to look up at him.

"I'm serious, Logan," she said. "I'm not good at not having a plan. You've brought out a different side in me here, a side I'm not used to, one that makes me feel vulnerable and open, but that's not the real me."

"I get that. You know I do," he said. "But I want us to be like this. When we're together, we need to be able to just be."

She stared up at the stars again, smiling when Ella whimpered to join them. Logan extracted himself from her hold on him and pulled on his boxers before getting down to help her up.

"Sorry, smelly dog coming in hot."

Angelina quickly reached for the sweater and slipped it on before pulling the blanket up just in time as Ella jumped on her and snuggled in. She sighed, arm instinctively going around the dog.

"You know, I'm the only one of my siblings who didn't collect animals as a kid," she told him. "Mia was always coming home with strays and waifs, but I was never interested."

Logan joined her, arm going around her as he settled back again. "Yeah, I remember you not being big into animals. But Ella's liked you from the moment she set eyes on you."

She stroked the dog's soft coat. "The feeling's mutual. I think I saw in her what I respect in humans. She's worked hard, she's smart, and she definitely doesn't suffer fools."

Logan laughed. "Sounds like someone else I know."

"Logan, let's give this a few weeks. If one of us hasn't jumped on a plane to see the other one by then, we'll know it wasn't meant to be."

"So I need to visit you within three weeks to show that I want you?" he asked.

"You only get on that plane if you can't wait another day to see me. We need to spend some time apart, to see if our feelings cool or if they intensify. What do you say?"

"I say I can't believe you managed to micromanage this, but yeah, I agree."

She lifted her hand, stroking his face, wanting to commit every angle, every groove to memory in case they were never together like this again.

"Whatever happens, Logan, this has been one of the best nights of my life. Thank you for showing me what love is, that I can be me and still be loved."

Logan kissed her—a long, lingering kiss that she greedily enjoyed, wishing it would never end.

"Why does it always feel like we're saying goodbye?" he murmured.

Because we are, she thought. Only she didn't say anything, preferring to kiss him instead.

All her life she'd been an overachiever. She'd refused to back down from a challenge, she'd worked longer and harder than anyone else to make sure she always had an edge, to be the one who won the biggest deals and made the most money.

But all this time, what she hadn't realized was how fiercely she'd guarded her heart. Maybe it was because she'd had her heart broken almost beyond repair when she'd lost her mom, and she'd hidden away from hurt like a broken bird, always feeling too fragile to come out of hiding, to let herself be vulnerable. Perhaps that was the reason she'd buried herself in work and believed she didn't need anyone. But in the end, work had broken her too, so whatever her subconscious plan was, it hadn't worked.

Perhaps it was finally time for her to be open to letting herself love and be loved, without being scared of that person being taken from her. Or that failure of any kind would break her. Because she'd risen from the ashes more than once now, personally and professionally, and she wasn't going to let fear guide her any longer.

"Wait, you gave him a weird timeline and that's going to be the marker of whether or not you guys should be together?" Penny asked. "Angelina, that's crazy! The man already as good as declared his love for you."

Angelina was wishing she'd never told Penny the truth. "It was the best I could come up with at the time. And I guess that I kind of believe it. If we're supposed to be together, then we'll find a way to be together. I really wanted to see how I felt once I had some distance, and whether he felt the same." She wasn't scared, she was pragmatic, and maybe she wanted to see what he did before she completely put her heart on the line.

"Hold up," Penny said, leaning back in her chair. "You were scared that he'd change his mind, so you came up with that bogus scheme to see if he came to you."

Angelina stared at her computer screen, pretending she was busy.

"Ange! You doubt the man actually loves you, don't you? You just can't let yourself believe it."

She sighed. "If it's too good to be true—"

"Why can't you just trust the man if he says he loves

you? I thought you'd known this guy since you were kids?"

Angelina looked up from her screen. "Hey, did you get any decent responses to the advertisement for client relations?" she asked. "We really need to put our energy into filling that position with the right person."

"A few actually, but only one guy who stands out from the bunch. I've scheduled him in for tomorrow."

"Great." Ange busied herself with checking over all the details for the launch. She had a few days until they were letting the world know who they were and what they did, and she wanted everything to go perfectly.

"There's actually something I wanted to talk to you about," she said, pushing back her chair to look at Penny. "My dad left me a letter, with his will, and I've decided to follow in his footsteps in a way. I'm going to set up a property development company, as well as continuing with his currency trading."

Penny looked alarmed. "But what about all this? We've worked so hard and—"

"Which is precisely why we need a good customer relations person to help our Executive Director," she said, trying not to smirk. "I know you think I'm afraid of love, but I'm not. I'm trying to be more open to new things, pushing myself to do more and try more, whether that's in business or my personal life. And one thing I've learned over this past roller coaster of a year is that people mean everything to me."

"Executive Director? Why are talking about yourself in the third person? And what people?" Penny asked, sounding confused.

"Because I'm not the CEO," Angelina said softly. "You are."

Penny erupted into laughter before her mouth slowly dropped open. "You're not joking?"

Angelina shook her head as she watched emotion ripple through Penny's face. "All I wanted was to sink my teeth into something real, something that would have an impact on the world in some way, and I've done it. But I couldn't do it without you at my side," she said, watching as Penny's eyes filled with tears. "You're special, and you're way too talented to be my sidekick, not to mention you stood by me right to the end when the shit hit the fan. This is your chance to prove yourself to me, and I'll be here whenever you need me. What do you say?"

Penny threw out her arms, leaping up to hug her. "I say you're the best damn boss in the world, that's what I say!"

Angelina hugged her back, but let go when Penny stiffened.

"I also say those are the biggest bunch of flowers I've ever seen."

She turned and saw a delivery man carrying what looked to be his own weight in flowers. He looked uncomfortable. "Um, are those for me?"

"Angelina Ford?" he asked.

She sprang into action and took them from him, setting them down on the big table they were working from. "Yes, thank you," she whispered, her jaw hanging open as she stared at them.

"If you were waiting for a big gesture to show he wanted to be with you . . ." Penny muttered from behind her.

But Angelina was too busy looking for the card to come up with a smart reply. *They're probably just from someone who's read about what we're doing.* She reached in, looking for the card, but there wasn't one. Just because she was thinking about Logan didn't mean they were from him. And besides, he didn't exactly seem like the romantic, over-the-top gesture kind of guy. *Serenading me the other night excluded.*

"Holy shit."

Her hand froze when she connected with a small black silk bag tied to a stem. She gulped, fumbling as she tried to untie it. There was something in it, and it sure as hell wasn't a note.

"What? Are they not from Logan?"

"There's a . . ." Her words disappeared from her throat as she stared inside the bag. She slowly reached in, pulling out the biggest diamond she'd ever laid eyes upon.

"Holy shit, that's huge," Penny exclaimed.

Angelina just gaped back at her, holding it. The big square diamond twinkled up at her, made to look even larger by the delicate platinum diamond band it was set on. It was easily the most beautiful ring she'd ever seen, and she couldn't take her eyes off it.

"Now do you believe he loves you?"

She slid it on her finger, turning her hand as she looked at the way it twinkled in the light. "Yeah," she whispered. "Maybe I do."

Penny suddenly cleared her throat, and Angelina looked up, freezing when she saw a very familiar, very handsome man leaning in the doorway.

"I hear this incredible start-up is looking for someone in client relations, and I'd like to apply for the position."

Angelina laughed. "You came all this way to apply in person?" she asked.

"Something like that. And because a beautiful girl

told me to jump on a plane if I felt like I couldn't wait another day to see her."

"Logan, I've only been home a day," she whispered, trying not to laugh.

"There's something else," he said with a grin.

"Oh yeah?" The weight of the ring was impossible not to notice on her finger as she stared back at him. But it was Ella who caught her eyes, trotting out from behind Logan toward her. She was carrying something, and when Angelina bent to take it from her, Ella sat and stared up at her. It was a card, with four simple words written on it.

Will you marry us?

Angelina laughed at the same time as tears slipped down her cheeks. "Yes," she whispered, shaking her head as she wiped at her cheeks. "Yes, Logan, I'll marry you."

He strode toward her then, gathering her into his arms as he swept her off her feet and kissed her, swinging her around as Ella barked and ran circles around them.

"I thought it'd take you at least two weeks to get here," she murmured as he kissed her.

When Logan's lips finally left hers, he smiled down at her. "Why waste another day to spend the rest of our lives together?"

Angelina's arms found their way around his neck, and she nuzzled into him.

"You do realize just because I said yes, I'm never going to be barefoot and pregnant on the ranch, right?"

"Let's just take this one step at a time," he said with a wink.

"Logan!" She punched his chest. "I mean it. My career means a lot to me, just like my last name does. It's always going to be Ford."

"Darlin', you can keep your name, and I'll settle with pregnant in heels."

"You're dreaming," she whispered as she gazed up at him.

"So do I get the job?" he asked.

Angelina shrugged. "You'll have to ask the new CEO, I hear she's got balls of steel."

Logan kissed the tip of her nose. "We spend half our time here, and half our time in Texas," he said.

"How about a sixty-forty split in my favor? I can't be in Texas half the year."

Logan laughed. "Done."

"Guys, get a room!" Penny called out.

Logan shrugged and strode back the way he came, not letting her go.

"I'll have her back tomorrow!" he called.

Angelina didn't even bother arguing. Logan had come for her, he'd *proposed* to her, and it was the best damn feeling in the world.

Epilogue

ANGELINA looked over at Logan and tried to hold her laughter in check. He was like a pig in mud—a month in California working alongside her, trying to blend in and be a city boy—it had almost killed him. Granted, to anyone looking at him, they'd never have known. He'd worked hard, he'd won over investors and helped launch her new business to the world without seeming to break a sweat, and he'd been by her side encouraging her as she found her feet again and listened to her intuition over her new property venture.

But seeing him back on the ranch, in his faded jeans and soft, overwashed plaid shirt, it was so obvious that he was home. That it was his happy place as much as California was hers.

"I'm liking that smile," she said as Logan strode toward her, his long legs eating up the ground.

"This place, it's just, I don't know how to explain it, but it's a part of me," he said, reaching for her. He took off his hat and dropped it on the veranda beside her before cupping her face as he slowly bent down. Everything slowed then—the beat of her heart, her breath, her movement—as Logan's lips found hers. He kissed her so tenderly, as if he could break her, and she loved how gentle he could be with her sometimes. For a woman who liked to take control and be in charge of everything, she'd started to crave the way Logan made her feel, the way he just took command of a situation, or of her. There was something to be said for submitting sometimes.

"Mmm," he murmured when he straightened, his smile drawing her into him, making her crave him. "With you here, this place is even better."

She looked past him to the green fields, seeing his horse tethered still by the barn, inhaling the fresh country air that was so different to where she'd been living. For years it had been her idea of a nightmare, the very thought of having to spend any longer than necessary on a ranch making her want to run in the opposite direction, but this felt different. The balance, it somehow felt right.

"What are you thinking?" he asked, arms scooped around her as he stared down. Logan had his hips tipped forward as he held her, their bodies connected, and she smiled up at him. "Is everything okay? You don't have the jet on standby, do you?"

"No," she said, shaking her head. "There's no plane waiting. I'm not going to run."

"Then what is it?"

"I'm just . . ." She laughed. "I'm happy. I mean, I can't believe that we've somehow managed to do this. Having you with me in LA was amazing, we worked so well as a team together, but we need this balance. *I* need this balance."

"Good," he said, his mouth kicking up into a sweet smile.

"I've worked so hard all my life, and I've never really stopped to just be. And I've never let anyone close enough to see what it's like to have a true partner, someone I can love and rely on, and actually trust to have my back."

She glanced at the ring on her finger, twinkling away, such a big bold statement of Logan's love for her. It was like a constant reminder to her that he was with her, that he'd made a huge declaration of commitment, leaving the property he loved to follow her.

"Logan, will you marry me?" she asked.

"Darlin', I'm fairly sure we've already agreed on that."

She laughed. "No, I mean now. Let's get married. Today."

His hands left her waist as he tapped gently on her head. "Um, I think we've got a problem in here. Has your brain been replaced by rocks? I thought you didn't even want to be involved in planning the wedding?"

She stood on tiptoe, hands on his shoulders as she kissed him. Angelina took her time, exploring his mouth, teasing him, tasting him, and loving every damn moment of it.

"You actually want to get married, *here*?" he asked when she lowered and let him go. "You're serious?"

She nodded. "Yeah, I am. I want to be your wife, and I don't need a big wedding or a fuss, I just want this to be you and me, for the rest of our lives."

He chuckled. "My mom would kill me if she missed it. Can't we wait a day or two just to make sure they can get here?"

She rocked back on her heels and grinned up at him. "I've known you most of my life, Logan, and I've probably loved you for most of it too. So let's do this. I don't want to leave this ranch until we're married."

Logan swept her up into his arms, and they both

laughed until he kissed her. And then, as usually happened between them, things started to heat up. Fast.

She tugged at his shirt, untucking it from his waistband, running her hands beneath to touch his smooth abs, excited about exploring his body even though she'd touched him a hundred times already. She just never tired of touching him, feeling him, being loved by him.

Logan's mouth was hot and wet at her neck as he walked her backwards. He pushed her against the side of the house as she hooked a leg around him, drawing him closer, feeling him hard against her as she yanked his head up, fingers curling tight around his hair, hungrily taking possession of his mouth.

His grin was wicked as his fingers hooked around her top, starting to lift it.

"Ahem," a voice said loudly, breaking through what was otherwise silence around them. "I hope we're not interrupting?"

Angelina's head shot back, smacking into the timber wall behind her as her leg snapped down to the ground. She looked up into Logan's eyes, filled with the same horror she was certain would be reflected in hers.

Crap.

As Logan mouthed "sorry" and took a step away from her, giving her a second to yank down her top and smooth her hair from her face, she felt like a naughty seventeen-year-old caught making out with her boyfriend.

"Mom, Dad, I wasn't expecting you," Logan said as he reached for her hand.

"Well, surprise!" his mom said, throwing her hands in the air. "I thought if you're not going to bring your bride to be to see me, then we'd make the trip ourselves."

Angelina held up a hand in a pathetic attempt at a

wave. She knew her cheeks would be flaming red, mortified from being caught getting hot and heavy with her man. *With this woman's son.*

"Ahhh, it's so lovely to see you again, Mrs.—" She stuttered, trying to compose herself as she struggled over the words. She was a successful, confident woman—why on earth was she suddenly so tongue-tied?

"Sweetheart, please, call me Mary," she said, walking up the steps and opening her arms. She kissed her cheek and held her at arm's length, smiling as she looked her up and down. "Frankly, I'd be worried if you *didn't* have your hands all over each other now. It's the sign of a good marriage, don't you think, Frank?"

Logan's dad groaned at the same time as Logan grabbed hold of his mom's arm and steered her into the house.

"Mom, that's totally inappropriate," Angelina heard him say, as she hugged his dad, kissing his cheek.

"You look as beautiful as you did when you were a teenager," Frank said, taking her arm. "I'm so pleased my son came to his senses. I always told him that if a woman too good to be true ever came into his life, then she was the woman for him."

"He's a good man, your son," Angelina said as they followed mother and son inside. "I think I'm the one who's ended up with a man too good to be true."

Logan found them then, eyebrows shooting up as he saw her arm in arm with his dad.

"I was just telling Mom that we're planning an impromptu wedding," he whispered.

"Aww, hell no!" Frank cursed. "That'll put her in a right tailspin."

Logan replaced his father at her side, his arm around

her waist, hand slipping into her back pocket. "Let's get married, baby," he said, kissing her head as they walked.

"Yeah," she whispered, turning in his arms and staring up at him. "Let's."

"I'm sorry about my mama just showing up like this," he murmured against her lips.

But Angelina didn't care. All that mattered to her was being in Logan's arms, taking time to enjoy her life for once, and letting herself just be with the man she loved.

"Come on, you two, enough making out already! We have a wedding to plan!" his mom called down the hall.

Logan groaned but Angelina just laughed, their foreheads pressed together.

"Hey, we can't choose our family," she whispered.

Logan held her tight. "Luckily we can choose who we fall in love with, huh?"

She let him hold her, loving the feel of his arms around her, the warmth of his body pressed the length of hers. And she didn't bother telling him, but she wasn't so sure he was right. She'd fallen head over heels in love with him, but she wasn't entirely sure that choice had had anything to do with it. Instead, she was fairly certain they'd been destined to collide, and she was only lucky they both hadn't been too stubborn to see it in the first place. Or give in to it.

Logan looked at the men gathered with him. They'd been resigned to the guest house while Angelina installed herself in his home, and he was having a precelebration beer with his new brothers-in-law. They'd decided to keep it as family only, with the exception of Penny, Kelly, and Lucy, just a small affair so everyone they loved could be with them, and he liked how comfortable he felt just sitting and swilling a beer with Angelina's family.

"You know this is your last chance to back out," Tanner said, raising his beer and draining it. "You hurt my sister after this day, and I'll break your legs, but you're not married yet."

Logan grimaced. "Yeah, I get that feeling. But I'm a big boy, I'm prepared to take that risk."

Cody laughed. "You're a brave man, because I'll break your arms once he's done with you."

They all laughed, but he noticed that Tanner looked more on edge, his beer bottle discarded as he stood. Sam smiled at him from across the room, though, and Logan smiled back. He knew Sam had no doubt been given the same talk before he married Mia.

"You know, I am sorry," Tanner said, running his fingers through his hair. "I know Cody's already apologized, but we were out of line from scaring you off all those years ago. Ange's been through a lot, and I wish she'd had you by her side all this time instead of doing it alone."

"Tanner," Logan said, standing in front of him and looking him straight in the eye. "You did the right thing. I was a boy and I would have had no idea what to do with a woman like Angelina. She still frightens the crap out of me with how successful and beautiful she is, but I love it. Back then, though, we would have both come away with broken hearts."

Tanner held out his hand and Logan clasped it.

"So, we're good?" Tanner asked.

"Yeah, we're good. We've always been good."

Tanner let go of his hand. "I'd better go get this bride, then. She's waiting for me."

Logan blew out a big breath and watched Tanner go,

before turning to look at the other two men in the room with him. Cody opened his arms up and gave him a hug, slapping his back, and Sam offered him another beer.

"You need one for your nerves?" Sam asked.

"No, I'm good. I just want to get out there and see my girl."

They waited a few more minutes before preparing to leave. Logan shrugged on his jacket, and soon they were walking across the lawn to the back of the house, where the ceremony was being held. His mom had gone all out, decorating the garden with white lanterns and fairy lights, and white rose petals strewn everywhere. A handful of white seats with oversize white bows tied on them were positioned at the foot of the garden, overlooking the ranch, and Logan walked over, stopping only to kiss his mom and then both Kelly and Lucy on the cheek before gathering with Cody and Sam by his side. Ella was with him, as always, but she was busy scratching at the white bow tied around her neck, looking less than impressed.

And then she appeared.

Angelina was holding her brother's arm, hand tucked to his elbow, carrying a single white rose. She was dressed in white, her dress skimming her curves and kicking out a little at the bottom. She had flowers in her hair, which was loose and flowing over her shoulders just like he loved it, and her smile told him everything he needed to know. *She's as happy as me about being here.*

Logan resisted the urge to go to her, watching as first Mia, Lexi, and Lauren walked toward him and gathered to one side, followed by Sophia and Lucy dancing to their own tune and throwing petals wildly like it was a competition to throw the most first. They giggled and collapsed onto the grass, busy chatting to one another, and Logan laughed along with everyone else at how darn cute they were.

But when Angelina started to walk toward him, everything else faded. All he could see was the woman he wanted to spend the rest of his life with as she neared.

"You look so beautiful," he said, stepping toward her and holding out his hands to her.

Angelina clasped them, tears shining in her eyes as she looked back at him.

"I'd sacrifice my own life for her, Tanner," he said to her brother, not letting go of her hands. "I promise you, I'll look after her forever."

"This girl is quite capable of looking after herself," Angelina interrupted.

Tanner shook his head at his sister and Logan just laughed.

"Darlin', sometimes it's okay to let a man look after you," he whispered.

Angelina kissed him, her arm around his shoulders as she smiled against his mouth. "I wouldn't be marrying you if I didn't already know that."

Everyone around them laughed, and Logan took his bride's hand again as they faced the officiant. Ella had trotted back over, her white bow around her neck long gone, and she sat and watched as Logan turned to Angelina.

"Are you ready to say I do?" she whispered.

Logan grinned. "Hell yes."

And before he knew it, it was time to kiss the bride.

Angelina looked around her at the group gathered, smiling as she saw all the people she loved. Her new mother-in-law had outdone herself, barely sleeping to ensure she could create something so beautiful in such a short time, and Angelina knew she'd be forever grateful for what she'd done for her.

She glanced at her man, his smile as big as Texas as he grinned over at her, before tapping his glass to stand. They were sitting at a big table on the enormous veranda of his ranch. Fairy lights hung above and around them, twinkling as the sky became inky, the ranch disappearing as darkness blanketed the valley.

"Speech, speech!" Tanner chanted, clapping as Logan stood.

Everyone raised their glasses and even the children, still excited about the day, started to clap. Logan just stood and waited them out, clearing his throat as he motioned for them to quiet down.

"I want to say a few words before the Ford brothers get too rowdy," Logan joked, and Angelina laughed as she watched him, loving that he was getting on so easily with her brothers. "First, thank you all for coming. I think we're all acutely aware that there's someone missing today, and I hope Walter's looking down on us and enjoying the festivities. If he'd been here, I would have gone to him to ask for his daughter's hand, but instead, I had to go to Tanner." Logan paused, shaking his head. "Let's just say that I've been reminded more than once what happens if I hurt his sister."

Angelina chuckled along with everyone else, even as tears twinkled in her eyes thinking about her dad.

"I'm the kind of guy who sees a red flag and runs," he said, turning to her now. She stared back up at him, suddenly feeling like it was only the two of them. "I've been in love with Angelina for a very long time, but even when I finally realized it, all I could see were the reasons why we shouldn't be together. I was scared, of losing her, of losing myself, of failing, of not being enough . . ." Logan's voice caught and he cleared his throat, but Angelina couldn't sit any longer. She jumped to her feet and held his hand, blinking away her own tears as he quickly wiped his cheeks. "I've lost a lot over the past couple of years, but this is a new chapter. This is about me and Angelina, being brave, and not looking for red flags anymore."

He turned to her and she cupped his face, stroking her fingers down his cheek as she stared into his eyes, knowing she'd just made the best decision of her life.

"Angelina, I love you so much and I always have. You scare the hell out of me, but I'm so pleased we're on this journey together."

She barely waited for him to finish, leaning in and kissing him, slowly, showing him just how much she loved him back. When she finally pulled away, she touched her forehead to his, staring into his eyes.

"I love you," she whispered.

"Right back at you, beautiful," he whispered back, wrapping his arms around her as everyone erupted into whistles and claps.

But as they sat down, Kelly stood, and Angelina touched Logan's hand to get his attention.

"I know I'm a stranger to all of you, but I want to say a few words."

Angelina nodded, keeping hold of Logan's hand as she watched a very tearful-looking Kelly stand in front of their family.

"Logan is, *was*, my husband's best friend. He is the strongest, bravest human being I've ever met, and without him, I don't what Lucy and I would have done. He's been our real life superhero, the person who's always there for us no matter what, and Angelina, I want to tell you how lucky you are to be marrying this man." Ange wiped at her eyes as Kelly gazed at her. "If you hurt him, I'll never forgive you, but if you love him like I know you will, then I will love you like a sister for the rest of my life."

Angelina rose and walked around the table to embrace Kelly, holding her as she cried, fighting tears herself. When she finally let her go, she carefully wiped away her friend's smudged eyeliner, before walking back to her seat.

"I'd like to toast the missing best man who should be with us here today," Angelina said, holding up her glass and taking a sip of champagne. "And to this superhero of a man I married."

"To Brett," Logan said, his hand pressed to her back as he raised his glass.

Angelina gazed into his eyes. Life sure had a funny way of turning things upside down and making things right.

"This is the happiest day of my life," she murmured to Logan as she sat back down, in his lap this time instead of her chair.

His mouth touched her hair, his fingers brushed her thigh, and as she leaned into the warmth of his chest, she knew she'd finally found her way home.

1579